BEASTS OF 42ND STREET

BEASTS OF 42ND STREET

Preston Fassel

CEMETERY DANCE PUBLICATIONS

Baltimore

❖ 2022 ❖

EARLY PRAISE FOR BEASTS OF 42nd STREET

Preston Fassel has proven himself as one of our most powerful upcoming voices in horror literature with Beasts of 42nd Street. Fassel simultaneously winks at past horror sub-genres while delving into new and innovative territory, creating both a love letter to 70s exploitation cinema while weaving a tight, contemporary, psychological horror tale.

—REBEKAH McKENDRY, PhD

Like the bastard lovechild of Paul Schrader and Abel Ferrera, Preston Fassel's Beasts of 42nd Street is a sleazy, audacious, razor-sharp slice of bloody exploitation...You may be able to wipe away the grime after reading this book, but the smile will stay for days.

—KEALAN PATRICK BURKE, BRAM STOKER
AWARD-WINNING AUTHOR OF KIN AND SOUR CANDY

You could sit around and moan about how they don't write 'em like they used to, or you could get acquainted with Preston Fassel. Beasts of 42nd Street is more reflective than you might expect from a book whose main character is a junkie projectionist...but it's as vividly drawn and engrossingly readable as any dog-eared paperback from the heyday of pulp fiction.

—KATIE RIFE; THE AV CLUB, ROLLING STONE

...one of the best detective novels to come down the pike in a long while. A rogues' gallery of great characters and a killer story mixed with New York City in all its 1970s sleazy glory. What's not to love?

—HARRY HUNSICKER, AUTHOR OF THE DEVIL'S COUNTRY;
FORMER EXECUTIVE VICE PRESIDENT OF
THE MYSTERY WRITERS OF AMERICA

MORE PRAISE FOR BEASTS OF 42nd STREET

Fassel impressively grafts a grimy, thrilling horror story onto the richly rendered true grindhouse setting of 42nd Street, using actual events and places to flesh out this exploitation nightmare. Demonstrating expansive research and knowledge of the era, Fassel's latest impresses on every level.

—MEAGAN NAVARRO, *BLOODY DISGUSTING*

You don't just read this book, you live it. A desperate love story of obsession and madness that could've only happened on 42nd street.

—MATT SERAFINI, AUTHOR OF *RITES OF EXTINCTION* AND *UNDER THE BLADE*

...a work of gritty, haunting storytelling. You won't be able to forget Andy Lew's descent into forbidden cinema.

—JOHN PALISANO; PRESIDENT, HWA

...a faithful yet imaginative transcription of one of the darkest times and places in our country's history...hedonistic, pharmaceutically inflamed, devastated by disease...Fassel captures it in all its inglorious glory: sick, violent, and propulsive as hell!"

—MICK GARRIS

FURTHER PRAISE FOR BEASTS OF 42nd STREET

If you get a thrill from classic exploitation flicks, Beasts of 42nd Street is like injecting one directly into your brain...the perfect book for horror-fueled mutants looking for their next grizzly fix. Just be careful what you wish for...

—ADRIENNE CLARK, *PHANTASTIQUE*

"A cast of maniacs, deviants and criminals- each more disturbing than the last. I was unprepared for what I learned at the end of this book—and you will be, too...Preston's writing is compelling, urgent, and loaded with intrigue...a brilliant storyteller.

—SADIE HARTMANN, *MOTHER HORROR*; *NIGHTWORMS*

Grabs you by the face and doesn't let go for its entire length. Fast paced, thrilling, and entertaining as Hell...Read. This. Book.

—JEFF HEIMBUCH, *HORROR BUZZ*

Beasts of 42nd Street
Copyright © 2022 by Preston Fassel

Cover artwork © 2022 by Justin Coons
Interior Design © 2022 by Desert Isle Design, LLC
All rights reserved.

Trade Paperback Edition

ISBN:
978-1-58767-853-0

Cemetery Dance Publications
132B Industry Lane, Unit #7
Forest Hill, MD 21050
www.cemeterydance.com

For Bill Landis (1959-2008)
and
Jacob Hacker (1985-2020)

You should not be reading this.

It was the jackal—Tabaqui, the Dish-licker—and the wolves of India despise Tabaqui because he runs about making mischief, and telling tales, and eating rags and pieces of leather from the village rubbish-heaps. But they are afraid of him too, because Tabaqui, more than anyone else in the jungle, is apt to go mad, and then he forgets that he was ever afraid of anyone, and runs through the forest biting everything in his way. Even the tiger runs and hides when little Tabaqui goes mad...

—Rudyard Kipling, *The Jungle Book*

COMING ATTRACTIONS

(PROLOGUE, 1977)

This inhuman place makes human monsters.
—Stephen King, *The Shining*

"SO, WHO'S Andy Lew?"

Chrissy asks this as Tony removes a crowbar from the waistband of his bell bottoms, slips it into the crack of the Colossus Theater's back door and begins to pry. Among a particular Times Square demographic, those who proudly count themselves amongst the pickpockets, burglars, confidence men, and run of the mill street corner delinquents, it is valuable knowledge what doors have been left open, which are never locked, which are loose. Worth even more is the knowledge when one of these unlocked doors contains a treasure; worth more still is the knowledge that the treasure is unguarded.

"Andy Lew? Andy Lew's the troll under the bridge, man," Tony says, twists the crowbar, pops the red steel door open with a mechanical groan. The two boys step into the yellow-lit stairwell of the Colossus Theater. The little space is an echo chamber; muffled cries and shouts boom around them from the auditorium just beyond the paper thin wall. "He's a burnout."

"What's a burnout?"

"Means he's fucked in the head," Tony says as the pair begin their ascent towards the projector booth.

"Fucked in the head, ok, yeah, but how is a burnout different from generally being fucked in the head? As opposed to everyone else we know."

"Well, here's how I heard it from Eddie: Some people aren't fit to see messed up shit every day. Some people, they're exposed to it long enough, they go nuts. It goes from them getting upset by it, to them enjoying it. Happens to some people. Not a lot of people, but some. They see messed up shit enough, it stops bothering them. Like a coping mechanism, from back in like, caveman days, or, like cowboy times, when people was dying all the time and shit, and you had to be tough. But burnouts, they stop being bothered by it, start liking it. And I don't just mean, like, horror movie shit. I mean stuff that bothers normal people, I mean, like, *really* bothers them, even bothers other people who're into messed up shit. They really start to enjoy it, and then they get hooked. And then they change. Most people, when they start to like messed up shit, they're still who they are, just kinda fucked up, you dig? Burnouts, they stop talking to their family— if they had one— their friends, fucked up shit becomes their life. And then they stop enjoying *it*, too. They don't even hate it because they *can't* hate anymore. They can't even *love* anymore. They stop being *able* to love or hate. And Eddie says, like a door opens in their head, that doesn't open in normal people's heads, and they start feeling something in the place of love and hate, except it's just one emotion instead of two, but it's the same thing, see? They love and they hate at the same time. And that's a burnout. That's Andy Lew."

"Fuck," Chrissy says. "How's Eddie know him?"

"Used to come into his place, back in the day. Buy shit, you know, just hang out, like a real human being."

The pair have ascended the stairs now, slipped into an access hallway and are near the projector booth. Chrissy glances down behind them; from their vantage point, the bottom of the stairwell is a black pit.

"And that was him, out in the crowd? With the camera?"

"Yeah."

"Fuck. Eddie better not fuck us over on this. Eddie better pay what he says."

"Eddie always pay what he owe," Tony says. "And if we get this for him he's gonna owe big, so move."

The boys open the door before them and survey their treasure: The twin projectors of the Colossus theater, and inside of them, their ticket to more money than either of them has ever held in his life.

"If anyone shows up," Chrissy says, "I can take him down. Just watch our backs."

"Yeah, you have fun with that," Tony says, casual, disaffected, by virtue of being born black in New York he has come up in an environment in which constant vigilance is the price of not getting mugged, shot, arrested for the crime of existing. His heart jackhammers against his chest, but his hands are steady and his breathing is leveled. Keeping cool is not a learned skill for him but an evolved instinct.

"I'm JROTC," Chrissy says.

"How old are you?" Tony asks.

"Sixteen."

"Your moms still around?"

"Yeah."

"OK then, don't get your ass killed, I don't want no pissed off momma gunnin' for me."

Chrissy approaches the projector not currently running and begins to unspool the reel. Each projector can only hold a limited portion of a film; it is the projectionist's job to remain vigilant as to when one reel is ending so that he can switch on the second projector and allow for a seamless transition. Fortunately for the boys, Andy Lew has decided to slack off tonight.

"See, Andy's the reason this movie is even here in the first place," Tony says. "They were supposed to get some other shit, Andy Lew convinces

Rod-Rod Tillman that the local element would really groove on *Last House*, tells him it's a real freakout film and Rod-Rod, he wants to be Mr. Bigshot with management so he ganks Andy Lew's spiel for his own, makes himself sound all hip to what's going on here when really it's Andy Lew's got his dick on the pulse of forty-deuce, gets it sent over. Ain't but a few prints of this thing in the whole wide fuckin' world and some people seen it are gonna pay a wad to have their own copy. You know what it's about, right?"

"Not really."

"Well it's just a bunch of fucked up shit, basically. And pretty much the guy in the movie is Andy Lew, or at least what Andy Lew wants to be. Or could be, I guess. Last night, saw a couple of brothers comin' out of this place sobbin'. Takes a sick scene to make a brother around here chuck his baloney in the gutter."

Chrissy peeks over Tony's shoulder, gets a glimpse of what *Last House* is all about, shakes his head and clicks his tongue.

"Twisted."

"It's supposed to be some evil shit," Tony says, and for the first time he notices that Chrissy is smiling, he is excited, he is enjoying this entire suicidal endeavor. "I read in a magazine that they don't even know who made the thing. Some people think it's real. Bullshit. *Snuff* wasn't real. CJ's girlfriend goes to high school with that chick they were supposed to have cut up at the end. Ain't no such thing as a snuff film. Just mondo bullshit and the six o'clock news."

Chrissy, done unspooling the unused projector, now moves to the projector still running and switches it off. Time is of the essence now. 42nd Street crowds do not take kindly to their films being interrupted. They have paid for a particular experience, of a darkened auditorium and muffled noise and loud, violent images projected onto a dirty screen, and whether they are there to fuck or shoot dope or drink or sleep or in some cases actually watch the movie, they have handed over their money in the expectation that this experience will be provided. Pushers and pimps and users and whores and runaways and two-bit gangsters and ice-pushing bikers are not in the habit of looking kindly on an interruption to their regularly scheduled program. It takes seconds before the first beverage hits the screen, followed by another, lit cigarettes fly, popcorn showers rain down from the balcony and people are rising and turning towards the projector booth, screaming and shouting, obscene gestures waved and threats howled at the tops of lungs, and somewhere in the shadowy, undulating array of bodies down below Tony sees someone produce a microrefrigerator and raise it above his head and hurtle it towards the screen. The fridge misses its mark, is caught by a second set of hands that passes it onto a third, and a fourth before the crowd surfing appliance finally soars with enough velocity to explode on impact, missing the screen by feet, littering the floor with debris.

Up in the booth, Tony's body goes rigid. There is an escape to be made; these are Andy's people and their cries of furious indignation and the sound of wanton chaos are like infernal prayers offered up to him, imprecations for him to arrive and strike down their enemies. If he has reentered the building, if he has heard the commotion in the auditorium, then at any moment a truly deranged individual will be returning and apt to do anything once he discovers two interlopers in his territory.

Tony jerks Chrissy towards the door, tries to tell him that they've got to leave now, that his instincts are flaring up and whatever nameless thing inside of him that has seen him through knife fights and beat downs and all of his desperate eighteen years on earth is telling him that danger is rapidly approaching. And then there is the sound of the projector door opening and booth boys freeze, Chrissy striking an attack stance, Tony, quietly, praying that God will show them the same mercy he did to Daniel when the prophet was cast into his own den...

OUR FIRST FEATURE OF THE EVENING:
HELL'S PILGRIMS
(1977)

There's something inherently wrong with the human personality.
—Stanley Kubrick

SHE HAS a birthmark.

Trembling hands switch off the projector, switch on the lights. For a moment, there is utter stillness in the apartment, utter silence, the projector growing quiet and the sound of the people in the units on either side growing quiet, the traffic outside and the clatter of the ceiling fan and the soft squeak and skitter of the mice nesting in the shredded newspapers around the floor all growing quiet until the only noise in the apartment is the noise inside of Andy's head, the great insistent tidal wave of revelation growing in his brain with an ever deafening fury that swells inside of his ears until he can't take it anymore, and all of that great pressure comes cascading out of him in a single, bitter whisper that is instantly lost to the resumed cacophony of the night.

"Oh, shit."

Andy rises, goes to the kitchen, retrieves a pair of cotton gloves from their plastic bag beneath the sink. Checks them for spots, dust marks, when he is sure they are pristine he returns to the living room and carefully begins the process of unthreading the film. Takes it to his work bench, sets it down, switches on the lamp. Skeletal fingers move across the film, Andy's eyes seeking out the frames he's just watched, the frames he has watched over and over again countless nights like this, studying, taking in every detail, every movement, every expression, watching, but, as he understands now, as he finds the frames and raises his magnifier to them, never truly *seeing*.

She has a birthmark.

Not a pit in the film, not a scratch—his beloved old Cinemeccanica *incapable* of scratching or tearing a print— not the remnants of some errant insect shredded in the grinding wheels of the projector, not a smudge on his glasses or a mote in his eye, but a *birthmark*. There, just above the jawline on her left cheek, visible for only a fraction of a second, here near the end when her head jerks to the side a bit. A birthmark, perhaps the size of a dime, perhaps smaller, not a cut or a contusion or even a large freckle. It is, Andy sees, *sees* for the first time in twelve years, that it is a birthmark.

Andy carefully sets the film down on his workbench, slumps into his chair and places a finger to his neck, looks at his watch. Like all small animals his pulse runs higher than the average human's, usually in the vicinity of ninety or so beats per minute, into the one-twenties when he is excited or threatened, up to one thirty as it is running now, in the wake of this most awesome and powerful of revelations.

She has a birthmark.

After he has secured the film inside of its canister, covered the projector, switched off the light at his workbench, Andy goes and lies down on his cot, checks his watch again. In the gray dusk of his apartment, the hands glow a soothing, ghostly blue. Still time before he has to be at work. He reaches beneath his cot, digs out his gimmick kit, opens it. He has performed the procedure so many times before that he only needs the most minimal of light to do it properly, just enough to hold

the lighter to the tablespoon, fill the syringe, ensure that there are no air bubbles. The track marks on his arms are so dark and clustered now, the veins so marbled beneath his jaundiced flesh, that Andy sometimes feels he can see *them* glowing in the dark too, as bright and sharp and clear as the hands of his watch. He slips the needle into his forearm; depresses the plunger. Once the smack has flooded into his system and he's popped the rubber band off his arm, laid back onto his cot, slipped off his glasses and put them on his chest, he puts a finger to his neck and feels his pulse descending into the sixties. Then he closes his eyes and dreams of her, the face he has seen so many nights for so many years rising up before him out of the darkness. Tonight, he adds a birthmark to her cheek.

RODERICK TILLMAN shifts nervously in his chair and tries to decide how best to position his desk.

What the manager's office at the Colossus Theater offers in coziness it lacks in basic security. There are no windows; no escape exit; the room is too small to offer any good hiding places. There is simply the wall safe, the filing cabinet, Roderick's desk and plush chair and a pair of metal folding seats before it for employees in need of reprimand or praise. So it is that now, as before every meeting with Andy Lew, he must consider what to do with his desk. He can pull it back closer to the rear wall of the office, creating a wider space for Andy to occupy when he comes in, give him more room to move around; create a nice, tight space for himself in the event of an emergency, flip the desk in front of him, barricade into the corner until someone hears his screams. Alternatively, he can push it further towards the door, give himself the space advantage, use his desk as an impromptu battering ram and drive Andy out of the office and into the lobby.

Someone knocks on the door; Roderick bristles. He pushes his desk forward, tugs it back.

Useless either way, really.

"Come in."

The door opens. Andy enters, stoop-shouldered in a denim jacket two sizes too big. One of the hottest years on record and the maniac is dressed like it's North Dakota.

"The fuck you want?" Andy asks. "I actually do shit around here." He slips his hands into his pockets; Roderick tenses, waits for one or both of them to come back out holding something deadly. They stay put.

"The new film's come in," Roderick says. He gestures to the canisters on the floor behind him. "We start showing tomorrow. Trevor will put it on the marquee in the morning."

Andy's mouth twitches beneath the sparse growth of hair that passes for his mustache. Aquiline nostrils flare. Once, years ago, Roderick had found him handsome, when his delicate body and sharp blue eyes had given him the appearance of a cocksure boy on the cusp of manhood. Now, looking at the filthy, sallow, pockmarked *thing* before him, cheeks sunken in, teeth yellowed and gums receding, black hair thinning in strange wisps and patches, horn-rimmed glasses wound together with masking tape, all Roderick can feel is fear tinged with a faint revulsion.

"It's here? Now?"

Roderick nods. "You can screen it tonight. Make sure it's ready... This is a big risk, Andy."

"It isn't a risk," Andy says.

"...a *big* risk that the company didn't want to take. That I had to convince them to take. These are the kind of movies we're trying to stay away from. We *could* have gotten *Other Side of Midnight*. If it weren't for the fact they were also going to force us to show some cheap space movie that would probably push everyone away, I probably..."

"It *isn't* a *risk*," Andy says again, his already shrill voice rising in pitch. Roderick takes the edge of his desk in his hands and gives it a quiet little tug towards himself.

"My point is that I'm taking your advice on this. *Yours.* Trusting *you*, God knows why, that *you* know what you're talking about, and that this is going to turn out a good crowd. My point, Andy, is that this is a desperate move, and if it bombs, it's on you as much as it is on me…So please, Andy…be right about this."

Roderick inhales. Wonders if perhaps he shouldn't have lead with assertive, assumed the role of the penitent from the beginning. Andy stares at Roderick; with the glare of the fluorescent lights on the lenses of his glasses, it looks to Roderick like he's gazing back at a pair of blank television screens, blaring silent static. Roderick waits; waits for the interminable minute that Andy Lew is completely, utterly still before him.

"Have you seen any of it?" Andy whispers.

"I haven't watched it, no."

"You looked at it?"

"I…took a glance, yes."

"And?"

"It's…disgusting," Roderick says.

"Then it's perfect."

Andy draws his hands out of his jacket. There is a moment, a single, suspended moment in time when Roderick sees the flash of silver, the flick of Andy's wrist, and knows that it's finally happening, that after all these years this is finally it, the knife, the gun, whatever he's got tucked away in there coming for him, and then the lid snaps back on Andy's lighter and he's sticking a cigarette clumsily into his mouth and lighting it up and Roderick doesn't relax until he's gone and the door has shut.

ONCE HE has threaded the film into the projector, Andy turns out the lights and settles into his chair. The concept of a screening room at the Colossus is one of his own devising. Once, long before his tenure, projectionists at the movie palaces on 42nd Street would preview the upcoming films on the Thursday night before their premiers, watching them in the Colossus' gargantuan auditorium after the patrons of the last show had gone home with dreams of Brando and Bacall in their heads. That was back when the patrons of the Colossus still wore ties and dresses; before the broken glass pipes and syringes started showing up in the toilets, before the concession stand had a bullet hole above it, before Zarek Baniszewski's girls started bringing their dates to the auditorium for $2 handjobs. Back when all of the lights in the lobby chandelier still worked and before "overdose" entered the ushers' vocabulary. Since the switchover to the current twenty-four hour format, designed to cater to the Colossus' new, more restless clientele, screening prints is ostensibly no longer a part of routine business. Old films go out, new films come in, and they are to be threaded up and exhibited to the public with no prior assessment of quality, the presence of scratches, warped audio, evidence of missing snippets of film pilfered by previous projectionists for their own collections.

Such a policy is, to Andy Lew, tantamount to blasphemy.

It took little convincing for Roderick to allow Andy to repurpose a long disused upstairs storage space and a Super Simplex projector of his own assemblage—cobbled together from spare sound heads and standing bases and film holding magazines—to create his own private screening room. The arrangement suits both men just fine: The enclosed room allows Andy to thoroughly study the sound quality of the films, lets him sit closer to the projected image and better assess it for the smallest of imperfections, the tiniest fragments of dirt to be cleaned from the print.

It gives Roderick more time that he doesn't have to spend around Andy.

Andy switches on the projector, makes himself comfortable, opens a bag of chips, begins eating them. Red and white credits roll over a black screen; the sound of a heart beating pulses on the soundtrack, intermixed with the stale crackle of noise. *Last House on Dead End Street*. Andy has heard stories about the film for months, in the darkest rooms and most secret corners of 42nd Street, where he goes to drink and rest and contemplate the greater matters of his life. No one knows who made it, he has been told; it is the most vile, disgusting piece of garbage ever committed to celluloid; the rough sex in it is real; it contains footage of actual murder; it was produced in Brazil, Venezuela, Zaire, Iran, Moscow, some other freedom-hating Commie hellhole; that the individual credited as the director, Victor Janos, is nothing less than Satan himself.

Naturally, Andy was intrigued.

The film is about a fey plug ugly named Terry Hawkins, who, recently released from prison, decides to vent his impotent rage by seeking vengeance against the world itself. Surrounding himself with a cadre of other poor pathetic sons of bitches and desperate young blondes, he sets about making his own snuff movies, filming the deaths of multiple, seemingly random characters who drift in and out of the film with dreamlike reason.

Andy smirks.

Onscreen, women in negligees and bandit masks frolic in blood; writhing bodies strapped to beds jerk and spasm in their death throes as knives are driven into them again and again, innards pulled from their still moving bodies; a man is forced to his knees as a woman unzips her jeans, tugging a deer's hoof from her fly and forcing it into the man's mouth before a power drill is driven into the back of his skull.

Andy smirks.

When the last reel has dropped and Andy finds himself sitting before the bright, white blank square on the wall, he wads up the bag of chips and rethreads the film. Checks his watch. Steps out of the screening room, walks down the corridor to the projector booth. Reality is pleasantly warped here, the tangerine lights and still air and sound of the film violently clacking, changing what is otherwise just a room into a place of incredible madness and violence. Stepping inside, Andy is comforted that there is another place in the world he can go besides his apartment or his clubs that reminds him of the inside of his own mind, that the ostensible civility of the world has not gotten a foothold everywhere. He likes, in particular, a small, softball sized hole in the wall at just about knee level, right outside the projector booth door. Andy likes that he can hear the Deuce through it, as though the hole is some kind of live wire hooked into a human brain, keeping him privy to all of the electrical discharges and firings across the synapses of 42nd's corroded mind; likes that he can hear the beseeching cries of pimps and the catcalls of young hustlers, the groans of whores and the shrieks of mugging victims, the occasional, euphoric explosion of a really fantastic car crash. Andy kneels beside the hole, runs his fingers over the thin sheet of plastic stapled there to keep out debris; he listens; the Deuce is quiet tonight— what passes for quiet.

Andy rises, moves to the booth window, looks out into the theater, at the film currently playing, the one that will be replaced tomorrow. Another disappointment. When the cue mark appears in the corner, alerting him that the reel is about to run out, he switches on the second projector; the movie continues. Once he's sure that things are running smoothly, he returns to the screening room. Puts on a pair of clean gloves, retrieves *Dead End Street*. Carries it back with him to the projector booth, lays the reel out on his work bench, switches on his fluorescent lamp and retrieves his splicing equipment. He winds the film out and out until he's found the sequence with the deer's hoof. Counts out twenty-four frames; a single second of screen time; virtually unnoticeable. Andy carefully cuts the frames out; winds the length of film into a tight coil and gently masking-tapes the ends together, dropping it into a plastic baggie. Once it's secured safely in his jacket pocket, he splices the film back together, replaces it in its canister. He looks out the booth window, at the film currently playing for the audience, some fat dipshit in a wheelchair getting disemboweled by a chainsaw while his sister screams bloody murder. In the auditorium, warm bodies loll like cold ones in the decaying seats, fading eyes glossed over in the reverie of their pipe dreams.

If the content of *Last House* is any indication of the character of its creators, Andy thinks, they're probably all dead by now, some by their own hands, the rest, most certainly, lined up against the wall and shot in whatever backwater hellhole they called home. Their names will be forgotten even among those who claimed to love them; memories of them will fade like newspaper left to bleach in the sun, and within a generation the only mark they will have left on this blighted world is a brutal, contextless sliver of unadulterated rage, distilled into pure artistry and captured for posterity on celluloid. It will never hang in a museum; never be discussed by a bunch of ghoulish, doughy-faced eggheads on a panel for needy, closet case coeds. The world will continue to venerate images of nude, fat women idling in their complacency and portraiture of dead Jews, and the planet will go on turning, never bold enough to lift the lid off the manhole cover of the world and realize that life doesn't happen on the street, it happens *under* it.

At least Andy can give it the next best thing.

ONCE HE'S left the Colossus, Andy stops at the first phone booth he can find, places a call, jiggles change in his pockets while he waits for someone to pick up. He glances down at his feet; there's a small scuff near the toe of his left cowboy boot. Will have to remember to polish it when he gets home.

Andy hears a click on the other end of the phone, followed instantly by shouts, screams, noise that might be music if the stereo were turned down a few decibels. Somehow, a groggy voice cuts through the din: "What?"

"Gator around?"

"Ain't no Gator here, man."

"It's Andy."

"Andy-man?"

"We need to talk. I just got off. Usual place?"

"Hey, Andy-man, I've got something going here…"

Somewhere beneath the noise, Andy can hear a woman's strained voice call out from Gator's end of the phone:

"Hey, baby, when you gonna come over here and fuck me, honey?"

Gator sighs. "You hear? *Busy*, Andy. Can't just drop my shit…"

"Hey. Gator. Come on. It's big."

"Maybe, like, tomorrow night?" Gator sounds as though he's asking himself the question as much as he is Andy.

"I saw something new," Andy says. He looks around; though the booth is sufficiently insulated against outside noise, he feels the creeping suspicion, as he often does when discussing these matters, profoundly watched.

"What, like, a new movie, man? "

"No," Andy says. "I saw something new…in *the* movie."

"*The* movie?"

A pause. On Gator's end, the noise momentarily cuts out and then renews as someone restarts the record.

"Fuck," Gator says.

"Tonight," Andy says.

"All right. Just give me like, thirty minutes, an hour. I've got to, like, come up with something to tell Sheila. You still be there?"

"Not going anywhere else," Andy says. He hangs up the phone, steps out of the booth, starts walking. Even at this hour the sidewalks of 42nd Street are so jammed full of human life, the street so congested with traffic, that movement at one's own pace is a near impossibility. Stepping into the crowd is like getting onto an escalator, the pace set, direction determined. Andy lets the sea carry him, drifting on a wave of tangled, sweaty limbs, irradiated beneath the yellow and crimson red neon signs like some great luminous beast from the deep sea, suspended in liquid blackness and waiting for its prey.

As he moves towards the subway, down into the dank, subterranean heart of the city, as he hops the turnstile, boards the train, Andy contemplates the information he has available to him thus far. Though it is easier in the presence of the film to meditate upon certain metaphysical particulars, when he is away from it, out in the world, especially on the subway, moving with electricity beneath him and the comforting, close smell of the car, he can make the necessary divorce from raw emotion and focus on the hard evidence. Though the birthmark is an exciting development, it is also potentially the kind of tail-chasing that has made the project difficult for so long. He once spent a year attempting to determine the girl's ethnicity, before realizing that identifying a single, blonde-haired woman would be virtually impossible, regardless of her ethnic origins. He must remember that, though the concept is counter-intuitive, it is information about things *other* than the girl that will yield the most about her.

The chair, for example.

Andy was able to identify it as a model offered by the Sanderson-Westville company, sold in their quarterly sales catalogs from January 1957 to April of 1959. It is precisely four feet high. Based upon this, Andy was able to determine that the girl is roughly five foot three to five foot three and three quarters, making exceptions for certain peculiarities of the film and her positioning on screen. Further, he was able to determine that the man is about five foot five; Andy is yet to identify the type of shoes he is wearing, and therefore unable to say for certain how thick the soles are. Andy likes to think that the soles are one inch thick, like those of his own boots. That would place the man at Andy's precise height.

Andy likes to think that there are many similarities between himself and the man in the film.

Andy is certain that the man in the film is also the director. His heart swells at the idea *he* could both make and star in something like that; that out there, someone very much like himself *has*. He wonders if the man and the woman spoke at all during the shoot; what they discussed; what intimate words were exchanged.

And now he's going off on a tangent again. Facts. Facts.

The film was made between 1957 and 1965, the year Andy obtained it.

The 35mm gauge, combined with the relative absence of shadow, indicates an individual with access to professional equipment and lighting.

The shadows which *are* present, relative to the height of the individuals in the film and that of the chair, indicate that the lighting implements which were used had to have been about six feet tall at most.

She has a birthmark.

Andy slips off the subway, ascends the stairs, back onto the street. It isn't much longer before he's slipping down another flight of steps, steep and narrow, into a concrete trench barely lit by a flickering blue sign reading "LAST CHANCE." The interior of the club is dark, noisy, and brutal; a smoky, unlit, cinder-block corridor barrels towards a cramped space full of writhing bodies made black by the deficit of light, the only illumination coming from the pale cobalt blue floodlights mounted above the bar. Andy pushes his way through the dancers, through rusty chains dangling from exposed rafters like doorway beads, over a bare concrete floor littered with broken glass and old safety pins and discarded needles and gauges, pauses to salute the tattered American flag hanging in the corner before he finds an empty spool table and sits down. The music here is almost as incomprehensible as that coming over Gator's phone, loud and pulsating and shaking the very foundations of the room, the lyrics little more than slurred profanities and angry, manic chants screamed into the microphone as the singer jams it into his uvula, the words pure, distilled rage, honest rawness from the blackest pits of this young man's soul, not the synthetic disco shit that's taken over the air.

For the first time this evening, Andy really feels himself really relax.

A girl in a leather halter top approaches him, a row of safety pins in place of either eyebrow. She leans down to ask him something; Andy feels himself reaching for his zipper, thinks better of it, sees she's not that sort of girl. Lets her take his drink order. Checks his watch. Still some time before he can expect Gator. True, what he said— nowhere else to go this evening. Might as well enjoy the show.

Andy is well into his fifth whiskey of the night when one of the black shapes on the dance floor breaks away from the crowd and descends into a lawn chair at Andy's table. Andy squints against the light. The man at his table is wearing a shredded tank top, decaying jeans, plenty of piercings, battered Elvis sunglasses, the sides of his head shaved to the scalp and what's left in the middle slicked back flat against his skull with either sweat or gel or some foul combination of human fluids. To the untrained eye, in the dark lit corridors and basements and warrens that Gator frequents, he looks to be another one of these kids playing dress up with their parents' nightmares. To Andy…

"Your sergeant know you're here?" Andy asks. "Captain? Lieutenant? Whatever the fuck your chain of command is?"

"Son of a bitch, Andy-man, the hell are you doing?"

"These freaks can smell a cop two blocks away, even through their own shit. They just don't give a damn. They know you're even more fucked up than they could ever dream of."

"Whatever, Andy-man. This is a risk, me coming to see you, in public. Always is."

"What risk? You got any other jackoffs on the force willing to come into places like this? I know any asshole who wants to put on that uniform got fucked as a kid, you're the only one I know who liked it."

"Now that there is inappropriate speech. You better have some good shit, Lewinski."

Andy bristles at the sound of his proper name. "She has a birthmark," he says.

"Bullshit. I been over that thing a dozen times."

Andy flips his glass upside down and claps it on the table. "On her jaw. Visible for precisely three frames. An eighth of a second. It's there. I checked it. I double checked it. It's *there*."

"Oh, Hell." Gator sits back; his eyes, wide and vacant in their relaxed state, bulge even more so that it looks like someone has just hooked a live wire up to him.

"Pictures," Andy says. "I'll need pictures."

"I want to see," Gator says.

"That's a big risk, bringing you to my apartment," Andy sneers.

"Bigger risk than you never finding out your dream girl's name?"

Andy stares back. "I can find her without you."

"That why you call me up? You want to meet me to let me know you don't need my help?"

Andy sits back, sighs, crosses his arms. "Shoulda let you take me in."

"You wouldn't have survived Rikers."

"Standing on my head," Andy says.

"That's exactly where they would've had you, sweet thing, once they found out how much you like showing what you got." Gator smiles; ought to grow a mustache, Andy thinks. Needs to cover up the buck teeth, balance out his face, offset the weak chin.

"Fuck you," Andy says.

"No, fuck you, Andy-man. Matter of fact, last time I saw him, those were Dick Valentine's exact words: 'Fuck Andy Lew.'"

"Why the hell is Dick Valentine talking about me?"

"Well, funny thing, you know, while we're on the subject of missing persons. Dick, you know old Dick, knows I picked you up, knows you went informant for me…"

Andy squirms; Gator rolls his eyes.

"…*thinks* you went informant for me. He says, 'hey, Andy Lew, he still one of yours?' I tell him sure, man, why not. Dick says, 'maybe you need to find someone else to rat out pipe heads, I don't think Andy's gonna be walking Forty Deuce much longer.' I ask him, well, why'd you say a thing like that? Dick, he says, 'well, you know Andy's brother?'"

Andy Lew goes rigid. Instinctually, he reaches for his glass, finds it empty; squeezes it.

"Yeah?" Andy says.

"Well, I say to ol' Dick, sure, I know Andy's brother, never met him but I heard of him. Dick, he says, 'well, you know he's a missing person?'

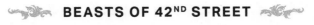
I say sure, Dick, might've heard that once or twice. Dick, he says, 'well, Steven Lew ain't no missing person no more.'"

"And?" Andy says. For the first time in the heatwave that has gripped the city, he begins to sweat.

"And now I want to see her," Gator says.

"LEMME ASK you something," Gator says, he and Andy slipping into the apartment, Andy hurriedly locking the door behind them, securing the deadbolt, each of the chain locks, the rim lock. "Personal question, if I may, don't gotta answer it, but on average, let's say monthly, how many things die in here? I'm talking rats, mice, whatever little things you pick up at pet shops to strangle in the bathtub or whatever it is you do when you're not working, what's the body count of this place look like?"

"The fuck do I know what dies in my walls?" Andy says. "I'm not eating any of it. Sit down."

Gator moves to take a seat on a plastic covered recliner; stops to admire a photo ripped from a magazine and nailed to the wall.

"This one new?"

"A few weeks," Andy says.

Gator whistles. "Oh, she's a real looker, now ain't she? Partial to redheads myself."

"Sit down," Andy says, uncovers the projector. He kneels beside his cot; beneath, a dozen film canisters sit crammed together, collecting rust and debris around their fluted edges. Only a single canister, meticulously polished, shines from inside of a clear plastic bag, the mouth secured with a rubber band. Andy retrieves the film; puts on his gloves, threads the projector.

"You got anything for me?" Andy asks.

"Aw, almost forgot. You enjoy this batch now, Andy-man, had to work extra hard for it. Just about got my nose bit right off while I was slapping the cuffs on." Gator reaches into his pants, comes out with a baggie of smack. Dangles it in the air for a tantalizing moment while Andy rifles in his jeans, brings out the cash. They make the switch off quickly, like a pair of cartoon villains each suspecting the other of treachery. Andy takes just long enough to inspect the baggie before stuffing it into his jacket. Then, he switches on the projector.

Once the movie has begun, he settles onto his cot, as far away from Gator as the room allows. Hates watching with Gator; hates that life circumstance forced him to share her rather than be separated from her. When Gator is watching her, Andy cannot watch her: he must be watching Gator. Does not want to; feels compelled; cannot move his eyes off of Gator's damp face glistening in anticipation as the numbers tick down; the twitch of glee when she appears on screen; the way that Gator writhes and twists in his seat, unable to keep himself still as she plays out her scene, each moment of her, every recorded memory reflected on the surface of Gator's filthy, hungry eyes; the way that he cranes forward near the end, knowing, as Andy does, the exact second of the money shot, stretching his torso and his shoulders and his neck as though his ass is glued in place; the way that, at the moment of the money shot, Gator lets out— always lets out— a long, low animal moan and collapses back into his chair, his body lax, collapses at the same time she collapses, spent, the part that Andy can stand the least, the way he mimics her, as though he's in the room with her, away from Andy, in some secret place together.

Andy rises, switches on the light.

"There. You saw it. Now tell me about Dick."

"Now, Andy, man, I don't think I seen that birthmark you been talking so much about tonight. Think you're gonna have to run it by me again."

"If you didn't see it then, you never will." Maybe she doesn't want you to see it, Andy thinks— something special, secret, that she's kept only for him.

"All right, all right. So maybe I did see it. Right about here?" Gator touches a finger to the exact spot on his own jaw. Lying bastard.

"Right there," Andy says. Gator should not have that spot on his jaw. Does not deserve to have that spot on his jaw, like her; should have nothing in common with her. Andy thinks about the straight razor in his bathroom; shaved this morning; it's still drying on the sink, the blade freshly polished, glistening and ready; could very easily remove that spot from Gator's facer without much difficulty, just sneak up behind him while he's seated and whisk it off.

"So it's there," Gator says. He bobs his head slowly, jaw slack, his tongue lolling around thoughtfully. "I'll start digging around. It's a nice piece of information. Good, strong identifying mark. Narrows the field."

"You'll bring me pictures?" Andy asks, tries not to let any hope slip into his voice.

"I'll try. I'll try. Gotta stay incognito, you know."

"I need pictures," Andy says. Gator looks around the room, at the collages and pinups littering the walls.

"Looks like you got plenty already, honey."

"Of *her*."

Gator smiles. Andy stares back. After a moment:

"And now my brother."

Gator smiles. "Right, right, right. What ol' Dickie's been talking about."

"You said they found him," Andy says.

"Aw, no, Andy-man, that ain't what I said. Ain't what I said at all, sir, that ain't gonna hold up in court at all. What I said was, he ain't missing no more."

"So they found him," Andy says.

"They found his *head*."

A moment passes. Andy reaches out and places his hand on the projector, on her; draws strength.

"Oh, now, Andy-man, no need to put the show on for me. I know the two of you weren't, uh, particularly close, what with you not giving two fucks where he's been for twelve years. Understand me, I completely sympathize. Little sister gone run off with the only kike in Beaumont back in '62, had the nerve to bring him to Thanksgiving. I haven't been back home since."

Andy takes a breath. He would like, very much, for Gator to be on his own Thanksgiving table, stuffed, beheaded, legs fried nice and crisp and sticking straight up in the air, waiting to be ripped from his torso and dipped in gravy. For the five years he's known him, Andy has made it a habit of not trusting Gator Hyatt very much. Theirs is a relationship of convenience; Andy, as a general principle, dislikes people, cops less. He takes much of what Gator says the same way he would consider the words coming out of a child's mouth: with great consternation and an urge to kill the source of the noise. If, in fact, Steven Lewinski has seen fit to come back into his life, Andy thinks, he really ought to have been one of the first to know. Been notified as next of kin; brought down to the morgue to make an identification. It could mean, of course, that this is a joke; that he's trying to get a rise out of him; that he is using another person's great tragedy as a source of personal amusement, as Gator finds most hilarious in life.

This is what Andy would prefer to think.

If he is wrong, though…if this is a situation in which Gator can be trusted, there are multiple considerations.

It means that Steven Lewinski has gone from missing person to murder victim.

It means that someone does not want Andy Lew to know this.

It means that *HE* has stuck his head out of his hole again.

"Where did they find him?" Andy asks.

"Some freak in Queens. Stopped showing up to work, neighbor called in a routine wellness check. Routine except for the whole severed head, you know. Don't have many details myself, but, uh, Peterson, now Peterson says that when they found him, he was in his tighty whities, had the windows blocked out with aluminum foil, dancing around…" Gator stops, cracks a bigger grin, stifles a laugh. "…dancin' around the head. Had it mounted on top of a coat rack."

Andy nods slowly. Somehow, this seems appropriate. "You got any names?"

"Nothing in particular yet, no."

"Draft?"

"Hmmm?"

"Has anyone said the name 'Draft'?"

For the first time this evening, Gator's face drops, and Andy is able to see the vestiges of the real cop that still lay dormant inside of him.

"Well, now why would you ask that?"

"Curious. If it popped up."

"I read your brother's case file," Gator says. "Name 'Draft' isn't anywhere in it. Not a known associate, not a person of interest, not that Ludo fella you said he was queer for. So, I gotta ask again, Andy-man, why you asking about a name that ain't in the case file, 'less you got something certain parties may want to know? You know me, there's particular indulgences I don't begrudge a man, but I also got lines I gotta walk in regards to who I let stay free in the world, you know what I mean?"

Andy shrugs. "Guy I used to score from back in the day…He was with me, the last time I saw Steven. Knew he wasn't involved. Wasn't gonna squeal, get anybody onto him." Andy stands, goes to the refrigerator, retrieves a full beer bottle from among the empties. Some form of rodent scurries over the toes of his boots. He returns to his cot, sits. Gator's face has regained its veneer of gleeful self-satisfaction.

"Dick is going to try and lay this on me," Andy says.

"In all likelihood," Gator says. "Dickie always has had a soft spot for you."

"I'm going to need some cash," Andy says, not sure if he's asking a question or making a statement.

"Bus ticket ain't too bad, even with the gas being what it is. Got a paycheck coming anytime soon?"

"I'm thinking one-way bus ticket, with luggage," Andy says. "Relocation."

Gator clicks his tongue. "Now that's a bit more difficult."

"I can always go back to…you know. I mean…You know anyone who needs anything?" Andy leans forward, lowers his voice, as though the world is listening. "You know…any *guys*, uh, who need…*something*?"

"The way you look now? Sure, maybe in a lights-off situation, but lights-on is what's gonna get you the bread you're looking for." Gator leans back, contemplates. Andy watches his eyes, the thousand thoughts racing through his mind. "You still working on your, what do you call 'em, little art projects?"

To the extent that Andy Lew can, he perks up. "Working on one right now." He reaches into his jacket, retrieves the roll of film. "From tomorrow's premier."

"Ever thought about selling?"

"Selling?"

"Awright, you remember Nicky Blayze?"

"The porno star?" Andy asks. "Yeah. Used to watch his reels. What about him?"

"I met him, man."

"Bullshit. He died of gay cancer in '75."

"Vicious rumor, man, vicious rumor. Pissed off all the wrong people, they needed to end his career. But get this: last month, I'm bustin' this broad, I'm giving her the usual spiel, you help me, I help you, and she tells me, 'If you like to fuck, baby, I can take you to a *real* party.' Well, I figure I'm getting pulled into something, that some pimp's gonna try to bash my brains out, so I think, why not? Could use some target practice. Next thing I know I'm in a loft in Union Square, and it is wall to wall freak, OK? I mean I am talking tattoos head to toe, black leather far as the eye can see, some guy in a beret setting his guitar on fire, chanting Latin or some shit. And there in the middle of it all, the man himself."

"So you fucked with a porno star. This pertains to me how?"

"I'm getting there, all right? So, I tell him I'm a fan, he says he loves the look, invites me to sit around, talk with him. I mean, *really*

talk. And things get real serious, you know? Like we're all passing the bowl, Nicky's tellin' us about art and culture and shit, how that's what he's been focusing on now, right?" Gator's voice takes on a wistful tone Andy is unused to hearing. He looks towards the ceiling, as though deep in contemplation over some profound matter. "He's a wise man. Tells us how he spent his life developing the physical, now he wants to develop the intellectual. Real deep, philosophical stuff, right? Told us about the Buddha, the I Ching, the Prophet. And he talks about how all this, the freaks, the loft, it's all about expanding his horizons, making himself the perfect being. Andy, I'm not ashamed to tell you, it was one of the most beautiful experiences of my life. Sittin' there, sun coming up over the city, talkin' about Picasso, snorting a line. Helluva night."

"*Me,*" Andy says.

"*So* he's some kind of weirdo art freak, right? Got a lot of money? What do weirdo art freaks do, Andy? They buy weirdo freak art."

"You think he would? Do *not* fuck with me, Gator."

"I can ask. Meant to stop by tomorrow. He's holding some kinda soiree, real sophisticated stuff, Peking duck, artichoke hearts, some kinda dessert only takes up the middle of the plate. I'll, uh, make sure to bring you up."

"You're a classic gentleman," Andy says. "And I'm getting tired." He gestures towards the door.

"Until the next time," Gator says, rises.

"Remember," Andy says.

"I'll ask," Gator says.

"I meant the photos," Andy says. "*Her.*"

"Naturally, Andy-man. And, hey…thanks for the show. A good way to kill a night." Gator slaps him on the back, moves to leave. "Really need to head out now anyway, sweet thing. Colored boys ain't gonna kill themselves. Well, guess they will, but won't hurt to give them a hand, now will it?" Gator makes finger guns, fires at Andy. "*Boom, boom.*"

Andy stares. Gator lets himself out; the moment the door is shut behind him, Andy scrambles for it, locks it. Sinks to the floor and sighs. *Alone.* At last, Andy is alone again, Gator's stench thankfully blended away into the natural musk of the apartment.

Alone, with her.

Andy rethreads the film, strips to his briefs, sits on his cot. He must watch her again; remove the taint left by Gator's drooling and leering and the thought of Steven's—

Andy runs his hands through what's left of his hair, is completely unphased when a small tuft comes out. He has to stop. Can't think of Gator right now; can't think of him, or Steven, or Dick Valentine; can't allow a single moment with her to be spoiled.

He presses play on the projector, and there she is. These are the moments Andy lives for: just getting to spend time with her, not doing anything particularly special, just enjoying the pleasure of her company; sometimes, as now, in stark silence; other times with the television on, Andy's head pressed to the stopped projector, not looking at her, but simply knowing she's there; listening to their song...

Andy stops the projector and goes to the record player. His collection is small and specific; before the punks came on the scene and gave musical voice to his rage, Andy had no real affinity for music, excepting a brief flirtation with jazz in his youth. Even still, there are few records he cares to own and indulge in on a regular basis. There is one in particular, though, which holds a place of reverence, the sleeve neatly wrapped in cellophane: *their song.* He'd heard it initially on the little stereo he keeps in the booth in order to pipe music into the auditorium between double features, tuned forever, by management decree and completely against his own will, to what they're calling *easy listening* these days. Andy has managed, for the most part, to block these noises out of his head; but on this particular occasion, while preparing *The Candy Snatchers* to play, a lyric had broken through his mental wall, a melancholy voice speaking of his love for a golden-haired girl who finds him neglectful. Andy had sat enraptured

despite himself, the soft guitar plucking and tambourines suddenly as gently melodic to him as the shrieking of an electric guitar or the explosion of drumsticks on cymbals. All he had seen in his mind was her, alive to him in a way she had never been before, and when he had gone out and purchased the album, brought it home, played it for her, he had seen why, that the song was perfect, that its rhythms are her rhythms, the slower parts of the song synching exactly with the parts of the film when her body is still and the man's movements careful and determined, speeding up as she begins to move herself, the final crescendo of the song coinciding perfectly with the final barrage of thrusts leading up the money shot, her body collapsing at the exact moment the song ceases. Since that first time, it has been Andy's custom, on special occasions, to play the song for her; for them; to stand swaying beside her, his hands on the projector, remembering their good times. The night that he first saw her; the night she came to live with him for good; the night of the blackout, so many years ago, when he had taken her to work with him, the two of them huddled together in the projector booth as the whole of New York went dark, and he had waited out the pitch black with her, shining a flashlight against her, knowing that if he emerged from the booth and found the world in ruin, only the two of them left, it would only be too perfect.

Andy drops the needle onto the record; "Sister Golden Hair" starts up. He sighs, returns to the projector. This might be one of the final nights they spend in this apartment, in this state. He wants to think about the good times now; everything they've done here together in this place he's occupied for nearly two decades now; their first home together. Andy switches the projector back on; there she is again, here, with him, just him, only him. Though the film is in black and white, Andy has been able to determine— by comparing the film stock to other motion pictures for which there exist color photos from the set— that her hair is the same blonde as Gene Tierney's in *Laura*, her eyes the same greyish shade as Clark Gable's in *Gone with the Wind*. Though her mouth is obscured, Andy imagines that it is small and delicate with little downturned corners that compliments the roundness of her cheeks. Her chiton both emphasizes and hides the contours of her body; it is cinched around the abdomen, displaying her narrow waist, but the bust is too loose for Andy to readily determine her endowment. Her shoulders are narrow but toned and speak to a power in the upper body that makes Andy whimper in desperate surrender. Andy wonders what thought went into the selection of the theme; is she meant to be Andromeda, Danae, Iphigenia? Or was there no specific myth being played out, the chiton chosen simply for its unspoken erotic elements? The man's costume, all chainmail and leather and, Andy believes, perhaps even nylon, certainly doesn't fit any ancient narrative. Did the director decide upon the story himself? Was it a commission?

A commission. A commission brought the film to him in the first place; brought her to him. A commission will make sure they stay together.

"Don't worry," Andy says. "I'm going to take care of it." He runs his hand tenderly over the projector case, rests his head against it.

"We'll never be apart. Never."

"IT'S...A REALLY good crowd," Roderick says, looking down onto the auditorium from the booth window. Beside him, Andy tinkers with the projector, runs last minute checks. Wants to make sure this runs smoothly; immortalize the moment in his mind. In a few minutes, *Last House on Dead End Street* will run for the first time on 42nd; a small sliver of the brutality that composes the inner life of Andy Lew will be blown up to mega-sized proportions and projected onto a screen for all of the world to see, and he will be the man running it, as though the film is pouring directly out of his own brain.

"They've heard the stories," Andy says. "Everyone wants to see if they're true or not."

"You screened it, right?" Roderick asks.

"Yeah."

"And?"

"And what?" Andy snaps around so violently that Roderick nearly loses his balance stepping away.

"And...are they true?" Roderick whispers meekly. "About...how bad it is?"

Andy smirks, leans in close to Roderick, cranes his head up so that their faces are inches apart. In spite of himself, Roderick feels butterflies in his stomach.

"It's awful," Andy hisses. He pulls back and returns to the projector.

A shudder runs through Roderick, feels like it comes from the groin but really knows that it's someplace deeper inside than that, somewhere situated in the bowels, the place where real gut dread lives. There's been a dark anticipation of this moment all day, the tug between disgust at show-casing such a monstrosity and the prospect of a really fantastic payoff, a full house and the food and drinks flowing like in the old days, when more people purchased from the concession stand than robbed it. What comes next, though, he hasn't looked forward to at all; has considered not saying anything; but through the layers of terror and loathing and curious disgust something resembling sentimentality still lingers for Andy Lew, and so Roderick thinks, really, that Andy ought to hear this from him.

"Hey, Andy... Have you listened to the radio at all today?"

"Barely."

"You...haven't heard the news?"

"Why, did someone die?"

"...yeah."

Andy's eyebrows go up. "Oh yeah?"

"Andy...I'm sorry to have to be the one to tell you. Michael Findlay died today."

Andy's eyebrows twitch just a little higher and then descend. Roderick looks for some trace of grief there; something human.

"I'm sorry," Roderick says.

"How'd it happen?"

Roderick bites his lower lip; had really hoped Andy wouldn't ask that.

"He was taking the helicopter shuttle from the roof of the Pan Am. Freak accident. The propeller broke off and cut through the cockpit. It... killed some people on the ground, too. Findlay..."

Andy, his face, Roderick thinks, almost hopeful, draws his thumb across his throat. Roderick nods. Andy whistles.

"I...wanted you to hear it from me," Roderick says. "I know his movies meant a lot to you."

Andy stares into some far away space, lost in reverie. "Mike Findlay made us what we are."

"I've never really gotten it," Roderick says.

"That doesn't surprise me. Gotten what exactly?"

"The movies we show," Roderick says. "I mean, I liked *Night of the Living Dead, Psycho*...I got that. They were weird and scary and they gave you the blood and guts and, I guess, tits...But...What we've been showing lately...The past five years...How...*sick* it's all gotten...The rape. Hurting women. Torturing them. How nasty...Not like, fun, play violence, but, how *real* it is...*Why*?"

"Why what?" Andy asks. The phrase "*fun, play violence*" is still echoing in his head like a stone trapped in a tin can, getting more aggressive the longer it remains trapped. What does Roderick consider "fun violence?" What brutalities could Andy subject him to, what dismemberments and vivisections and amputations, before Roderick no longer considers it "*fun?*" Andy sits back in his folding chair, kicks the front legs up off the ground and leans against the wall. "Why what, Rod-Rod? And why are you asking me?"

"Why do people like these things?" Roderick says. "Why do *you*?"

"You mean instead of some Lon Chaney, Dracula, Wolfman bullshit? Monsters from the deep, ghosts, killers in black coats running around haunted mansions? Why does the shit we play draw a bigger crowd than all of that, is that what you're asking?"

"Yeah," Roderick says.

"Because it's real," Andy says. "And I only truck with what's real."
Andy checks his watch, turns to the projector, and flips it on.

"Showtime."

AS THE elevator doors open, Andy straightens the lapels of his suit. He
wonders if the beige, three-piece windowpane was the correct choice.
He spent nearly two hours standing before his closet this morning, sort-
ing through the plastic dry cleaning bags again and again, trying to
determine what would be the proper outfit. He had initially considered
his blue birds' eye or his gray pinstripe; this, after all, being a business
meeting. Then it had occurred to him that, while his purpose here *is*
to make a business transaction, it would behoove him more to present
himself as an artist; and that, after all, the meeting is to take place
concurrently with an informal gathering. His mind had turned then
to the browns in his wardrobe. Despite the idiom, he has always found
the color an appropriate choice for in-town gatherings of a more casual
nature, or for those situations in which one wishes to present himself as
having a greater personal ease and natural charisma; blue and gray, he
feels, demand power, while brown subtly encourages it. The tan, he'd
decided at the last minute, in a frenetic rush to make it on time, is close
enough to the color of sports jackets that have become fashionable in
recent years. It recalls the casual while presenting the formal; the addition of the vest adds a hint of the stylish, showing that he isn't above
making slight, subtle modifications to keep up with the times while still
maintaining a classic aesthetic.

Andy steps out of the elevator; hard to imagine Gator in a place
like this, in his leather and chains, on the top floor of some fantastic
apartment building with ankle-deep carpets and a rubber plant in every
corner and a muzak version of *Summer Samba* on an eternal loop on the

building's sound system. He double checks the address on the card Gator gave him, looks for the apartment number.

He should've gone with the brown glen plaid. He just knows it.

At the apartment door, Andy straightens his tie—rust-colored, knit, four-in-hand knot, of course—and knocks, trying to retain a secure grip on the film canister beneath his arm. Though he has been working on his art projects for as long as he has been at the Colossus, he has always conceived of them as private endeavors—meant for his own consumption and to entertain company, on the rare occasions he has ever had any company he cared to keep entertained. Standing here now, a faint glimmer of something rises up in him. Though his intention tonight is to secure enough funds to leave the city, perhaps there is a future for him in today's brave new art scene; perhaps the world will look upon his creations not with disgust but awe, drop to their collective knees and commit ritual *seppuku* in reverence of the power of his art. Perhaps they will one day look on him as he has always looked on the man in the film.

The door swings open to the sound of a sustained, metallic screech from inside of the apartment. Before Andy there stands a man the size of a soda machine, his shirtless torso bulging with muscles on top of muscles. He stares down at Andy with a pleasant, blank look on his face. Andy sees that one of the man's swollen, bouncing pectorals is tattooed with a massive orange swastika.

"Yeah?" The man smiles giddily.

"I'm here to see Nicky." Andy hands the man the card given to him by Gator, containing the apartment's address and, on the back scrawled in blue ink, "Nicky Blayze cordially requests the pleasure of Mr. Andy Lew's company!"

The man takes the card, studies it. His grin widens. "Are you wearing a selection from the Summer 1976 Phoenix Clothier's Catalog?"

"Yeah," Andy says. "So?"

"Most men with your complexion would've gone for the slate blue. Couldn't resist the rust, myself." The man steps fully into the hallway,

and Andy sees that he is wearing a pair of pants identical to his own, save the deep, ruddy color. He extends a gigantic hand towards Andy. "Chad Montgomery. I think we're gonna get along just fine." He slaps the swastika tattoo on his chest. "Let me ask, you down with the Buddha?"

"God is dead," Andy says, and steps inside.

Even after all his years ensconced in the projection booth and the dim, pitiful lighting of his own apartment, he's unprepared for how *black* it is. Black paisley wallpaper lines the place, buttressed by black lacquered wainscoting descending down into black shag carpet that itself slopes into a sunken living room adorned by a massive cracked black leather couch. With only sparsely placed, red-bulbed track lighting casting occasional spotlights down onto the floor, and the bodies illuminated in them, some intertwined and writhing, others prone or supine and stationary, more still—particularly those on the couch—sitting idly and dully passing around the mouthpiece of a gigantic hookah that towers above them, spewing pale smoke, the overall effect is not that of a complete living space but a series of desolate plains suspended in an infinite void, populated by a degraded lifeform on its last legs before extinction. Presiding over it all, on a black lacquered stage nearly touching the ceiling, a spindly, long-haired freak in a ruffled shirt and wire-rimmed sunglasses pounds out the same six notes on an electric guitar over and over again, a rhythmic cycling of noise, meditative in its repetition, tuneless and discordant but insistent all the same, hypnotizing the crowd, providing them a soundtrack for their cosmopolitan debauchery. Beside him stands another longhair, somehow even thinner than the first, his anorexic frame emphasized by his nudity, rocking quietly on his heels, hands raised high above his head, gripping a mesh-wrapped candle. Periodically, as the music continues, the dumbass with the candle tilts it down towards his own head, allowing wax to drip into his hair, onto his face, down his sparsely haired chest, restrained little shrieks of agony rising up out of the base of his throat like the strangled pleas of an asphyxiation victim. There is no response from the crowd, no applause or gasps or cries of encouragement: the atmosphere of the whole place, it seems to Andy, is like a funeral service for someone especially loathed, the family and alleged friends of the deceased gathered together out of duty rather than a sense of loss, and, having congregated to pay their obliged respects, have given themselves over to something more entertaining for the duration of the ceremony, going through the motions of drinking or fucking not because they derive any joy from the activity but because it beats the alternative.

Andy bites the inside of his own mouth; he sees, in his mind's eye, the boys' spectacular and blood-soaked deaths, strapped writhing to an altar as a man with a goatee raises a bejeweled dagger in the air. He hears the crack as the blade penetrates their breastbones...

"This way. Nicky's waiting for you," Chad says, grins, slaps Andy on the back, too hard. Andy winces. One of Chad's giant hands grips him by the shoulder, begins leading him deeper into the apartment. As they pass the stage, Andy glances up at the duo, the guitarist casting his own gaze down at him, never missing a beat as his head turns and he looks over the rims of his sunglasses and their eyes meet, and a look of recognition passes between them, like this is their hundredth meeting, their thousandth, as though they have come together and clawed at each other's eyes and torn at one another's tongues again and again and collapsed bloody and exhausted on top of one another on mountainsides and beaches and in city streets all throughout history, and it's not Nicky that Andy is here to meet, but him, to kill and kill and die and die again and live out whatever fantastic nightmares they've been experiencing throughout the ages.

"Andy-man!" Gator's voice cuts through the noise of the guitar. Andy looks around, sees Gator reclining in a lounge chair, watching the stage show.

"What do you think? Thing I love about this place," Gator says, gesturing around them, "Got all types here, Andy, uh all types. It's a real Ellis Island. Take Chad here, I see you already met Chad. Chad's a bodybuilder, like those fellas in the movie with the Austrian boy. Keeps an eye on the door, makes sure no unwanted elements get in. Hey, Chad, do that thing for Andy, that, uh, thing you do, with, the, uh, you know..."

Chad nods, strikes a most muscular pose, and in an Austrian accent barely audible beneath the noise, says, "Franco is a child." Gator cracks up.

"Aw, hell, I never get tired of that, let me tell you."

"This isn't a social call," Andy says. Beside him, Chad continues to strike poses, muscles rippling and bulging as he transitions smoothly from a double biceps shot into a crab.

"Sure, sure, of course not. Let's go ahead and see about making you a star."

Andy trails behind Gator to a darkened corner of the living room, drifting down an elongated, unlit hallway, placing his hand to the wall and shuffling his boots along the carpet to keep pace, an eternity passing, it seems, before they enter a red lit chamber, more black, black walls, black sheets on the king sized bed tucked away in the corner of the endless room, shapeless forms writhing on it in the half-dark. Above it all, perched in a director's chair, his expression bored, tired, contemptuous, the simian form of Nicky Blayze, gone to pot in middle age, shirtless and barefoot, clad only in a leather vest and matching pants, arms longer than his tucked-in legs, staring vacant-eyed at the bed, puffing disinterestedly on a fetid smelling black cigarette.

"Hey there, Nicky-o," Gator says, grins wide, reaches out a hand; Nicky raises a finger to his lips, shushing him, never taking his eyes off the bed. Silence permeates the room, the dipshit on the stage having either put down his guitar or this chamber too sequestered for the music to reach this far. There is virtually no sound in here, no rustling of the bedsheets, no moans of pain or pleasure coming from the forms they all watch continuing to move on the bed, hypnotic in their liquidity, rolling and shifting with such fluid motion that Andy wonders if there are any bones left in the things beneath the sheets at all.

"Andy Lew," Nicky says, his voice sandpaper. "Gator's been telling me about you. You come here to *fuck*, Andy? Gonna have to get in line to do that." A rasping, joyless chuckle escapes Nicky's throat and he takes another puff of his cigarette, eyes still fixed on the show unfolding on the bed. Andy tenses, grinds his teeth, says nothing; doesn't want to blow whatever potential opportunity awaits him here.

"Kidding," Nicky says after a moment. He casually flicks his cigarette at the bed; it lands, triggering a soft shriek. The forms briefly pause as they fumble at the smoldering butt, one or the other putting it out before they resume their coupling. Nicky chuckles again, retrieves another cigarette from inside his vest, lights up. "You see a line right now? But if you want to fuck, you've got to pay. Nicky Blayze is only gay for pay. Gator tells me we've got that in common."

"I'm not here to talk about your sex life," Andy says. "I'm here"

"You're here to talk about whatever the fuck I want to talk about," Nicky snaps. "When *I'm* ready to talk. For now…we watch."

Andy opens his mouth to make a protestation, that he hasn't been summoned here to play games, that, regardless of what his pay stubs may say, his time is more valuable than this. Before he can speak, the room is lit up with a bright, white flash, Andy momentarily blinded, seeing, as the spots fade from his eyes, the dumbass with the guitar standing before him, clutching not his instrument but a Polaroid camera. The guitarist stares at Andy through his sunglasses, still perched on his nose, stares through the dark as the mechanical whir of the camera fills the air and a photo emerges. The guitarist shakes it gently, his partner appearing behind him now, draped in a flimsy bathrobe; Andy can see in the dull light of the room the slowly developing image of his own face in the photo, eyes half-dazed in mid-blink, lips curled into a sneer. The guitarist studies the picture, turns to his partner, the taller boy leaning down for them to converse in whisper; the guitarist looks away briefly, back to Andy, nods to his partner, the spectacle unfolding unseen by all but Andy as Nicky and Gator continue to fixate on the bed.

"The fuck are you saying?" Andy says, addressing the guitarist. He turns to Gator. "Who are these assholes? The fuck are they saying about me? Give me that." Andy snatches at the photo of himself, the guitarist permitting it to slip out of his fingers, raising his hand in silent submission. Andy wads it into his pocket, turns to Gator.

"Is he high? I mean too high to talk. I didn't come here to…"

Abruptly, with no buildup—no slow tensing of the forms, no building groans or sighs—the shapes on the bed go rigid, one seemingly hunched, the other bolt upright, both statue still as a pair of shrieks emanate, impossible to tell if they're masculine or feminine, too pained and agonized to be sexed, piercing the silence for what seems to be minutes before they degenerate into a long, low, shared wail that grows lower in register by the second until it abruptly ceases and the figures collapse, the sheets seeming to deflate as they sink into the darkness. The guitarist and his friend applaud; Nicky reaches back, punches a button; a wall-mounted fluorescent light strip flickers to life, dull grey at first, at last casting a swath of the room in a pillar of stark white light.

"I'm not high, Andy. I like to enjoy myself when I'm high. And already…well, already I don't enjoy being around you. I like beautiful things, Andy. Beautiful people. And you, well…From what Gator tells me I'm at least going to give you the benefit of some self-awareness, hmm?" Andy bites his tongue; his eyes adjusting to the light he sees for the first time the extent of Nicky's degradation, the sunken eyes, the caved-in stomach, the telltale skin flakes and mouth sores of a man who came to narcotics too late and too quickly in life and thus never learned to pace himself properly, to mediate the speed of his own deterioration.

"But I am curious," Nicky continues. "Tell me, Andy, you ever been to the Australian Outback? Ridden in the back of a jeep, watched a pack of dingoes rip apart a kangaroo through a pair of binoculars? Stood on the bow of a yacht around the Horn of Africa while one chick sucked your cock and her sister jiggled your balls?" Nicky smirks, knowing the answer already, taking a puff of his cigarette; moves to flick it at Andy, Andy flinching, regretting it immediately, the test failed, Nicky making that dry, empty chuckle in response. Another camera flash, another

Polaroid from the guitarist, staring blankly at Andy as he retrieves the photo from the camera and begins shaking it, Andy snapping it away before it can develop.

"Of course you haven't. I have. I've done all those things and things you couldn't imagine. Gator tells me you've spent your life here in this city. How far've you gone outside your zone? How small is your world? Going to work every day, coming home, the same ten blocks, year after year? I've gotta give you this: I'd have slit my wrists a long time ago. Heh. Man's gotta leave behind a good looking corpse when he dies, right?"

"This some kind of sick joke?" Andy asks, turning to Gator.

"Hey, c'mon, Nicky, you hazed the man enough, huh? Maybe time we bring it around to a point, uh, pull everything together?"

"Sure, Gator." Nicky's eyes never leave Andy's as he speaks; Andy notices for the first time that—since he came into the room—he doesn't believe he's seen him blink once.

"I've been on a lot of quests, Andy. Lot of quests. Quest for the perfect pussy. Perfect food. Perfect beach. And believe me, I succeeded in every one of them. But you know what they all had in common? They were out *there.*" Nicky points a finger at Andy, as though he's played some part in some great, unspoken failure. "What about the perfect *me?* I'm already the best lay in the business; best *looking* lay in the business; that's two for two. Six months ago, I'm in a chateau in the Alps—you know where the Alps are, Andy?" Before Andy can respond, Nicky cuts him off: "They're in Switzerland, Andy. Ever skied down a Swiss slope? Ever seen a Swiss woman? They sound French, and they fuck like them, too." Nicky smirks. "Nah, you haven't. We been over this. But I'm waking up six months ago underneath this Swiss bitch, rolling her off me, wiping her pussy juice off my cock while I'm staring out the window at the sun coming up over the Alps, and I realize—what about the *intellectual?* What about the *spiritual?* I've fucked and come a million times, but, if I don't know what any of it was about—what any of it was really *about*—then was it worth it? Was it *really* worth it, if I could've been the perfect man but I blew it? So that's why I'm back here. That's the name of the game: self improvement.

Mental, spiritual, physical. I've been studying. Tai chi, the Koran, *Jonathan Livingston Seagull*, *The Tibetan Book of the Dead*. To achieve the union of sensual, spiritual, physical, and emotional. The total fusion of body, mind, art, and God."

Andy wonders what he would look like taxidermized, stuffed and mounted in a pink tutu on the wall of some rustic lodge.

Another flash, another whir as the guitarist's Polaroid produces another picture.

"I see you've already found the perfect assholes," Andy says, snatching at the latest photo.

Nicky smiles. "Gator tells me you're an artist. Well, I think you'll appreciate this. Wilson and Aaron are artists, too."

"I thought they were comedians," Andy says.

"It is not *comedy*; it is *art*," the boy with the camera snaps.

"They're very serious about music," Nicky says. "Used to be roadies for Sabbath. Smoked ice with Ozzy."

"I don't care if they sucked Ozzy's cock," Andy says.

"Mr. Blayze is providing us a place to live while we work on our opera, in exchange for providing him artistic and spiritual enlightenment," Wilson says, ignoring the slight. Aaron nods, crossing his arms over his chest.

"Culture has stagnated," Wilson continues. "Our opera will be the first true composition of the century. Everything since Mozart has been mere imitation. We shall change that!"

"By making everyone kill themselves?" Andy asks. Gator snorts. Wilson's eyebrows raise behind his sunglasses.

"It is the story of John Sybarite," Wilson says. "He returns from the jungles of war to a city of horror. All around him, the filth and decadency of the city threaten to consume his very soul. But there is nothing left of his soul! So he trudges unscathed through the depths! He looks into the heartless heart of the city; and, when it stares back into the space where his own heart used to be, he stares back! Ultimately, faced with the true implications of his own existence, he kills everyone, and commits a grand act of self-sacrificial suicide at the foot of the Statue of Liberty, shedding his blood in a noble effort to bring about the rebirth of our nation."

Andy sneers. "*Taxi Driver.*"

"Beg pardon?"

"That's Taxi Driver," Andy says. "Except he doesn't actually kill himself. He just puts his hand to his head and goes 'Pow.'" If only he had pulled the trigger, Andy thinks. Had loved the film up to that point; loathes sappy endings.

"Do not confuse our hard contemplations about the state of the world with some…*Hollywood* drivel," Wilson says. He looks to Gator. "You said that you were bringing us a *real* artist, not some plebeian imbecile who spends his time watching mass-market *swill*."

Andy's head pulses. His hands twitch. One arm grips the canister tightly; his hand itches to move towards his zipper.

"Hey, hey, now, Andy-man is the real deal, ain'tcha? This here's just all part of the package, man. Andy here, he tells you exactly what's on his mind. Don'tcha, Andy?"

"Fuck off," Andy says. "Why the fuck did you drag me out here, to put me on display? I'm not here for your fucking amusement, assholes."

"I thought you liked to be on display, Andy," Nicky says. Another chuckle; another flick of a cigarette towards the bed; a slight frown when its landing elicits no response. He addresses Wilson and Aaron: "Gentlemen. Andy here is a different type of artist. See, Gator tells me that Andy here is fond of public displays of the male physique. Now, this is something we've got in common. I also feel that the world should not be deprived of the visage of my manhood. Gator also tells me the law has made him suffer greatly for this; and again, I sympathize. See, in spite of everything else, as soon as Gator told me how the two of you met, I felt a certain…simpatico; and I was *very* pleased to learn that you're an artist, too. See, Wilson and Aaron here, they're musicians. The visual arts, though…well, let's just say I'm no regular at the Modern. I'm eager to see your work, Andy. Gator tells me it's very unique. That it's very *of* the City. And fuck, man, do I love this city. I want to discuss it with you. Meditate on it. Consider it."

Andy stares at Nicky; one of the corners of his upper lip curls. "I'm not here for small talk," he says. "I'm here for money." He taps the canister beneath his arm. "This? This is my art. You either like it and pay me, or you get the fuck out of my way."

IT TAKES a few moments for Nicky to dispatch Chad for a projector and screen, for him to return with them, Nicky sitting stock still as the musclehead tries to set it up properly, fails, Andy stepping in and completing the task for him, perturbed to see that it's another Super Simplex, a newer model, nicer than his own; takes moments more, still, for Andy to prepare the film, his cassette player, take his seat on a folding chair beside the projector. The door is closed, the fluorescent light switched off, Nicky becoming animate as the room is once more bathed only red, stretching his legs, leaning forward towards the screen. His movement seems to trigger an energy in the room, Gator rubbing his hands together in anticipation, Wilson and Aaron crossing and uncrossing their arms in front of themselves, shifting back and forth; even the shapes on the bed rise up like ghosts in a shoddy William Castle picture, still anonymous in the darkness, seeming to gaze out from unseen holes in the death shrouds of the sheets still draped over them.

Andy hesitates as one finger hovers above the play switch on the projector, the other on the cassette player. He previewed the film last night in his apartment, came away with mixed feelings. As he anticipated, the deer's hoof scene was exactly what was needed to maintain the film's rhythm;

still, he is displeased with the soundtrack. The samples he's obtained are too stilted, too slow. Their authenticity is undone by their mundanity, and he would like to get more black and white footage, something to act as a palette cleanser after periods of oversaturation, segments of the film when the reds and oranges flood the senses, risk numbing the viewer.

Andy sighs. An artist, he has always felt, ought never compromise; yet he knows of few artists who've ever had to make a quick buck to flee the city.

He presses play. The projector whirs to life; white light floods the screen. On the cassette player, the soundtrack kicks in: Explosions. Gunfire. Furious dogs snarling and snapping at some unseen threat.

Onscreen, the pure, white light is replaced by an explosion of color. Heads explode. Eyeballs are gouged from their sockets. A woman runs screaming through an orange-lit corridor.

On the soundtrack: A dump truck backs up; a man shouts; more gunfire; more explosions; porn jazz from a multitude of sources, the beat occasionally underscored by the artifact of a gasp or moan.

Onscreen, red painted fingernails claw at wet, hungry lips. Buildings incinerate and smolder. Living corpses dig their way up out of moldy graves, worms pouring from their orifices.

Andy sinks his fingers into his palms; he feels himself on the brink of sweating, his heart rate reaching infarction levels, his eyes feeling like they're about to burst from their sockets. Nervous; so nervous.

Onscreen, at last, the hoof. The hoof. Andy closes his eyes. In the darkness behind his lids he sees women frolicking and Andy leans forward, studying their faces, focusing on them, their contours, the black voids behind their person masks where their eyes ought to be, the birthmarks on all of their jaws.

On the soundtrack: artillery fire; more porn jazz; Richard Nixon declares that he is not a crook.

Andy imagines himself prone, hands bound behind him with barbed wire. The deer hoof is presented; he cranes his head up in supplication, his glasses cracked and streaked in his own blood. His mouth opens; he casts his gaze upwards, up to her, gazing back at him serenely, her mouth tight but kind, her hair all mottled with blood and gore and a single scarlet drop rolls down her forehead, down her cheek, comes to rest for a moment perfectly on her birthmark, suspended in eternity before it plummets, her blood falling through space and time to land on Andy's forehead, mixing with his own blood, joining it, disappearing into it, and Andy takes the hoof into his mouth and the drill is driven into the back of his skull...

Andy's eyes snap open. He is surrounded by darkness and quiet, punctuated only by the sound of the whirring projector, out of film, and the slow hum of the cassette player. In the residual light of the projector's beam, he can just make out the staring faces of his audience. Andy rises before the group, sweat dripping from his chin onto his tie, stains spreading from his armpits. He switches off the projector; red light ensconces them all once more.

"Predictable," Wilson shouts from the darkness.

Andy's eyes bulge behind his glasses.

"I could see the direction it was going from the first frame," he continues. Andy didn't realize anyone's voice could be shriller than his own.

"It was garbage," a voice mumbles from somewhere, and Andy realizes it must be one of the shapes from the bed.

Wilson snorts. "In our travels, Aaron and I have seen countless so-called 'films' of this nature. Most of them much better accomplished than this. The moment I saw the man's head explode, I knew immediately that the deer's hoof would soon follow. It would be an amusing twist...for a child."

Aaron nods eagerly.

"Certain drive-ins in the American South might consider this good material for a double feature with particular hardcore pornographic films," Wilson continues, making a circle of the room now, hands folded behind his back. "Though they'd be overstating its intelligence."

"How the fuck is this any worse than your bullshit?" Andy asks. "What the fuck does that say? This—this *says* something. What the fuck is your statement?"

"If you consider your film to be of any artistic merit, I'm afraid that the meaning of Aaron's and my own endeavors would elude you," Wilson says.

Nicky stands up, strokes his chin, walks around in a small circle, muttering quietly to himself, as though trying to urge himself on towards some sort of conclusion. He passes by the bed; as he does, a frail, hairless arm shoots out from beneath the sheet and grasps his wrist.

"Nicky," a voice whispers. Nicky spins around and brings a fist into the shape on the bed; immediately it collapses with a whimper, the hand retracting.

"Shut up. I need to think," Nicky says. He stares at the bed; looks back to Andy; stares at the bed a long time. Finally, he turns back around and moves to Andy; stands looking over him, staring down at him, the dull luminescence of his eyes taking on the same red sheen as the lights.

"I don't like to be fooled, Andy. A lot of men have tried. Lot of men got burned right out of the business trying to fool me. They're still putting salve on those wounds. Gator told me you were bringing me something *real*."

"It doesn't get any realer," Andy whispers. His hands are vibrating at his sides.

"It doesn't?" Nicky asks. "You sure about that?"

A long moment passes; responses ricochet around inside of Andy's mind; scenarios unfold before him, different answers leading to different conclusions, different outcomes: Andy on a bus riding out of the city, a fat check in his wallet, *her* riding beside him; Andy in the darkest, filthiest pits of Rikers, Sing Sing, some prison the world has never heard of, trapped forever in one of the dark, damp, subterranean chambers where the filth of the world is locked away when there's no one to plead their case; when their repugnance is such even the bleeding hearts want to see them rendered into fat. At last:

"No. It doesn't."

It's Nicky's turn to hesitate; there's a second—a brief second—in which the veins in his neck bulge, his breathing quickens, when Andy can see his pupils constricting even further, a second in which Andy thinks he's about to pounce forward on him and throttle him there, use his meaty paws to crush his windpipe and choke the life out of him right here in front of Gator and everyone. Then; nothing. The dead chuckle. A pat on the back devoid of any friendship or affection.

"Well, that's too bad, then. You can get the fuck out of my apartment now."

"HEY, ANDY-MAN!" Gator, jogging down the hallway as Andy goes to the elevator.

"Thanks for putting in your two cents back there," Andy says. "Nice support, asshole."

Gator chuckles. "Hey, now, Andy, I don't know good art when I see it."

"You've liked all my other shit."

"Yeah, man, but, I wouldn't exactly call that art, now." He giggles.

"You son of a bitch."

"Aww, just having myself some fun. You, up there, in front of those freaks?"

Andy hisses. "You knew exactly what the fuck was going to happen. You son of a bitch."

"Hey, hey, now. I did think, maybe, for a second, that there was the possibility fruitcake back there might actually like your stuff. Wasn't a total waste, now was it?"

"I'm not fucking around, Gator." Andy steps into the elevator, touches his forehead; he'd like to be alone right now; the prick of thin, rigid steel in his arm, the cool, slow descent of the smack flooding his veins, driving away all of the ills of his life, her sweet light shining down on him…

"The mug books," Andy says. "Pictures. Have you gotten those, at least?"

"Well I haven't…"

"Get them," Andy says. Gator is just opening his mouth to respond when the elevator doors shut, trap Andy in gentle solitude. *Summer Samba* plays softly through the speaker in the ceiling. A failed night; another humiliation in the long chain of humiliations that are Andy Lew's interactions with the human race. He plays the night's events over in his mind; tries to find some redeemable moment, something accomplished, something that brings him closer to her, to escape; can find neither. Precious time wasted with the second hand ticking extra fast, the march towards midnight on a downhill slope now. How many hours, days, til he returns home with squad cars circling his block, yellow tape everywhere, uniforms with shotguns and binoculars scoping out every street corner, waiting for his return? Will they try and bring him in, Andy wonders, or take "the direct route," as Gator calls it? Two quick shots, one in the gut, one in the head, drop a scrubbed pistol on his corpse and call it self-defense. No; won't be that dramatic. They need him. He's more valuable alive, in the wake of Steven's discovery. The name has come up now, Andy is sure; another person of interest in the twisted post-mortem life of Steven Lew.

Draft.

He's sure the freak in the tighty whities has dropped it to Dick Valentine by now, if not a dozen other uniforms. Knows that it's only a matter of time before he himself is strapped into an interrogation chair, berated, beaten, harangued and threatened until he can answer for the New York Police Department where they can locate Mr. Samuel Draft.

If he were a talking man, Andy would love to tell them that he's been wondering the same fucking thing for twelve years.

THE FIRST rays of sunlight are just beginning to corrupt the vibrant electric kaleidoscope of the 42nd Street night when Andy reaches his destination. After last night's failure, he needs some time outdoors, inhaling the scent of the city, to reinvigorate him. He's meant to make the pilgrimage here for some time now; has kept putting it off; can't figure out why. This morning, though, seems as appropriate a time as any. He stops and stands in quiet awe and shuts his eyes and imagines the buildings around him quivering in the shockwaves of an atomic blast, windows exploding into a showers of glass that lacerate the screaming, burning puddles of humanity melted to the pavement below by the power of the bomb, Andy among them, his boiling eyeballs cast upwards to gaze while they can at the awesome mushroom cloud enveloping the city.

Andy opens his eyes and peers up at the Pan Am building.

This is the spot where Michael Findlay died.

It is a shame, Andy thinks, that Findlay's passing has had so little an effect on 42nd Street. He and his contemporaries did, after all, come of age watching his films; survived their twenties hunkered down in theater seats not yet gone over to age with protruding springs and festering upholstery, eagerly chewing their popcorn in anticipation of Findlay's next masterwork. It was old Mike Findlay, after all, who made the Deuce what it is. Before Findlay came on the scene, those who flocked to 42nd Street for their fix of vice had a choice in films: those violent or those carnal, bodies hacked apart with construction implements, impaled on ancient weaponry, blown apart by artillery; or splayed nude on concrete blocks, stretched on crosses, displayed in loving detail on tropical beaches. Yet for all the years the template survived and pleased the crowds, it was Mike Findlay who finally came along and asked, "Why not have it all?" So it was that sex and death finally wed on 42nd Street, and their unholy union has only strengthened since; Findlay bestowed upon the masses films churned directly from his own fevered mind, monochromatic nightmares of one-eyed men stalking whores through an endless night, balling couples driven from their beds by knife-wielding maniacs, striptease artists attacked upon the stage. Forevermore would a single film permit the denizens of 42nd to fulfill all of their desires in a single sitting; and, for a while, the masses rejoiced. The next Findlay film was an event on 42nd in the last decade; he was one of the few directors to earn his name on the marquee, one of the only auteurs that the Deuce knew by name. Andy himself remembers the sensation in his own trembling hands when he would open up a canister and try to sneak a preview of what was to come from a few individual frames.

Yet Andy Lew stands alone in his vigil before the Pan Am building. No theaters have hung wreaths in his honor, hosted retrospectives of his life; no mourners have gathered in black; no girls have congregated at his death site to open their own wrists in acts of mortal solidarity. There is only Andy Lew, thinking about the demise of the world, about how he wished he had been able to make it to the building in time to snap a polaroid of the chopper all chewed up and gory; thinking, finally, about the future.

Last night's failure is a major setback in the flight of Andy Lew from New York City. He has, at last inspection, $47.51 in his bank account. Though a bus ticket is cheap and would get him away tonight, Andy realizes that fleeing now would be an impulsive move. California seems, to him, the only logical destination; the only place big enough to hide comfortably, the only other state offering a vice culture nearly as decadent and densely interwoven and impenetrable as the Deuce's. He will do well in the Tenderloin, Andy has decided; yet getting there, *surviving* there, will be a matter of much greater financial burden than a simple bus ticket. He will need money for lodging upon his arrival; food and drugs for the journey; enough extra cash to grease the wheels once he's ready to establish himself on the scene, a new identity, new social security card and driver's license, a forged work history with references. Can't afford to purchase those here; doesn't want to leave behind anyone who could point the screws in the right direction.

Another consideration; the biggest. *Her.*

Andy has rarely taken her beyond the confines of his apartment, other than occasional trips with him to the Colossus; does not like to consider the risks inherent in bringing her across the country. While he is content to relieve himself in bottles and rarely experiences bowel movements, while he will watch her like a hawk every step of the way, Andy knows that, eventually, he will have to sleep, out in the open, with her vulnerable to prying, greedy eyes and lustful hearts; that while he dozes between here and San Francisco some hot young stud might take her away from him, whisk her away to a life in corners of the world Andy will never be able to find...

Andy kneels down and places a hand flat against the sidewalk; though he wasn't able to confirm it from the scant news photos, he likes to imagine that this is the spot Findlay's head landed, rocking back and forth with momentum from its descent, smack dab in the middle of a bullseye of his own blood. There is, of course, a sentimental cord tethering Andy to the city, further slowing his delay. Travel to California means he will never set foot here again; never place his hand on the spot where a generation's hopes and dreams evaporated into a red mist; never settle into one of the theaters of 42nd Street again and inhale familiar odors and listen to the particular, muddy echo of the soundtrack off of cavernous auditorium walls. Worse still: he may never *know*.

Andy has considered from the beginning that the film was not produced here in the city. Though it is speculative, he has long supposed that, based upon its nature, it was made in a room that would be difficult or impossible to see from street level, and that had to have been relatively—if not completely—soundproof. This, Andy believes, rules out most apartment blocks in the city, certainly all hotels and motels. His best guess: A basement somewhere, perhaps a private office building. Yet since he first laid eyes on her, Andy has known, felt it, that the key to her identity lies somewhere here, in New York; that no matter how far away she was born, no matter how far her travels, no matter what remote destination she came to shoot the movie in, that all of the answers to her riddle are buried somewhere in the piss-stained sidewalks and festering alleys of his hometown.

Andy holds his palm to the cement another moment, takes strength from it, feels Findlay's steaming blood flow into his own fingertips, reinvigorating him. To know her or to lose her. Andy rises; heads home; doesn't know if he has quite enough strength to make that choice.

"WHAT DO you think she did? I mean, before." Andy asks. A thousand angry and desperate faces stare back at him from mugbooks and missing posters and last known photos, a buffet of the damned laid out for his ravenous consumption. Here are all the city's wayward souls, vice workers and runaways, addicts and hustlers, everyone of record who has ever made the fatal shuffle off of the city's narrow beam of righteousness and taken the head-on plummet into the vast and hungry sea below.

"That really matter?" Gator asks, reclining on the floor, idly playing with one of his nipple rings. "I mean, great scheme of things, all things being equal, whether she bussed tables, sucked guys off, crunched numbers, that really matter anyway, once you get down to it?"

"It tells you what she was like. What she did. What've you got if you don't got your job? Then you're either a bum or some fucking commie socialist bastard."

"Well maybe our little miss was a certified Red. Got herself mixed up into some trouble."

Andy shakes his head. "Not someone like her; not then. *Today*, maybe, as fucked up as the kids are. You even got fucking Stalin lovers in the suburbs now... But this is older... No, she... She *did* something. She was someone."

"Aww, Andy don't wanna believe his honey could be a Red." Gator sits up, grinning. Andy glares at him over the rims of his glasses, goes

back to perusing photos; every criminal and missing person in the city of New York with a facial birthmark recorded as a defining feature. "Let me tell you something, Andy-man, I don't know what hole you were sucking shit out of back in the day, but every sweet young thing at City College got it up for Papa Joe behind closed doors. Went to a few meetings myself, just for the easy pickings. All you had to do was drop your drawers and you could have a pack of pinko bitches on their knees sooner than you could say, '*Ooooh, Mother Russia!*'"

"Lemme ask you something, why the fuck you want to know anything about her if you don't give a shit, huh? Or are you really just hanging around so you can keep looking at her and drinking my beer?"

Gator shrugs. "Call it general curiosity, I suppose. Also figured you might find out she has a sister, know what I mean? Imagine, another one of her walkin' around out there? Aww, I'd love to pay her a visit, give her the same treatment as Big Sister."

"*There isn't another one of her!*" Andy snaps. His body involuntarily rises from the cot and he pulls himself back down. For a split second, he sees a flash of something unfamiliar in Gator's eyes: Fear.

"She's the only one," Andy says.

"All right, chief, you got it. Only one." Gator nods, looks around the room. "Aw, hey, speakin' of something special, you shoulda seen me this morning. Got up nice and early, went hunting. Ain't nothin' like hitting it in the early morning, sun's just coming up, everything round you's all dark, you're just aiming at shadows, really. Bagged me a big one, had to have been at least two-fifty, three hundred pounds. Got one in his throat, didn't think he was gonna go down, put another one in his gut and *boom, boom!* Finally hits the dirt. Think his girlfriend called him 'Tyrone.'"

Gator's cackles drift through the fog in Andy's mind; staring at the photos, he has long since taken himself to his special place, to better concentrate, to fully study each and every picture. He has only seen her in black and white, only under particular lighting, only from very specific angles, only at one exact moment in her life. Cannot bear the thought of coming across her picture taken under bad lighting, when she was very young, at an awkward angle, and missing her. Andy pictures himself deep in some cavern, so close to the bowels of the earth that the walls glow dull red with the heat of magma; it is very quiet here, with only the soft hiss of escaping subterranean gasses to break the quiet. The ceilings are vast, the halls wide; Andy enjoys walking this place in his mind when he needs to exercise particular concentration, or when he needs to relax and the needle isn't an option. It is his safe harbor; his happy place. He can see anyone here, all the people from his life who're gone now, those he's lost touch with, those he's never had the opportunity to exact revenge upon, girls he's had thoughts about on the subway. His brother is here, and his old friend Ludo, too, situated atop squat red pillars, their ribcages splayed open by thin wires descending from the ceiling, arms dangling above their heads like fleshy marionettes; his cousin, Saskia, isn't too far away, her jaw wired open, pretty chestnut hair sheared to the scalp, her ankles bolted to the floor. Down another corridor is his old family priest, and, down yet another, Roderick, mounted to the projection booth workbench, bound with splicing tape, blindfolded with film, a variety of surgical instruments laid out across his bare and quivering abdomen. And as Andy moves through the halls of his happy place, stopping to marvel at each exhibit in turn and listen to the quiet, he can feel, just beyond his grasp, see, just out of the corner of his eye, the subtlest of movement; a flash, a shadow, a sigh; and he knows that she is here, too, walking the same halls, gazing at the same wonders; waiting for the day that Andy will speak her name and call her forth...

Special.

The only one.

No one else like her.

"Hey Gator?" Andy asks.

"Huh?"

"I need you to talk to Nicky again. It's about that art project."

"Yeah?"

Andy's mouth hangs open; money, an escape, guaranteed safe passage with her. They all await him on the tip of his tongue; to speak the words; to take the risk.

"I need to tell him to fuck himself," Andy says; sighs; goes back to looking at photos. Has another idea. Needs to talk to a pinko of his own.

"HELLO?" THE voice on the other end of the phone is lightly accented; Andy figures she'd have tried to get rid of it completely by now. Wonders if that's chic these days, if all the liberal scum who've taken over the campuses get a thrill out of a real live Polack teaching them how to undermine the American way of life.

"Saskia?" Andy asks. His voice is slower than usual; had to shoot up just the right amount to make this call, is afraid he might've miscalculated, taken a hair too much.

"Andy?"

"Who the fuck else?"

There's a brief pause before: "I thought you were dead."

"The hell, Saskia?"

"We haven't spoken in years, Andy, and the last time I saw you...I thought you'd have been buried in some shallow grave by now."

"I've been doing really fucking well, thanks for asking." Andy sighs. "How about you? You still a commie?"

It's Saskia's turn to sigh. "You call me out of the blue to insult me? I got a second doctorate, what the hell have you been doing with your life?"

"I've been working a real job, making a real living," Andy says. "Shit's a lot harder outside of the ivory tower. I've been working and...I've been looking for my brother."

A faint giggle on the other end of the line; Andy feels the hairs on the back of his neck go up, a roller coaster feeling down in his gut. "Andy, I know my own cousin. You've spent as much time looking for Steven as you've spent looking for God."

"I found him," Andy says.

"What?"

"If I gave a shit I'd ask if you were sitting down, but I don't, so, he's dead. Got his head chopped off by some freak. Probably some kinda pinko black mass shit; you know, *your* scene."

Andy waits for some sound from the other end of the line; a sob, a cry, anything to adequately convey his cousin's pain at this news. Disappointed when there's only silence, followed by:

"So, he's dead?"

"You cold blooded bitch. What the fuck is with you being fine with everyone being dead?"

"Runs in our family, doesn't it, Andy?" That giggle again.

"A lotta shit does," Andy mumbles.

"Will there be a funeral? It might be nice to come back to the city. See how things have changed. I've been working on a paper on the semiotics of modern urban decay. Manhattan as the death of the Jet Age Fantasy. We had a visiting sociology lecturer here last week from the University of Liverpool. Do you know that the English think Manhattan will destroy itself by the end of the decade? 'The people there have all become desensitized and depraved by poverty and broken dreams,' he said. I told him I'd known that for years, that he should meet my cousin."

"Actually, that's what I'm calling about. I haven't set the funeral up yet and...I need some cash. To pay for it. I was hoping you could pitch in."

Saskia sighs. "Andy, darling. We really don't change, do we?"

"You wanna bury your cousin or not? They'll put him in potters field."

"Because his brother shoots all his money into his arm and buys dirty movies? We both know that if I send you money it wouldn't go toward a casket."

"Because funerals are fucking expensive," Andy says. Tries to keep the pitch of his voice under control. "I...don't have exact costs but...I figure around a grand should do it. Maybe two grand, I don't know… That'll cover expenses, all the shit that needs to be taken care of."

"The prodigal brother wants to make amends by giving his murdered kin a proper sendoff? I know you Andy, this is not your style. You would have done better to have asked me for bail money, to put you into a clinic. *Those* things I'd have believed; you might have even gotten something out of me, if you caught me in a sympathetic mood. But this? I'm not going to pay to pump more poison into your arm, Andrezj. If you want money for that, you can keep doing what you do best."

"I *learned* from the best, didn't I, bitch?" Andy asks. He sucks in a deep breath; thinks he hears Saskia doing the same.

"What're you wearing?" Andy asks. A hand drops to his crotch and he begins to tug his zipper up and down.

"Andy…"

"That slutty little Eisenhower jacket?" Andy whispers. "The one your mother always used to put you in before she sent you over?"

"*Andy. Please.* We aren't teenagers anymore."

"Whore," Andy whispers. "Fucking cunt. Slut. Feel your tits for me."

"I'm at work, Andy. This isn't the time. I've a class to get to in ten minutes."

"You're going to let them put your cousin in a potter's field? I don't have shit to my name, you're going to make me put my last dime towards a pine box to bury what's left of my brother?"

"If it was just his head," Saskia says, "They might let you use a shoebox. If you ask nicely, they might even let you be the one to put it in. Save the undertaker's fees."

Andy groans, helpless. "You listen to me, you fucking ingrate. Who bought your books when the scholarship money ran out? Who bought your fucking cap and gown? You wouldn't even have your fucking dyke-whore job if it weren't for me, so give me some fucking respect and you pay me back."

"I've already done enough for you," Saskia sighs. "Not that we haven't had our fun. Steven was a monster, Andrezj. I'm not sorry to hear he's dead. I won't shed any tears tonight. I might shed one when you're gone. But I won't help you do it to yourself."

"I don't need smack, you fucking bitch, I just need fucking money!" Andy shrieks.

"*Dasvidanya, Jędruś.* I probably won't hear from you for another few years, will I? If I do at all. I'll remember the sweet, nervous boy in the back seat of his mother's car. Not the animal he turned himself into."

The click of Saskia's phone hitting its cradle sounds to Andy very much like his projector switching off. He quietly slips his hand out of his jeans and zips them up. Looks around; no one watching. He slams the phone against the wall of the booth, lets the receiver drop, leaves it swinging like a pendulum as he storms away, abandoning it to swing, swing, swing, until it's finally run out of momentum and comes to hang like a dead snake in the violent summer heat.

LONG NIGHTS into long days. Coffee keeps Andy awake to work; the needle, beer, and whiskey put him down. A few stray playable records net a handful of dollars at the pawn shop; so does a spare switchblade, parts from a broken cassette player, a few sterling cufflinks he's never cared for that much. The sum in toto: Not nearly enough. Might get him as far as the Midwest; doesn't want to end up stranded in the Bible Belt with his reel and the clothes on his back and an even greater chance than in New York of getting picked up in the event he needs to make a few spare bucks the old fashioned way. Missouri, Kansas, Oklahoma; they'd burn him alive down there.

The one thing deflecting complete madness: the absence of Dick Valentine. No phone calls; no unwelcome visits. Andy turns his eyes to the back of his skull on his walks home, his trips out to the Last Chance;

no unmarked crawlers follow him, no plainclothes broadcasting their status to the world with their cop struts and smug looks. The biggest danger in thinking yourself safe, Andy knows, is acting like it. He begins taking long routes back to his apartment, staying on the subway two stops past his destination, hopping off, backtracking on foot. Keep the pigs guessing; can't rely on Gator's intel, that he knows nothing, sees nothing; can't trust that Gator isn't working alongside Valentine on the whole thing, that the little fucker's put aside his racialism to take Andy down, be the first one in to search his apartment once the arrest goes down; Gator Hyatt, alone in Andy's den, his filthy hands all over her, right there in Andy's own living room...

ANDY LEANS back in his chair, drops forward, leans back, drops forward. Not enough caffeine this morning, too much smack last night. He can feel his eyeballs sucking moisture from the rest of his body. Through the booth window, *Last House* is a fuzzy mess of bloody splotches and bad clothes, the soundtrack no different than Nicky's in-house fuckboys pounding on their guitars. He's too on edge; needs to let the steam out; find a way to relieve the tension of waiting, working, waiting. Has been considering a trip to the Port Authority. Wishes it were a cooler season; can walk through the crowds virtually unnoticed in a trench coat at the Port Authority in the wintertime, all the men in their plaid jackets and peacoats milling about and Andy small enough to vanish into a particularly large crowd, can very easily fling his coat open at just the right moment, for just the right group, the college girls with the hungry eyes and tight-lipped mouths, aching and needing but too shy to say it, too repressed to give speech to their desires, broadcasting with little twitches and glances what they want to see, what they really came here for; and then, once he's given them their show, belt it back up and keep moving. Can't operate when he's wearing pants; learned that the hard way back in

'72, trying to jam it back in and pull the fly up at the same time, moving one hand too slow and the other too quick, ended up on his knees on the pavement shrieking and that's where he was when Gator found him, bleeding and shrieking and with no way out but either go to the Tombs or think of something suitable with which to bribe the cop staring down at him with a grin on his face and a pair of cuffs in his hands...

"SO HOW we gonna do this?"

"I'll think of something."

"You been thinking of something for five days."

Tony and Chrissy stare at the marquee of the Colossus, sweat dripping down their faces, wet hands dampening their pockets, stare at the marquee to the point that they've ceased to see the blinking lights moving round and round but have begun to see the illusion for what it is, one light after another switching off and on in unison, like a nervous housewife checking and rechecking the garage for an intruder.

"Colossus ain't gonna have this thing forever," Tony says. "Then it's on to who knows where, and that's money out of *our* pockets."

"We're gonna get it."

"Ain't gonna get it standing here watching the lights."

"OK, so, let's bust in and get it."

"This ain't a dice game," Tony says. "You can't just bust and run. Not on the Colossus. Not on Andy Lew."

"So what then?"

"Gotta think of something. Or wait for something to go down."

"What's gonna go down that's gonna let us lift some reels?"

Across the street, a scream, a screech, the quick, rough sound of blood and flesh against tempered glass and the multitudinous shrieks and cries and gasps of an impromptu peanut gallery drawn together by the most fascinating of all the shows on Earth: human tragedy. Tony and

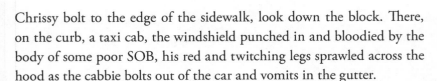
Chrissy bolt to the edge of the sidewalk, look down the block. There, on the curb, a taxi cab, the windshield punched in and bloodied by the body of some poor SOB, his red and twitching legs sprawled across the hood as the cabbie bolts out of the car and vomits in the gutter.

"Damn," Chrissy says.

"Perfect," Tony says.

IN THE Colossus projector booth, Andy's ears prick up. Something has happened—some noise has come to him through his hole in the wall, some catastrophe beckoning to him, reassuring him that all is wrong with the world. He moves to the hole, squats, places his ear to it. Yes, something is going on; he can hear the commotion rising, that peculiar blend of human sounds that accompanies very public disasters, equal parts excitement and revulsion, mixed with a dash of concern and, beneath it all, a healthy foundation of titillation.

Andy's breath quickens; what has the Deuce, in all of its infinite wrath, bestowed upon him tonight to ameliorate his suffering? He has been listening to noises coming through to him long enough that he become able to determine, like a sommelier tasting from unmarked bottles, the exact nature of a given calamity by the sounds that waft up through his hole. He can successfully differentiate between mugging and a murder, a stabbing and a bludgeoning, a car theft and a carjacking. What is it he hears tonight, though? What fantastic misfortune is unfolding now— as Andy can tell by the proximity of the shouts and the intensity of horn honks— no more than a block outside his very theater?

A car accident. Yes. There's been a car accident— specifically, someone has been *hit* by a car. He hopes it's a taxi. The image of bright, streaked red on dirty yellow is particularly striking if seen in the right light. Andy checks his watch. He has ten minutes before the next reel switchover.

Hurriedly, he leaps to his feet, bootheels skidding across the concrete floor as he moves to his workbench and digs out the battered Polaroid camera he keeps there for just such occasions. He casts one last glance over his shoulder at the film playing out in the auditorium before he's out the door and down the stairs, skipping down them two at a time, three, letting his momentum carry him, not even pausing to feel the pain when one foot gives out on him at the bottom of the steps and he crumbles awkwardly onto one ankle; and then he's out the door and into the dark, neon signs reflecting colors off of his glasses and turning the whole world yellow, orange, yellow, red for seconds at a time as he dashes towards the crowd, growing in numbers, drawn out from the whorehouses and theaters and bathhouses by the siren smell of blood and death. Andy jerks to a halt, feet away from the crowd, frozen in place by the sight, a dozen or so bodies gathered around the cab, circling it, others passing by, aware that their privileges have already been taken, stealing passing glances as they drift on.

He raises the camera, snaps a photo, waits the agonizing seconds for the camera to grind it out. Andy studies it a moment, satisfied. He comes closer, inching his way in, weaving between bodies to get a better shot, not of the crowd now but the legs, making little jerking motions on the hood; swerves around to the driver's side to get a picture of some black kid still in his sunglasses kneeling on the seat, trying to talk to the pulverized mess that was a man seconds ago; ducks to the curb to get a snap of the sobbing taxi driver, covered in his own vomit, green faced and bug eyed, taking occasional pulls from the flask settled in his lap. No one molests Andy; no one interferes with his shots; he lets the others be and they return the favor, all of them here for the same reason, all of them drinking in the same thing, separated only by their lack of a means to capture the moment for posterity.

When he's gotten what he wants, Andy floats away from the crowd, transfixed by his photos; shuffles them in his hands over and over as he makes his way back to the theater, his own private slide carousel, already playing the last few seconds back to him; as sirens cry and flash behind him, an ambulance pulling onto the scene, the pack dispersing, the moment gone, except in the memory of those who experienced it, those who will forget it in minutes, hours, weeks and months from now until it exists only in the photos of a theater projectionist...

Noises. Noises up above. Andy stands in the doorway of the Colossus stairwell, listening, unfamiliar sounds drifting down to him, miniscule but apparent through the din of the film. He looks at the Colossus door, at fresh scrape marks along the jam; jerks his head back to listen; is straining to hear clearly when the sound of the film cuts out. Andy's heart goes into overdrive; slings his camera around his neck, is charging up the steps just as the crowd erupts into a wave of fury, the violence in the air palpable, hitting Andy like electrical shocks as he moves upstairs, stuffing the photos into his jacket. If he were a praying man he would be praying for an electrical failure now, a projector malfunction, even a reel breakage, but the non-deity he has not been praying to does not show mercy upon him tonight as he staggers through the door of the projector booth and finds a pair of dipshits gathering up his reels.

There is that singular instant, as between cobras and mongooses, when the combatants survey one another, poised but motionless, not hesitating but contemplating, instinct and experience joining together to form the perfect method of attack. Age and surprise put Andy at the disadvantage: he has not been a teenager for over twenty years. There is still too much residual smack in his system. There is only one of him. All these things collude to form the circumstances in which Chrissy lunges forward and, with the kind of clumsy strike found in the very young and the very confident, knocks Andy into the doorframe. Andy staggers, loses his balance, comes down on his injured ankle but he feels it this time, a crumpling, icy pain shooting up into his calf and hip and groin, and as he stumbles about on one foot, trying to keep his balance, grabbing onto the door jamb. Tony attempts to make his exit, less dexterous than Chrissy, not able to bolt and carry a reel at the same time, and as Andy goes down to the ground he reaches up and grabs the boy around the waist of his jeans, yanking him back, snarling; he can feel the flecks of spittle catching in his moustache and the saliva beginning to run down his jaw, can feel the Polaroids crumpling in his jacket.

"Lousy fucking cocksucker!" Andy hisses, and rather than have the desired effect of intimidation this somehow spurs the boy to spin around and hit Andy across the face with the film canister, knocking his glasses off, sending Andy into abject darkness. The world blurs; his own foul myopia cripples him. Andy releases the boy, still snarling, turns over onto his hands and knees and scampers across the floor, feeling for his glasses; finds them; puts them on. He leaps to his feet, adrenaline dulling the pain in his ankle, comes barreling down the stairs after the boys, taking the same two step, three step descent as before, down the Colossus' dank stairwell smelling of cheap sex and stained with dried menstrual blood smeared there by desperate whores, down towards the door and out into the chaotic night, still abuzz with the fervor over the taxi-hit, the ambulance still on the scene and the paramedics still trying to extract the pedestrian from the windshield, and the boys are grunting as they run, away from Andy, towards some abject freedom, Chrissy looking back over his shoulder, Tony looking straight ahead, knowing exactly what threat is behind him and so only focusing on the unknown that lay before him. So it is that Tony is fortunate enough to see the police cruiser coming up the street, lights flashing, sirens off, it is Tony who is fortunate enough to veer away from it, and as he does so he sees Chrissy turn his head over his shoulder to look back at Andy.

Tony's mouth opens. In his mind he shouts a warning, tells him to stop, tells him to dodge. In reality: Nothing. His mouth gapes. His trembling hands drop the reel canister; it splits open, spilling film across 42nd Street. Chrissy darts forward, head still turned back, eyes still fixed on Andy Lew, is still staring at Andy Lew and congratulating himself on a successful evasive maneuver when he runs into the path of the police cruiser and it strikes him in the hip; sends him rolling into the windshield,

spiderwebbing it, rolls up onto the roof where the lights slam into his ribcage, his body crumpling into the fetal position for his descent down the back of the cruiser and into a bruised and bloody mess into the street behind. As Chrissy flies through the air the canister he is carrying takes a similar arc, traveling with him over the hood, opening in midair, the film bursting out like a celluloid confetti snake, spiraling and pirouetting through the night air above the cruiser, cascading down in a tangle over the car and over the sidewalk and over Chrissy's mangled form.

Andy freezes; his breath catches in his throat. He stares at the whole tableau, the ambulance, the taxi, the cruiser, the boys, one in a messy heap, the other staring dumbfounded, his gaze drifting bac and forth between Andy and the boy in the gutter, and then one of the cops opens his squad car door and the boy takes off like a shot, and Andy watches him go, leaving behind the wounded, and as the officer moves around to the rear of his vehicle all Andy can do is unsling the Polaroid from around his neck and aim.

ANDY DOES not bother to look at his second set of photos of the evening as he ascends the Colossus steps to the projection booth; has them safely secured in his jacket, for perusal and study at a later date. He simply stares at the steps, moving up, slowly, one at a time; injured ankle notwithstanding, he has no particular desire to make it to the top. The auditorium is quiet now; knows that the silence came courtesy of the second, third, and fourth squad car that followed the first; watched officers filing into the theater as he made his slow and deliberate trek back unnoticed, unobserved. Knows, too, what awaits him at the top of the steps.

Roderick Tillman sits perched on a stool, flabby asscheeks hanging off the back. Everything around him looks small, Andy thinks, Rod-Rod so massive and doughy that even the projectors and his workbench and his chair look tiny beside him; had never considered before how big the man has gotten over the years. Wonders what would happen if he were dropped down one of these water slides they have down in Florida, if he could gain enough momentum that the surface tension of the water would explode him, blow him apart into a soppy shower of bloody gruel onto all the little kiddies in the park.

"Where's my movie, Andy?" Roderick asks. His voice quivers. Hadn't expected to shout that loud; had thought he would try and reason with Andy; walk him through what happened, figure out what went wrong; surprised at himself that his anger surges so readily. His breath catches in his throat. He thinks to apologize; to beg; almost braces himself for the impact of Andy's bullet. He rises, means to raise his hands above his head, offer surrender. His buttcheeks flop back into place; his shirttail rides up out of his pants. Andy steps back, wheezes.

"It's not my fault. They.... They broke in. They took it. There were two of them. What the fuck do you expect...expect me to do if.... If two little shits want to come in here? Look at what they did to my ankle!" Andy shrieks, tries to hold his foot forward as proof of his bravery, as though Roderick can see through the leather to the swelling beneath.

Roderick stares at Andy's cowboy boot, looks back to Andy, back to the boot. All fear of the tiny man is gone from him now; had never realized how much smaller Andy is than him, how frail, how *weak*. Watching him hobble into the room, the little lowlife who's cost him thousands of dollars, is responsible for the destruction of one of the theater's most profitable films of the last three quarters, he can't believe how many years he's wasted in terror of someone he could easily crush between his thumb and forefinger.

"They never would've tried to break in if they knew someone was up here guarding this shit! Like you were supposed to be!" Roderick is surprised at the bellow escaping his throat; hadn't realized he was still capable of such resonance. A bolt of excitement runs through him, seeing Andy cowering before him, at the realization that it could've been this way all along, that there are no knives in Andy's jacket, no guns waiting

to be drawn, no power behind his threats; that Andy Lew is not a hunter but a scavenger, picking on the scraps of filth that litter this street, and that, like any vulture, all that's ever been needed to drive him away is a good swing of the arm and a shout.

"You're a fucked up piece of shit I should've fired a long time ago!" Roderick shouts. "Sick fuck! Degenerate! Get the fuck out of my theater!"

Andy freezes. His legs slip out from beneath him; catches himself at his work bench. The room has become suddenly even more familiar than he thought possible; this room where he has worked and thought and watched movies and eaten lunch and masturbated for the majority of his adult life is suddenly not just his home away from home but it is his home, missing only *her* feminine touch to make the comfort of the place complete.

"I…can't go. I belong here," Andy says.

"You get the fuck out of here before I jam your cock into a light socket!" Roderick moves to lunge forward; Andy whimpers, raises his hands up in front of his face. Roderick lunges again, smiles to himself, lunges a third time before Andy scampers around on his hands and knees, regains his footing at the top of the steps, and for what he thinks will be the last time in his life, departs the Colossus Theater.

THE TRIP home is fevered, the pain in Andy's ankle vacillating between crippling and non-existent, icy chills and unbearable sweats overcoming him by turns, the marquee lights and signs of the Deuce more hallucinogenic this evening than usual: neon phantoms and electric demons swooping down from on high with their luminescent wings spread and ready to swipe him up, goateed men in cassocks ringing bells on street corners and bellowing "Satan lives," hobos with fakir beards on their cardboard matts cackling at him and chanting curses in strange tongues. Andy pauses a few times to collect himself, to cower behind trash piles or huddle into the fetal position and rock for a few moments to calm his nerves, to snap his mind back to reality. This cannot be happening; cannot have his beloved Colossus taken from him; cannot imagine that he will never again sit in the booth and watch a film play out in the auditorium, that he will never again snip frames from a print on his workbench. What's more: without a regular paycheck, flight from the city is both more imperative and less possible. Must get home. Must be with her. Must slip the needle into his arm and forget tonight for a while.

Andy stops in the hall outside of his apartment door; sees it open; presses himself to the wall, looks both ways. In the past twelve years, has never experienced a break-in; has never had to worry about it; found that shortly after Steven left, shortly after *she* came into his life, his neighbors began to regard him differently, tenants stepping away from him in the hallway, whispering about him as he passed, pulling their children out of the stairwells when he came home; learned that stories about him drifted throughout the building, mounting in brutality over the years until the point that he has come to be regarded as something approaching Dracula. Two break-ins in one night; had figured that the kids in the projector booth were just a couple of hopheads blazed out of their minds and looking for a quick hock; wonders now what sort of mad conspiracy is working against him, working against *her*. Her. But for her, he would bolt, go hole up in some café or at the Last Chance, come back when he was sure the coast was clear; can't bear the thought of her in there alone with some intruder; digs his nails into his palms and slowly approaches his open door.

"Come on in, son, ain't here to bite you." The rich basso coming out of Andy's apartment is strikingly gentle, perfectly regulated in the speaker's voice box to soothe the listener. Andy's muscles relax as others tighten and in spite of himself he steps into his apartment. There, situated on Andy's cot, lit only by the light coming in from the hallway, is the ursine figure of Dick Valentine. Sleepy eyes regard Andy with something between whimsy and pity.

Andy freezes in the doorway. "You'd better have a warrant." His voice trembles. "Is that why…do you have a warrant?"

"We can talk in the hall, you want, but people gotta pass through. You standing there's gonna make it damn awkward. Think you'll be more comfortable in here, too, anyway." Dick looks around the room, at Andy's photos decorating the walls, shakes his head. Andy steps in, closes the door behind him, shuttering the men in darkness. Andy switches on the light; the walls of the room are greyer than he remembers.

"Looks like you had yourself a rough night," Dick says. "I'd usually say I'd come back another time, but…" He looks down at a rat sitting hunched in the corner, nibbling on the remnants of some long-ago discarded pizza. "…but I'd rather not come back."

"You can't go through my shit without a warrant," Andy says.

"Ain't here to go through your stuff. Ain't here to bite you. See my suit? This here's my talking suit. I was here to bite you, it'd be a lot darker. Don't like the blood to show up." Andy studies the outfit; looks familiar; realizes to his horror that it's the same design as his beige three-piece.

"All right then," Andy says. "Let's talk. And then you can get the fuck out of my apartment."

"Officially you haven't been notified of your brother's death yet," Dick says, leaning back on his elbows. "But unofficially I know that you run with Gator Hyatt, so I understand you've probably known for a while now."

Andy stares.

"Like I said. Unofficial. I've seen your jacket. You been a CI for Hyatt for five years now. According to him, you've given him sixteen collars. Bullshit. I know you, Lewinsky. You're a rat, but you ain't *that* kinda rat."

"Know a lot about rats, huh?"

"I do. Biology, zoology, they're hobbies of mine. Man in my line of work's got to have his hobbies. Keeps your brain from turning into…" Dick trails off, gestures to the room around him. "Scientists got it right, see, studying rats. You learn all you need to learn about people, studying rats. This city for instance. I heard some college professor—say, your cousin's one, ain't she?"

"Fuck her," Andy says.

"Uh-huh. So I heard some college professor is trying to figure out, 'Why's New York City got so bad? What's wrong there?' And he's hollering about all of this social, political bullshit, and I just wanted to be able to ask him, 'Son, you know what happens when you stick a bunch of rats in a cage?' Do you, Andy?"

"You're wasting my time."

"You stick some rats in a cage and everything's fine. They live together. Form a community. Hell, you got enough space you can have an entire city of rats. But you start to put more in than what it can handle and things start to change. See, rats look out for theyselves. It's where the term comes from, though it ain't that apt. Now, a rat...a rat can look out for other rats, too. Care for them, support them. Make families with them. But then you start to take things away. Take away their space, their food. Rat stops thinking about the other rats so much. Keeps looking inward. Keeps trying to figure out, what do I gotta do for myself? And the more the rat asks that, the crazier he gets. Cause that's all he's thinkin' about. Not about gettin' away, not about makin' more space. Just his own damn fixation. Finally, not enough space, not enough food, whole bunch of rats lookin' out for number one, you know what happens? Rats start to eat. One another. Alive. And you got one rat chewin' on his neighbor while another rat's chewin' on him. Then 'fore long, you don't got any rats left at all. So, see, you learn a lot about people studyin' rats. And that's how I know you, Andy Lew. You'd eat a man sooner than turn him over to a group of people you hate more than life itself. So I know you ain't fed no one to Hyatt all these years. Which means you been givin' him *something* to keep your narrow ass on the streets..."

"I am a law-abiding American citizen," Andy says.

Dick chuckles, a deep, hearty bellow. "Sure, son. But here's the thing. Whatever sort of sicko arrangement you got, there's only one party I'm interested in, and it ain't you. Say what you will—or don't—but there's two men in this room who know that Hyatt's a sick piece of shit. I know there's boys on the force turn they backs on a lot of stuff. Man's gotta do what he's gotta do. I don't worry myself over that, we leave one another alone, cause they know their lines, don't step over 'em. Hyatt ain't got no lines. We both know that. Men have a habit of turning up dead 'round him, lot more than any other boy on the force. The dope he brings in and the money he brings in from deals he busted up always seems like just a little too *little*, dig? And, too, you gotta look at the company he keeps. No offense."

Andy shrugs.

"There's a difference between a vice boy going undercover and going native, you know."

"Me," Andy says. "Why it matters."

Dick smiles. "'Course. You. You and Teddy McCarn."

"Who?"

"The man we found with your brother's head, son. Hyatt not tell you that?"

"Not the name," Andy says. He wonders if Gator's been holding out on any *other* names. "You gonna fry him?"

"Now, see, that's the interesting thing. See, I remember your brother going missing, remember it very well. One of my first cases, you know, you never forget your first. Twelve years ago."

Andy tries not to breathe too quickly. Could really use the needle right now. Wonders if Dick would mind so much; seems serious about this not-on-official business thing.

"Twelve years," Dick continues. "Now, you say the boy went queer, ran off with his new boy-toy. Talked to his buddies, seems like the sort of fella who'd have some hidden proclivities. Good for him. I got a few of my own. Story never sat right with me, though. Always seemed off.

Keeped seeming off, every year goes by that no one hears from him. His wife, his buddies. You. That little cousin of yours. Most boys decide to open up about that lifestyle, they decide, sooner or later, to try and reach back out, try and make some kinda amends. Especially these days, cultural climate being what it is. Not Steven Lew, though. When he disappeared, boy really disappeared."

"So?" Andy says. "Now you know. This freak killed him, this McCarn."

Dick smiles again, shakes his head. "Twelve years, Andy. Remember? Teddy McCarn got discharged from the United States Army last August. After *sixteen* years of service. Boy was in Saigon when your brother went missing. Whereabouts accounted for every...single...day."

Andy inhales raggedly. "So? He gets out of the Army, comes back here, shanks my brother. All the shit they got when they came back from the suck, what do you expect? These fucking hippie sons of bitches spitting on them in airports, I'd want to kill a bastard, too."

"Aww, I forgot what a flag waver you are. Always got a kick out of that."

"Ain't nothing funny about loving your country," Andy says.

"Not at all. It's just that you..." Dick looks around the apartment. "Well, you wouldn't *expect* it from you, would you?"

"What's that supposed to mean?"

"Nevermind. Point being is—and I can't keep stressing this enough—science is a wonderful thing. See, science can't nail it down exactly, but it can tell me this: Your brother's been dead a lot longer than since last August."

"Meaning what?" Andy says. Something clicks. He reaches into his coat, comes out with tonight's photos. Starts thumbing them rapidly, like a scrap book. Feels his breathing steady, his nerves calm.

"Meaning I'm not having Teddy McCarn held on charges of killing your brother. Improper disposal of a body, maybe. Not that."

Andy glances up over the rims of his glasses. "What?"

"Teddy McCarn ain't a killer. Sick fuck, though. See, I don't like him for whacking your brother, but I damn sure like him for the twisted

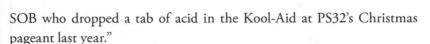

SOB who dropped a tab of acid in the Kool-Aid at PS32's Christmas pageant last year."

Andy can't help but snicker; stifles a full-blown laugh. The pity in Dick's face is temporarily replaced by rancor.

"You *would* think that's funny, you nasty little fuck, wouldn't you? A bunch of little kids freaking out like damn hippies at Woodstock?" He stares with an intensity that even Andy finds unsettling. Both men recompose themselves. The gentility returns to Dick's voice.

"Teddy McCarn, though...Well, it don't make sense coming from him. Seen a lot of boys coming back from the other side as different men...Was in Anzio myself and...Say, your old man was in the Big One, too, wasn't he? Think your cousin said that. Eastern Front?"

Andy stares at Dick; for the first time this evening he makes eye contact with him, Andy's ice blue eyes burning through the lenses of his glasses.

"Yeah," Andy says.

"Real sorry to hear what happened. I mean that. Your cousin says you're the one who found him?"

"Moving on."

"You're right. I'm sorry. For both of you." Dick pauses a moment, considers his own hands; looks apologetic. When he looks back up at Andy, he's business again. "But you know these boys comin' home done some awful stuff. I get that. Get the rage. The flippin' out, hitting the wife, the bar fight. Don't condone it. But get it. But dopin' a bunch of kids? Where's it come from? What makes a man drug school children... The same man we find months later dancing around the severed head of a man he almost certainly didn't kill? Like he's a brother in some old cracker horror story, trying to conjure some spirit?"

Maybe he was, Andy thinks.

"Not that we don't got a motive from him. Mr. McCarn, he ain't a shy one, no sir. Some boys like that, you bring 'em in, they get real quiet. Clam up. Go all spooky on you. Shrinks call it 'catatonia.'

Other ones, they can't shut up, for all the damn sense it makes, babblin' about little green men, vampires, whatever kinda sick stuff they got bouncin' round in their brains. Mr. McCarn, though, he's all business. Can hear the military man in him. Yes, sir, no, sir, sits up straight in his chair, respects authority. Now, we ask him about PS32, you know what he says?"

"I'm assuming you're going to tell me."

"Says, 'Yes sir, that was me, sir.' Not accustomed to gettin' a confession so easy, myself. Not in a case like this. Man finds out his wife was having an affair, gets hot, puts a slug in her, realizes what he done, that's the kinda man starts sobbin' when you stick him in a room, spills everything. Something like this? I'm used to grilling loonies four, five hours without shit. 'Yes sir, that was me, sir.' Wild. Figure I'll press my luck. I ask him, 'Well, Teddy, why'd you do it, and why'd you have that head?' And you know what he says? Don't answer—I know you don't know. He tells me 'Sir, I went into the suck to kill commies for the good of this country, and I never got to put a bullet in a damn one.'"

"Sounds like a good man."

"Oh, just you wait. Mr. McCarn, he ain't done talkin'. Says he ends up back Stateside, steamed he didn't get to put a bullet in no Charlies, says he's even more steamed he didn't get a souvenir. That's what he called it. A souvenir. I ask him, what kinda souvenir you want to bring back, Teddy, you want a post card, one of them flower necklaces—though, come to think of it, maybe that's only the Hawaiians. And Teddy, he tells me, 'All I wanted to bring home was a dead Red's head.' And then, he gets happy. Real happy. Ain't used to seeing a man smile that big in the hot seat. And he says, 'And *he* got me one.' And I ask who *'he'* is. And Teddy McCarn, he didn't stop smiling. But he *did* stop talkin'. Teddy McCarn ain't stopped smilin' and ain't talked again since that day. Boy even smiles in his sleep now."

"This is all very fucked up," Andy says. "Thank you for completely ruining my evening. Can you leave now?"

"See you got some pictures there," Dick says. "Think I can guess it's not anything I'd want to see. Now, me, on the other hand…" Dick reaches into his own coat, produces photos of his own. "These here, my pictures, I think *you* wanna see." Dick extends the photos; tentatively, Andy moves forward, snatches them away, scurries back. He looks down at the photos. Looks back to Dick. Back to the photos.

"What the fuck is this shit?"

"Same thing your sister-in-law wanted to know, when she brought them to me…two years ago? Maybe three. Things like this slip your mind. Was getting set to move out of her place, knocked a baseboard loose moving the couch. Found her a nifty little stash. Couple of vials of morphine, couple of porno mags. Those."

Andy squints to make out the details in the pictures. Dick's pictures are much older than his Polaroids, monochrome and grainy, yet taken with more precise care than Andy's hasty snapshots. He recognizes the place in the photos as his own apartment years ago, slightly cleaner, fewer holes punched in the walls, fewer photos pinned up. Recognizes, too, his brother's old friend Ludo, head to toe black in his beatnik getup, mugging for the camera; here, spread across the old couch, smoking a joint; here, holding a pair of candles over his head like devil's horns; and, here, in the last three photos of the series, his jeans down around his ankles, mounted on top of a half-nude figure, its eyes lolling in a narcotic stupor…

Andy tears the pictures in half, in fourths, in eighths, until they litter the ground like the multitude of mouse nests that already dot the apartment floor, then recoils from the shredded remnants.

"Fella in the pictures— though I'm figuring you know— *used* to be an asshole named Ludomil Dombrowski. Got hisself shot ten years back, trying to push baking soda to some boys in Harlem. And I'm figuring that you know who the other fella in those pictures is."

"You don't know shit," Andy says. It comes out as more of a whimper than he'd intended. "What've you been doing with those, huh? Three years, you fucking degenerate? Is that how you get off?"

"What I been doing is thinking," Dick says. "About what kinda man keeps those kinda pictures of his own brother. What kinda man keeps hanging around with the other fella in the pictures. Thought I'd come up with a few answers. Which is exactly why you ain't seen my face for a good, long time."

Andy stares.

"But, see, another thing I been wondering about a lot too, is what to do about Gator Hyatt. Cause you see, when the rats start eatin' one another, it's gotta start somewhere. Gotta start with one rat. You got yourself a whole cage of 'em, just crammed in there, just right there on the brink...And then one gets it into his head that this is what he's gotta do. Just one, chowin' down on the nearest thing he can sink his teeth into. And then maybe he gets another one, and another one, but eventually he's bitten enough, eaten enough his own damn self, that it gets everyone else on the move. But maybe, you stop that rat. Maybe you reach into the cage and you yank his ass out. Maybe you delay things. Maybe just a day. Maybe a few days. But you still keep things going the way they been going for a little while longer."

"Maybe all the fucking rats need to eat one another," Andy says. "Maybe that's what's meant to be."

"Don't wanna find that out for myself," Dick says. "What I do want is for Michael Hyatt's racist ass to end up the same place as your brother's."

Andy loses track of how long both men are silent; Dick keeps his gaze fixed on Andy; Andy's eyes move between the floor and Dick's forehead.

"Yeah?" Andy says. "And why the fuck would I help some pig get what he wants?"

"Cause those pictures you just tore up? Those are the copies," Dick says. "Those pictures are motive. Someone sees them, those pictures take your ass to the electric chair. But the thing is...I don't want no one to see them. No one besides you. I want to burn them to ash. Because doing that lets a man walk away who maybe isn't a good man...but maybe he's a man who don't deserve to be punished for *every* bad thing he done. You still like to play with yourself while people watch?"

"Why, you wanna see?"

Dick nods. "Thought so. Hyatt, he's a wily fuck. Lotta fucks on the force, not so many of them wily. Any of them leather-wearin' circus clowns tried to throw down on him, I know he'd see that comin' down the block. He don't let his guard down with them. He don't spend time with them… alone…in their apartments. But, if he did. And maybe they got into it. Maybe things got nasty. Maybe Gator ended up with a bullet in his punk ass. Maybe I'd tell anyone who asked that it was self-defense, open and shut. And maybe I tell those same people that we never gonna figure out who did Steven Lew. That Steven Lew was a sad, lonely, fucked-up man who went into some dark corner of the world and never come out. And you know a cop's always gonna listen when another cop's talking."

"And if your buddies on the force found out what you were talking about?" Andy asks.

"Who'd believe you?"

"Gator," Andy says.

"Aw, son. Gator know I got it out for him. Don't waste your breath telling the boy something he already know." Dick checks his watch, rises from Andy's cot. His head nearly touches the ceiling, has to stoop his shoulders to avoid bumping it. "You think it over, son. What you want your future to look like. Whether you want the rats to start biting sooner or later."

Andy is surprised at himself when he opens the door for Dick to leave. Listens to heavy, trudging footsteps fade down the hallway. When he's sure that Dick is gone, he drops the record on the player, starts up "Sister Golden Hair;" squats by his projector and sobs as he holds the lighter to the spoon. Is still sobbing when he slips the needle in and drifts away to a place beyond memory.

ANDY AWAKENS to the hiss of the record player, the hum of traffic, the insistent pounding of fists against decaying wood. He feels around for his glasses, puts them on, blinks to clear his vision. Someone at his door, knocking fast and hard but not too violently. Has a pretty good idea who's there. Reaches into his pants, finds his switchblade, keeps his hand on the trigger in case he's wrong.

"Well damn, ain't you looking pretty?" Gator steps past Andy into the apartment, looking a little too happy at the same time he's looking a little too disappointed.

Andy rubs his head, plunks himself down onto his cot. "What the hell do you want?"

"Heard what happened, came to offer my sincerest apologies, deepest regrets, all that touchy-feely bullshit you're supposed to do when an acquaintance has fallen on hard times."

"Learn that from Nicky?" Andy asks.

"Learn a lot from him," Gator says. "Chakras, tantric shit. Oughta stop by sometime, you're not feeling too sorry for yourself, expand your horizons. Might even get yourself laid, you show up with a bag over your head."

Andy shakes his head. "Not my scene."

Gator smiles. "Course not. You're a one-woman man, ain'tcha?" He slaps the side of the projector; Andy stares.

"So it's curtains at the Colossus then, huh?"

Andy stares.

"Can look into getting you some piecemeal work, til you're back on your feet," Gator says. "The department, you know, they're real eager to bust some queers, show the good, clean people of the world that the Big Apple ain't down with the sin of sodomy. Could catch some real doozies with you, know what I'm saying? Not the pretty boys, you know, the Redford looking homos with the wife and kids in the burbs, sorta fella who pops up on the six o'clock news and gets the whole world feelin' sorry for him. I mean I want some real nasty sons of bitches to frog walk.

I'm talking sarcomas, abscesses, the whole shebang. What do you say, Andy-man? Put your old skills to work for the good of the people. Old Gator will give you a nice new Mr. Jackson for every nasty queer you bring to him."

Andy shakes his head. "This…isn't the time, Gator."

"Come on, Andy-man, how many toilets you had your face shoved in? How many times have you had you had the shit beaten out of you by a trick didn't wanna pay? You are forty-one fuckin' years old, man, I'm surprised your ass hasn't gotten itself canned or killed two, three dozen times over, all the shit you pulled over the years. I'm amazed it took two of Eddie Lawler's bitch boys trying to rip you off to finally bring down the curtain, know what I mean? Figured it woulda been, uh, a little more freaky, ol' Rod-Rod walking in on you with your stick in your hand."

Andy's eyes prick up at the mention of the name. His body remains still but his eyes slowly rotate in their sockets towards Gator.

"Eddie Lawler?"

"Yeah. The little shit stain who got run over trying to make off with your reel didn't kick it. Got his ass in traction up at Bellevue, came to a few hours ago. Says Eddie Lawler offered him and a buddy a c-note each to rip you off, supposed to have some buyer wants to pay top dollar for a print of that little dick flick you were showing."

Andy's eyes rotate down to look at his hands. Eddie Lawler. A name unspoken for twelve years, rising up out of the muck of 42nd Street at the same time all of the other phantoms have finally decided to slip back out of the shadows.

"Take me to him," Andy says.

"What, the kid?"

"Eddie," Andy says. "Now."

IF ELEPHANT graveyards are where pachyderms go to die, and Florida is where Jews go to die, then Eddie's House is where good taste goes to die, withering and convulsing on semen splattered floors beneath blinding fluorescent lights. As he pushes through the blacked out door, Andy's nostrils flare, assaulted by a barrage of scents and odors strikingly familiar to him these twelve years on: bleach and semen, ammonia, sweat, desperation. Little has changed here, from the damp muskiness of the air to the stickiness of the floor, the wire racks with their fading porno books, ancient sex toys gathering dust in crumbling cardboard boxes. Time moves slowly here, he supposes, or Eddie Lawler has seen to it that his business is a monument to lechery in the 1960s, a living museum for future generations to indulge in their grandparents' hidden desires.

"Attention, meat-beaters and taco eaters," Gator shouts, pulls his revolver from its hiding place at the small of his back and raises it over his head. A half-dozen heads turn towards him, weary, glazed eyes staring in no particular shock. "Don't mean to alarm you, but if you keep your hands and other weapons right where I can see them, there won't be any trouble. Aw, you and me might have a little bit of fun. But right now I'm looking for the owner, so if Eddie Lawler would kindly pull up his jeans and join me in the lobby of his lovely establishment, I won't have to go putting any more holes in the ceiling than there already are."

The customers return to their indulgences, eyes going back to magazines, hands back to work inside coats. From the back corner of the room, Andy can hear rustling coming from one of the booths, followed by the heavy, strained sighs and grunts of a weary man carrying around just a little more bulk than he'd like. A second later Eddie Lawler appears through the curtain, shirt undone to his waist, mangy hands zipping up his pants. Balder than Andy remembers, but his torso just as hirsute. As he approaches the front of the store he stops, sees Andy, his whole body going rigid.

"The fuck did I tell you?" He asks. "You come in here again, I kill you. You think there was an expiration date on that?"

"I'm here with him," Andy says, points to Gator. Eddie looks from Andy, to Gator, to Gator's gun, aimed straight towards him.

"You sick fuck," Eddie says. "Fine. I'm not surprised. Fine. Should've fucking killed you the last time I saw you, little rat shit. Go ahead and do it, punk asshole. Don't waste my time. I'm just where I wanna be."

"Now let's not get too hasty with the threats, and the promises, and the swears and so on," Gator says. "My friend and I are just here to ask you some questions. I think after certain events that transpired at the Colossus Theater, he has a right to ask a few, don't you?"

"I don't know what the fuck you're talking about," Eddie says.

"He lived," Gator says. "Bout yea high, skin the color of shit? Yeah, he came to, and he's got himself a big ol' mouth."

Eddie's face reddens. "Back here," he says. "Not around my customers."

Eddie waves the pair into the back office; in all his years of patronage Andy never set foot inside of it, doesn't know if it's as well preserved as the rest of the establishment. The walls are covered in porno mag cutouts and movie posters, a dozen topless blondes staring down at a hobby horse desk and a cluster of folding chairs.

"You send some dumbfuck kids to rip me off, get me fired?" Andy hisses the moment Eddie's ass has hit his chair.

"Now, I'm the one asking questions here," Gator says, slipping his gun back into place. "Go on. Answer the man."

"It wasn't personal," Eddie says.

"It was my job," Andy says.

"It's *my* job," Eddie snaps back. "They're practically showing skin flicks on Saturday Morning now. I gotta compete. Law of the jungle. So I had a guy come through here last month, said he heard I knew how to get my hands on things. I says yeah. Guy says if I ever get my hands on a print of *Last House*, he's got a chunk of change to drop on it. Collector. Only a few prints of it floating around out there and he wants one for himself. I'd have sent my boys after any theater. Trust me...I wasn't thrilled when I heard who had it. Chrissy gonna be OK?"

"Now, can the American negro ever really be OK? I guess that's a question for the philosophers," Gator says.

"Company you keep degraded over the years," Eddie says, staring at Andy, Andy shifting his eyes this way and that to avoid contact. "But I'm not surprised. Who else you trucking with these days? White slavers, child molesters?"

"Myself," Andy says. "Only company I need. Me and my girl."

Eddie shudders. "Any girl trucks with you I don't wanna meet, if the broad's even real."

"She's real," Andy says. His voice rises in pitch. "More real than you." Andy composes himself, adjusts his jacket. "That's why I'm here."

"What?" Eddie asks.

"You helped me find her," Andy says.

Eddie stares at Andy a moment, confusion turning to recognition turning to horror, Gator watching the transformation, his sly little smile itself giving over to bemusement.

"You told me if I ever came back you'd kill me," Andy says. "As far as I'm concerned you broke the truce last night. But I'm willing to go back to the arrangement. If you answer some questions I've had for the past twelve years."

Eddie's breathing grows ragged. Sweat starts to trickle down his forehead.

"What do you want?"

"Where'd you find him?" Andy asks.

Eddie shakes his head, looks at the ground.

"Hey, Andy-man...the Hell we talking about here?" Gator asks.

"Twelve years ago I came here with the same request. To find me something. And he gave me a number..." Andy turns back to Eddie, wringing his hands in his lap. "But I never figured out, and I always wondered... Where did you find *him*? Where did you find Samuel Draft?"

Silence fills the room. Eddie sits shifting like a fly in the web.

"I didn't," he says after a moment.

"Bullshit," Andy says.

"It is the truth and fuck you," Eddie says. "I didn't find *him. He* found me."

Again, that silence, Eddie rocking sideways, the fly trying to escape. "I put out some feelers for you. Foreign shit, I think, mostly, figured maybe you'd get a thrill out of what they were watching in Germany. I was waiting for a call back from a distributor I knew in Toronto. Instead I get a call two, three in the morning. At my place. Couldn't tell if it was a chick or a guy. Think a guy. Had a deep laugh. But a soft voice. Says he hears I'm looking for the next best thing. Almost shit myself. Only my family has that number. Don't give it to my contacts, nobody."

Eddie goes quiet, looks down at his hands. His face has dampened; Andy can't tell if it's more sweat or tears. Gator's jaw goes round and round, looking back to Andy, Eddie.

"Andy, man, the hell is all this?"

"Keep talking," Andy says.

"I'm set to ask the guy how the hell he got the number, he says, 'Let me cut out the middleman,' some shit like that, tells me to write down *his* number. Says he can take care of it for me. I say hold up, that I want my cut out of whatever it is he's got going, that this is about one of my customers. Guy says, 'Andy's not your customer anymore.' I'm ready to shit myself again. Never mentioned your name to anyone I put out feelers to. Guy laughs. Says, if I want, he can hook me up with some new product for my place, on the cheap. I'm curious. I ask what he has. Guy says I got whatever you want. I ask what he wants for it…"

Andy can see that they are tears now, fat, sloppy, sweaty tears rolling down the cracked and saddened face of a man who only thought he'd seen and heard it all.

"The things he said … He didn't want money. He said he had enough money. He said he wanted… He wanted other things. He said that he wanted to be…*entertained*… And he said… He said, 'There's a family with a little girl lives right under you… Just one unit down,' he says. And he asked me…"

Eddie puts his face into his hands and sobs.

Gator looks between Andy, Eddie, back to Andy, grabs Andy by the bicep and hustles him back into the hall, leaving Eddie Lawler bawling like an infant at his desk.

"What the hell was that?" Gator asks.

"A pantywaist son of a bitch on his last stop before crazy town," Andy says.

"Nah, nah, fuck that, man. I seen some shit in my day, you don't live in one of these places for that long and cry like a sissy for no damn reason. That back there, that was a man who's seen some shit, and I want to know what the hell it has to do with you. Plausible deniability, man. I cover my own shit, I don't need to go down because of some-body else's."

"Hey," Andy says.

"What?"

"Twelve years ago, Eddie gave me Samuel Draft's phone number. And we talked. And we made an arrangement. And then *he* gave me *her*."

Gator shakes his head, shakes it again, eyes rolling around in his skull. "You told me that it was an accidental shipment, distributor sent you the wrong canister. Said you tracked that lead down, that someone somewhere mixed up some reels, then the trail went dead. The fuck are you telling me, Andy? All the shit we been looking into, all the research, the birthmark, all of that's bullshit? You know who fucking made the thing, you know who she is?"

"No," Andy says. "I know who I got it from. And I haven't seen or heard from him for twelve years. If anyone has answers, *real* answers, it's him. And he's gone. Or he *was* gone. Until now…" Andy turns, walks out of Eddie's, into the blinding-white light of daytime on 42nd. Andy feels his body shrivel, his eyes burn. He puts a hand over his face and looks for shade. Gator follows, barreling out of Eddie's at double-time.

"You get your ass back here, Lewinski. Now what the fuck is this shit? This about your brother? Huh?" Gator grabs Andy by the shoulders, spins him around, thrusts him into the nearest wall. Andy grunts; his jacket absorbs most of the shock.

"Get your hands off me."

"On paper, you been my CI for five years. That means five years of knowing all your bullshit, keeping you on a leash. It turns out that I have, what, some kind of freak killer on my hands, going around, chopping his brother up, turning him into the fucking Mummy, you know how that shit's gonna come down on me?"

"My brother…killed himself," Andy says. The words stick in his mouth, reverberate against his tongue and finally escape his lips in a dull trickle. "And I found him."

"And?" Gator asks.

"And my brother was worth more dead than he ever was to anyone alive." Andy slips out of Gator's grip, checks the corners of his jacket for stains. Gator turns, puts a hand to his forehead.

"Son of a bitch." He turns, points a finger at Andy. "And, what, this guy, this Draft, he's where you got it from?"

"Yeah," Andy says.

Gator puts his hand to his head, walks in a little circle. "I did not hear that. I did not hear that, and I do not know that…Aw, your little missy just about got you into a world of trouble."

Andy shrugs. "Yeah? Well, now she's going to get me out."

THE HASH smoke is thick in the air as Andy and Gator enter Nicky's apartment, and with the deep carpet and black walls it seems to Andy that he's trudging through some nightmare warzone, that at any instant the sound of human chatter and faint bossa nova music will be replaced with screams and gunshots and the scented smoke will become mingled with the thick aroma of gunpowder and blood and death. Only the picture window breaks the illusion, the curtains drawn back tonight to reveal the sparking Manhattan skyline, the lit windows and signs a multitude of artificial stars.

Tonight the apartment's inhabitants are congregated around a television set, a newer model, Andy sees, but looking ancient, the wood of the cabinet warped and cracked and covered in stains that might be water or blood or some other human fluids, a smear across the screen where someone attempted—unsuccessfully—to clean off something long ago congealed. Playing on the set, broadcast in from a massive VTR attached to it by a multitude of wires tangled around it like predatory jungle vines, is one of those nature shows they broadcast on Saturday mornings for, it seems to Andy, no other apparent purpose than traumatizing whatever poor idiot kids whose mothers might turn it on thinking it's a funny show about animals: Lions on the Serengeti converging on fleeing antelope, hyenas feasting on the carcass of some discarded wildebeest. In the center of the group sits Nicky, his legs tucked up beneath him.

"Well, see now, *my* favorite animal used to be the whale," Nicky says to Chad, continuing some ongoing conversation. "Obvious reasons, you know? Then, one time, this bitch I'm fucking on set, she's a marine biology student. Know what she tells me? The barnacle has a cock fifty times the length of its own body. Seriously. Lets it fuck every female in, like, a ten foot radius. Stick a male barnacle in a tank with a hundred females and it'll stretch its cock to fuck every last one of them. Told her, 'Well, guess my favorite animal's a barnacle, now.'"

Nicky's mouth opens a sliver and a stale, cracking sound comes out that Andy supposes is the closest thing he can muster to a belly laugh. The circle laughs approvingly, Chad, seated directly beside Nicky, elbowing him jovially in the ribs. In the midst of the revelry Nicky looks up, sees Gator and Andy at the door.

"The fuck did you bring this cocksucker back for?" Nicky stares at Andy, his mouth closing, tightening, any joy gone from his face. "I was having a good night. Watching some good, quality entertainment." On the television set, the picture rolls, breaks up; when it becomes visible again, some sort of big cat Andy doesn't recognize is in the process of eviscerating something too bloodied and masticated to identify.

"We come in peace," Gator says, raising his hands above his head, giving a playful little spin. Andy stands his ground, eyes locked with Nicky's; waits for him to blink; keeps waiting.

"That so?" Nicky asks. "Well, if that's the case, I'm feeling pretty peaceful myself. Tell me, you boys fans of animals? Can't trust a man doesn't care for animals. My mother used to call them one of God's greatest amusements."

"Perfect timing, Nicky-o," Gator says, slapping Andy on the back. "I brought my favorite animal right here." Andy sneers.

"You brought the dallier back into our artistic sanctum? Against the wishes of our patron?" Wilson shrieks. "This is a forum in which one can expand one's horizons, contemplate great matters." He rises; tonight he is wearing a red and white striped shirt and a little black beret. "What horizons does he have? He has the intellectual depth of a tide pool. Your favorite color, black? Your favorite animal, some clichéd, intelligent predator, like the gorilla or the ocelot? Some beast that fulfills your fantasies of virility and wisdom?"

Andy stares back at Wilson. "Gator's right," Andy says. "I'm my own favorite animal. And that's why you should shut the fuck up and listen to me."

The circle goes quiet; all eyes move to Wilson and Andy. Nicky slowly rises, a thin smile spreading across his lips.

"You ride in a hippie van around the country with a bunch of slap-happy dope smokers, sucking cock and jamming to The Dead?" Andy says to Wilson. "Party with guys who knew a guy, think you're experts on the city? This Sybarite bullshit, rage against the world, decadency of the Big Apple on the eve of destruction? What the fuck do you know about that?"

"We know …" Wilson begins.

"You know jack shit," Andy says. "Because you're up here in this braindead party palace with your punk boy love club trying to figure out the world and chanting 'Namaste.'"

"Namaste," Chad says, offers a little bow.

"See, Andy here's the real deal," Gator says. "Maybe shoulda been a little more up front about that, not taken the whole fancy-pants arty-fart angle. Naw, Andy-man, he's seen it, he's done it, he's lived it. You boys really don't know your shit, do you? You wanna write about your little Sybarite fella, kill crazy psycho hates the world, wants to end it all, wants to rage against the system?" Gator slaps Andy on the back perhaps a bit too hard, jerks him forward. "This here? This fella here *is* John Sybarite."

Wilson leans forward, as though studying the scratched and pitted lenses of Andy's glasses for some sign, some indication of truth to the statement. Mirroring his partner, Aaron leans in as well, nearly pressing his nose to Andy's in his assessment.

"Prove it," Wilson says.

"What I'm here for," Andy says. "The true John Sybarite experience. For a price."

Wilson looks to Aaron, back to Nicky. He puts his sunglasses back on.

"Won't regret it, fellas," Gator says. "I taken the ride myself. Honest Injun, Nicky, don't know why I didn't think of in the first place. Andy-man, his little art projects, now, I grant you, they're essentially shit. But the mind they come from, man? That's what you really need to study. There's your window into the world. Can't live in the light without the darkness, all that zen bullshit, right?"

"Hey," Chad snaps.

"No offense, man-o-mine. But you little fellas here, you wanna write your big rock opera, talk about the state of the city, state of the world? It's all right up there in Andy's place. All the research you could ever hope to conduct in one, tiny, convenient location."

"Five hundred dollars," Andy says. "Cash. Up front."

Nicky smiles, shakes his head. "Don't get me wrong. I appreciate aggression. Hell, I've used it plenty of times to get what I want. Usually works, if you got the cock and the fists to back it up. But I don't pay for shit I haven't seen. That's a rookie mistake. Made it too many times myself. Reason I make a bitch undress with the lights on now."

"It could, perhaps, be a risk worth taking," Wilson says. Aaron nods. "Who, after all, knows how to identify the quivering underbelly of a city better than those sworn to protect it? And Dear Gator has so exceptionally entrenched himself in this milieu that perhaps he alone is qualified to identify the true heartless heart of the city." Wilson walks excitedly around Nicky, stroking the tiny little tuft of hair on the tip of his chin. "Five hundred dollars is a pittance to your acquired wealth...*right*?" He asks.

Nicky looks back and forth between Andy, Gator, Wilson. He reaches down into a glass bowl full of ash on the coffee table, fishes around; comes up with a half-smoked cigarette, still smoldering. Takes a drag off of it, his fingers dusted black like a chimney sweep's.

"Mmmm. Sure, sure," Nicky says. "Maybe."

"You must go fetch it then. We are intrigued. Though I am skeptical that this apparent philistine has anything to offer the world in ways artistic, evidence is mounting that perhaps he may be a worthy subject of *study*."

"I don't keep cash lying around my apartment," Nicky says. "Had my wallet and my weed lifted too many times on set. Got tired of getting calluses on my palms slapping around assholes to get it back."

"Don't believe in checkbooks?" Gator asks.

"Is that acceptable?" Nicky asks Andy.

Andy sighs. "We gonna do this or not? I don't have all night. Grab the fucking thing and let's go."

NICKY, CHAD, Wilson and Aaron must squint to adjust themselves to the dim light of Andy's apartment, the filament in the two clear ceiling bulbs beginning to decay, diminishing the level of illumination in the room and casting swaths of shadow as they flicker and blink. Gator and Andy move smoothly through the little place, stepping over rodent nests and other assorted debris, their eyes more well acclimated to the dark.

"Close the door behind you," Andy says as they enter, slips back around as Chad comes in so he can move all the locks into place. As everyone becomes accustomed to their new surroundings, Andy watches them, a little smile on his lips as he sees their expressions change, curiosity becoming confusion becoming horror on Chad's face as he studies the myriad photos tacked and nailed and stapled to the walls, Andy's carefully assembled and steadily growing shrine, only the most graphic and detailed photos clipped and torn from the pages of true crime books and detective magazines, both famous and infamous, a monument to violence dating back decades, Elizabeth Short transforming into Kitty Genovese transforming into Sylvia Likens, the stark black and white as vibrant as any color against the drab gray walls.

"Oh shit," Chad says. His voice trembles. His muscles seem to bounce involuntarily beneath his t-shirt, quivering. Nicky stares around him; Gator chuckles. Wilson and Aaron seem nonplussed, slowly making a circuit of the room, studying Andy's pictures, lifting their sunglasses, putting them back down. Andy watches them a moment before he sets about uncovering his projector, setting it up; retrieving the film; threading the reel.

"What you're seeing, now, boys," Gator says, flopping down, "this here's the appetizer. The, uh, what do you call it, the prologue. The Coming Attractions. Now, what Andy's got here... This is the feature presentation."

"Sit down where you can," Andy says. "Just not on the floor. Try not to fuck anything up. Anyone want beer?"

There are no takers. Andy shrugs, goes and retrieves one for himself. When he returns, everyone has found a place for themselves to sit,

Nicky's head tilting back and forth curiously, Wilson and Aaron studying the projector as though deep in thought. Only Chad seems ill at ease, his head bobbing around the apartment, eyes moving between the front door, the window, the bathroom door, the bedroom door—long ago boarded up, a dozen two-by-fours nailed in place across it and blocked off by a tattered lawn chair— like he's considering an escape plan.

Andy goes to the projector. Thinks to put *their* song on, to enhance the experience; thinks better of it. Too intimate. This is a formal introduction; nothing else.

"You want life?" Andy says. "Well, boys, here it is."

OUR SECOND FEATURE OF THE EVENING:

THE PASSION OF THE DAMNED

(1965)

> *Protect me from what I want*
> —**Jenny Holzer**

ANDY LEW, twenty-nine, sallow, slumps back in the darkness and lets the feeling wash over him. It is not an unfamiliar sensation of late, neither here in the solitude of Eddie's back rooms nor in the projector booth where he works, nor in his own home, nor any other place he may settle in for the activities he once found fulfilling.

The feeling is complete and utter emptiness.

Andy rubs his face in bony palms and rises to exit the booth, draws his trench coat tight around his narrow body. Freezing in here. Air conditioner, full blast; winter outside and sleet beating hard against the storefronts of 42nd Street and ice patches threatening to send pedestrians tumbling into traffic, tumbling into one another, tumbling through glass doors and into businesses in bloody pulpy messes that will be summarily mopped up before the authorities are notified…Always, Eddie Lawler sees fit to keep the air conditioner on full blast.

"Well, whattaya think?" Eddie, husky, goateed and bursting from his clothes, calls from the lonely counter that sits center-store, perched precariously atop a teetering wooden stool as he peruses the *Times*.

"That was it?" Andy sneers. Makes his way to the counter, sticks his hand out palm-up. "I seen shit more hardcore in the funny pages. Gimme back my fifty cents."

Eddie swats Andy's hand with the paper, focuses in on an article. "Buyer's remorse ain't refundable. I got more important things to worry about. See this? Germ warfare, man. Fine, go ahead, nuke the fuckin' Commies, all I gotta say. Germs, though? All it'll take's one VC slipping away from the lines, infect the whole fuckin' world. You own a gun?"

"No."

"Consider it. Way things are going, the world's never gonna see 1966."

"Oh yeah?"

"Don't look so fuckin' excited."

"I gotta get excited about *something*. The shit you're showing me don't do dick."

"You never had a problem with any of it before."

Andy looks around, the sensation that someone is watching him, feels it in the back of his head like a pair of pins digging in. Turns to face the door, no one there, just passerby outside, just the electric signs of the strip shows and theaters and bars burning dully through the midday snow-haze. Turns back to Eddie, rolls his shoulders, adjusts his jacket collar. "The problem is the stuff you got now is the stuff you had before."

"And?" Eddie turns on his stool, almost topples, seems unfazed by this near humiliation, surveys his fiefdom of marital aids, books in paper wrappers, bustiers, leather jockey shorts, returns his gaze to Andy with a renewed sense of satisfaction, the old world sensibility of a man justified through work, through the construction of a business with which he supports himself. "What I got is either titties or blood, son. What more you need?"

"You fucking serious? Titties are for high school boys who can't get any action at the prom. I need something for a *man*."

"When I was your age, two chicks and a bubble bath was plenty enough for a man," Eddie says, looks over in the vicinity of the booths. "So was Bogie gunnin' down gangsters in Largo. C'mon, Andy, nothing? You really telling me that was *nothing*?"

"*Kiddie shit*," Andy spits.

"Don't say 'kiddie' in here. Bad for business. You want me to get sent away?"

"Who the fuck's gonna hear you? I'm the only one in here."

"*I* can hear you and that's enough. Now I given you everything you ever come in here and asked for. Everything. What more you want? You sit on your ass all day long watching that sleaze you show over at the Colossus. You fried your fucking brain."

"It's the real world," Andy says, eager, desperate. "A hell of a lot better than Doris and Rock. The real world, Doris'd be shoving a coat hanger up her cooch and Rock would be taking it in the ass in the Oracle mens' room. Life ain't technicolor."

"It also ain't a twenty-four-hour rape fest. Whips, whores, twenty dead bodies in every film. You done this to yourself, Andy. You're a fuckin' burnout, is what you are."

Andy, indignant: "I ain't no fuckin' burnout."

"You are and that is the truth. You're a fuckin' burnout. You can't feel jack shit anymore, you're so fuckin' dead inside—"

"Dammit, I am not-"

"And it ain't my fault. Don't you lay that shit on me. No. Don't you dare."

"I ain't no fuckin' burnout," Andy, more insistent now, incapable of hiding the pleading desperation with which he says this. "Eddie...My tastes just changed. They're more...*sophisticated*. People's tastes change. Everyone's tastes change. They see something when they're younger, they don't like it anymore when they get older because they're smarter now.

They're more civilized. I just need something different. Come on, man. We known one another ten years. You *know* me. I just need something different now is all."

Eddie looks Andy up and down. "Ten years. No shit?"

Andy taps the masking-tape mended arm of his grey and silver browline glasses. "Same frames."

"Well, you need new ones. A new wardrobe, too. You ain't as big as you used to be. Shit." Eddie rocks back and forth on the stool; Andy on some base level amazed at the dexterity with which Eddie manages to do this in spite of his mass. "Your *tastes* changed?"

Words spill out of Andy Lew like pearls from a broken necklace, directionless, frenzied, the only purpose to trip up anyone who might stumble across them: "Sure, I watch the stuff we show at the Colossus, but it ain't trash. Just because it shows what it shows don't make it trash. It's art, it's aggressive, it makes you think. I've...matured. I see things more clearly now. I know that the stuff we used to show and the stuff you're still showing isn't *real*. I see things the way they are now: that the world's a shithole full of shitty people, that it's rough and real and violent and *raw*. And I need...*entertainment*...to *satisfy* me...that reflects that."

Eddie raps his knuckles on the countertop. "I don't know what that is. A man needs a challenge now and then, though. Keep himself sharp. Hell, maybe the burnout crowd is the market I need to be looking at after all. Gotta have some cash somewhere, more of you people turning up every day."

"Dammit, I'm not a-"

"Shhh. It's OK. Listen. You give me a while. I'm going to have to make some phone calls on this."

Andy's lip, twitching, his best approximation of a smile. "Really?

"Some people who know people. Feelers. But, listen. Understand something here. I find what you're looking for...it's going to cost you."

Andy Lew says, "Anything."

ANDY LEW enters his apartment, grocery bag cradled in one arm, loaded up with all the spoils that his salary can afford. The apartment is only slightly warmer than Eddie's, by virtue of the multitude of candles erected like a shrine on the coffee table in the center of the living room, greens and reds and yellows liquefying into a rainbow on the sheet of glass set beneath them. Andy breathes deep: The smell of smoke and sweat and whiskey and empty beer bottles fill his nostrils; the smell of home.

"Andy?" Steven Lew lumbers from the bedroom, looking frailer than he should, three-hundred pounds straining at a tattered cotton robe two sizes too small, a naked lamp held in one plump hand like an electric lantern. He wheezes, coughs, squints against the dying light of the bulb. "That you, Andy?"

"If I was someone else, I'd have killed you and robbed you already."

"I didn't think you were a robber."

"Who did you think, then?"

"Someone else."

"Who?"

"I don't know. Anyone else. You're late."

"I stopped someplace on the way home from the Colossus."

"Where?"

"The fuck does it matter, where? I stopped someplace. I got my own damn life."

"I know. But I'm hungry."

"You got enough fat on you to last the winter." Andy puts down his grocery bag and rummages through it, comes out with a canned ham, a bottle of beer. Steven sets the lamp down on the floor, opens his arms; Andy tossing first the ham and then the beer, allowing Steven a moment to catch each one. Steven misses the ham, gets the beer, hunkers down there in the doorway beside the lamp, opens the ham and begins to eat it with his fingers.

"That's disgusting," Andy says, taking out a copy of the *Times* from his grocery sack. "Use a fucking fork." Andy carefully tears out the story about germ warfare, trying not to lose letters to frayed edges. When he's finished, he tacks it to the wall beside the door, steps back to observe this addition to his slowly burgeoning shrine of news stories he finds to be particularly fascinating: The Kennedy Assassination; the Bay of Pigs; Kitty Genovese; along with innumerable small snippets detailing deaths in Vietnam, muggings in Central Park, rapes in Queens. Satisfied, he sits down on the couch, opening a beer for himself. "Use a fucking fork," he mutters again.

"If I used a fork…I'd have to wash it," Steven says between mouthfuls.

"You lazy bastard. You're thirty-two years old. You live here for free. It gonna kill you to wash a fork, pick up after yourself? This place is getting filthy. I keep a nice, clean home. What do you do all day here but lay around and get stoned and eat my food and watch my television?"

"I don't watch television. There isn't anything on." Steven opens his beer with his teeth, spits the cap into a nearby pile of old newspapers and empty tin cans. He drinks down half of the bottle. "Besides, you can go on and kick me out anytime you want."

"Mom wouldn't like it," Andy says, takes another drink of beer.

"Mom's dead. So's dad."

"No shit." Andy guzzles his beer, pops open another, a quixotic attempt to add weight to his spindly frame.

"I could go stay with Cousin Saskia."

"She'd kill you."

"We always got along."

"She'd do it for fun."

"At least I'd die warm."

"Your fault in the first place," Andy mutters.

"What?"

"Your own damn fault you're here. I'm doing you a favor and don't you forget that. Your fault and Ludo's. That fucking pinko should be the one taking care of you, not me."

"You can still kick me out."

"Then you'd freeze."

"Probably." Steven wipes out the inside of the now empty can with his fingertips, turns to his beer. "You got another?"

"In the bag. Get it yourself. I'm tired."

"Tired from what? Pulling your pud up in the booth? I don't feel too hot. Come on. Gimme another one."

"I'm tired from working a real damn job so neither one of us freezes, that's what I'm tired from. Awfully fuckin' convenient you get 'sick' right after you move in here. Awfully fuckin' convenient. So sick that 'just a few nights' turns into a week, turns into a month, turns into three months. Three months later and you're still fuckin' sick. Go lay down in front of the hospital. Be *their* problem."

"Ain't my fault I'm sick. Can't lay that one on me."

"I'll lay that and a whole lot more on you. Some fuckin' brother you been."

"I paid you back good."

"Sure, the first time. The first hit's always free, ain't it?"

"Gotta make a dime somehow." Steven lifts himself up on the door frame, wheezes with every step, makes it to the bag, lifts out another beer. Moves to open it with his mouth but stops, stands there a moment, small eyes growing large behind folded lids before a coughing fit begins to rack his body. Andy rises from the couch, moves to Steven, brings him back to the couch and sits him down. The fit goes on; Andy kneeling beside him on the sagging cushions, breath shallow, hands extended before him in some futile gesture, the hope that his body will somehow know how to react in the event that he must pull Steven back from the brink. Moments pass. The coughing subsides. Thick wheezes taper down into a volley of staccato breaths.

"You OK?" Andy asks.

"Get...me something."

"You're sure?"

Steven's eyes still bulging, he nods, sweat beginning to bead up on greasy hair tips.

"You're breathing shallow anyway. It'll fuck you up."

"Make me…feel better."

Andy rises. He makes it halfway across the room before Steven groans out after him, "No sneaking."

In the bedroom, Steven's gimmick kit: Little glass vials, filthy syringes, fleshy rubber hoses twisted and retwisted to the point of breaking. Andy fingers one of the vials, lifts it up, casts a glance over his shoulder and slips another of the vials into one of his many pockets.

On the couch, Steven, heaving, mouth open in a small, slack 'u'. Andy approaches, prepping the needle, one of the rubber hoses slung around his neck.

"C'mon, man."

"Gimme a minute." Andy turns Steven's arm around, wraps the tube, ties it, starts searching for a vein amidst the field of lesions and track marks that populate his masticated flesh.

"My guts are on fire, man," Steven groans.

"Because you eat too much and what you eat is shit. Dammit, where are your veins?"

"Sleeping. Happy." Steven coughs, flecks of spittle hitting Andy's glasses. Andy, at last, finding a sweet spot, angles the needle, penetrates Steven's flesh, a little twitch of excitement in Andy's bowels as he draws blood out to ensure he's hit his target before he mashes the plunger down. Steven closes his eyes tightly. Andy watches, his tongue grazing back and forth across his upper lip.

"Good?" Andy asks.

Steven nods. Andy moves to rise up from the couch, Steven's hand reaching out to snag the cuff of his jacket. "Wait with me, man."

"Wait for what?"

"Watch me breathe. Make sure."

"Son of a bitch, I fuckin' warned you beforehand."

"I needed it, man. Shit. I needed it. Just a few minutes, man."

"Fucker."

"Tell me about Eddie's."

"What?"

"Tell me what you saw at Eddie's."

"You sick bastard. That gonna get you off? That your scene now?"

"I just wanna hear something. What else you got to tell me about?"

"We got a new movie coming in to work," Andy says, turning over his shoulder to grab at the grocery bag with his fingertips. He lifts out a beer, pops it. *The Whip and the Body.* I'm optimistic."

"Sounds sexy," Steven says. "Who's in it?"

"Christopher Lee."

"Groovy."

"What's the second feature?"

"*Cannibal Orgy.* Lon Chaney's kid and a bunch of inbred chicks in negligees."

"Mmmm. Think you can get me in?"

"Sure. I'll pretend I'm sneaking you in. Like when we were kids."

"Even if this shit's tame, nothing you ever got us into was that nasty."

"We could only hope. *Cannibal Orgy*'s probably the better bet. A title like that, it's gotta live up to it, right? *Whip and the Body*, that could be anything, you whip a horse, that's still a whip and a body; they don't say it's a *human* body. But, *Cannibal Orgy*…"

"Doesn't mean…you get to see anything."

"Don't jinx it," Andy says.

"Even if it's awful, you'll get something new in a week," Steven says. "Always something new."

Andy thinks a moment. Steven's breathing becomes more shallow, little gurgles echoing out of his throat every other breath. "Eddie's going to be getting something new soon. Something better soon."

"Yeah? What?"

"I don't know. He just said it'd be something better. Better than what he's got now."

"Better," Steven whispers.

Steven drifts off. Andy watches, ten minutes, fifteen, decides that's enough, removes his jacket and slips beneath the heavy burlap blanket on his cot. Leaves his shoes on for warmth; wads the jacket up beside him and nestles his glasses on it, the world around him becoming a blur, the light of the candles kaleidoscopic across a ceiling of whorling browns, aged paint and water spots and dried blood and what else? He stares at this a good long while, waiting for sleep to overtake him. An hour passes. When he realizes tonight will be just like all the other nights since the first time, he puts his glasses back on and rummages in his jacket for the vial, the needle he pulled out of Steven. Andy rolls up his shirt sleeve, ties the hose, squints at his arm against the now dying glow of the candles; sees he won't be getting anywhere in this light. On all fours he shambles over to Steven's lamp, sets up on his haunches. Looks over at Steven; makes sure he hasn't woken him. Steven gurgle-snores. Andy, satisfied, finds the vein, administers the shot. Fire burns through his veins, floods his heart, pounds battering-ram style against the base of his skull until his defenses fall, until the elixir begins to take effect. On the cot, curled beneath his blanket, Andy slips into the sweet, peaceful nothing.

"ENJOYING THE show?"

Andy, feet propped against the projection booth wall, turns around in his folding chair; there behind him, Roderick Tillman, newly hired manager of the Colossus Theater, blonde and square-jawed, a pretty boy in the final years of his natural beauty working on a spare tire gut and a receding hairline. "Yeah," Andy says. "Not bad. I seen better. They lie to you, in the advertisements. 'See the terror that crippled the Amazon's most fearless explorer.' 'Hear the screams of the doomed virgin'. That shit's on a poster, it means you've never seen anything like it before, right? That's why it's a big deal? But then you come in here and you see the movie, and, it's the same shit you seen a dozen times before but with different chicks."

"I thought it was pretty bad," Roderick says, shifts his weight from foot to foot, hands stuffed into the pockets of too-tight pants, wrinkling up his too-tight vest in the process, all of Rod-Rod's uniform too tight, a chain reaction of dishevelment whenever one article of clothing goes out of place.

"This the first theater you managed?" Andy asks, pops a chocolate into his mouth. Stale: the kids at the concession stand always give him the expired stuff.

"Yes."

"You seen many of the movies on the Deuce?"

"The Deuce?"

Andy rolls his eyes. "Forty Second Street. Where the fuck you from, Tillman?"

"Topeka."

"Well, you seen any gnarly shit down in Topeka? Shit like we show here?"

"I went to the drive-in a few times."

"Drive-ins. Fuck." Andy continues to watch the film. A moment passes; Roderick clears his throat.

"I was just hoping to get to know you. I was told when I was hired that there's not much turnaround with projectionists. I figure that the kids downstairs are going to come and go, but you and me will probably be working with one another for a long time."

"When is this bitch going to die?" Andy mutters. "Yeah, it ain't popping popcorn and scraping shit off the auditorium floor. Sound goes out, reels don't get changed over on time, not to mention the fuckin' print catches fire, people get pissed, things go wrong. You don't wanna see things go wrong."

"Gosh," Roderick says. "It sounds so…intense."

Onscreen: Dissatisfaction defined.

"Fucking Steven. Fucking jinx."

Roderick clears his throat. "So…How long have you been at it? I mean, working here. I haven't had the chance to read everyone's employee dossiers yet."

"Since '55."

"Any…special reason?"

"It was a job," Andy says. "And I wanted to see the stuff they wouldn't show on TV."

"I do enjoy it when a job comes with perks," Roderick says.

"Yeah," Andy says. "Free shit's cool."

"Perks, not free," Roderick says, "After all, you work for it, don't you?"

"Damn straight I work for it," Andy says, sighs. "Fuckin' kids these days expect to show up and get paid for walkin' in the door. It's the socialist bullshit they're feeding them in school now, you ask me. My old man found out I had that kinda work ethic he'd have come down here and shoved a reel up my ass himself."

"He sounds like a real son of a bitch," Roderick says.

"Fucking straight," Andy says.

"But you can't let that bother you."

"I don't," Andy says.

"That's good. I had to learn that the hard way. My own father was the same. His answer to everything was his fists."

"And?" Andy asks.

"I was terrified of him."

"So?"

"It took me a long time to ever feel secure around other men," Roderick says. "That they weren't going to hurt me." Andy tensing more, now completely unsure what this is.

"Little fear's a good thing," Andy says. "Keeps you sharp. Stops you from fucking up."

"I guess," Roderick says.

Andy sighs. Which the greater indignity: the third degree from this shmuck, or the complete and utter failure of the film to live up to even a fraction of what it promised?

"Reel change in a minute," Andy says.

"Oh," Roderick says.

"You gonna stand there and watch?"

"Sure." Roderick shrugs. "I've never seen it before."

"You never seen a reel change? The fuck you do before this?"

"College," Roderick says. "Business."

"Good for you." Andy Lew rises; waits for his cue; a white donut appears onscreen in the upper righthand corner, the signal to switch on the second projector. The transition must be done correctly to ensure an even flow, for the action to continue, for no dialogue to be missed. Roderick watches, transfixed. The second projector comes to life; the first dies; the film continues.

"Wow," Roderick says. "That's pretty cool."

"You don't gotta blow smoke up my ass."

"No, I'm serious. I've seen movies all my life, I never realized that you had to do that. I just thought you hit "play" and it went all by itself." Roderick approaches the projectors now, bending over to inspect them. "Huh."

Andy sighs, crosses his arms. Roderick stands. "Well, anyway. I have to get back to work downstairs. Hey, Andy. Just remember, if you ever need to talk, about your dad, anything— I've been there."

"That's great."

"OK then."

Roderick leaves, a final glance back at the projector. Andy watches him go; turns back to the machine, with all of its whirring cogs and rapidly spinning gears, the film churning through it at the flesh-blistering pace of twenty-four frames per second, eye-blinding light bursting through it to transform a tiny, transparent square into a massive image on a wall a room away, and tries to figure out what the big deal is.

"EDDIE?" ANDY hisses into the receiver, cradling it in two hands, snow beginning to build up on the booth, turning it into a little rectangular igloo amidst the yawning skyscrapers of 42nd Street.

"Andy? Andy, what the fuck?" Eddie, sleep groggy, husky voice even thicker than usual. "What the fuck time is it? Where you get my number?"

"You gave it to me. When I asked if you'd be my emergency contact? Hey Eddie, listen. *Eddie?* You come up with anything yet?"

"Andy, it's been a fuckin' week." A long pause; Andy wonders if Eddie has fallen asleep holding the phone. "I'm doing my best. Listen, you gotta call me again, you call at the store, during business. I got my own life."

The line goes dead. Andy hits the phone with the receiver, hangs up. Hugs his jacket tight around his body; stands there and watches the snow dance in little cyclones in the sky, illuminated in the blue-white glow of a sign advertising what Andy knows to be the vilest coffee on the street. After a moment he turns towards the diner, sees a pair of girls exiting, nineteen, maybe twenty, little college girls up far past their bedtime. He strains to listen to their conversation through the sound-muffling panes of the booth; failing to hear the words coming from their mouths, he begins to formulate his own: tests to be taken in the coming days; hopes for the future; plans for majors; plans for careers; plans for vacation. Arguments with hard-headed fathers and temperamental mothers; pestilent younger brothers; crushes on boys in class; crushes on professors. Whispered fantasies that haunt their nights, secret yearnings exchanged not in their words now but in wry little smiles on weary faces, secret hand signals, darting glances directed first towards one another and now towards Andy. Andy, looking them in the eye and sure they are looking back at him, calling to him to exit the booth and deliver, beckoning to him, he can hear them now and their words are clear and they are beckoning to him, and Andy is frantically working his belt buckle and the door of the booth flings open with a sudden metallic sound that startles the girls so they are completely motionless and staring at the booth when Andy exits, chinos around his ankles, hands on his ass as he thrusts his hips out towards them.

First one girl screams and then the other and then they are running away, fast, faster than he can move, and the rage and the confusion build up inside of Andy quicker than he can understand and he is screaming, *sobbing*, "Isn't this what you wanted? *Isn't this what you wanted!?*"

The girls disappear down the street, into a sea of lights. Andy stands there, stares at the point on the muted rainbow horizon where they vanished, the little cyclones growing larger around him.

"WE'RE SPECIAL." Steven says this as he and Andy lie side by side beneath the coffee table, heat from the candles radiating down, ensconcing them in a darkened shell of muted flame.

"What?" Andy asks. His voice has already begun to slur from the effects of the drug.

"You…and me. No one is ever going to have this moment. Because you're you and I'm me. And we're here, man. We're here, right now, doing this, and no one else is because no one else is you or me. And us being here right now…this is us…so you're me…and I'm you. And no one else is us."

"Shut the fuck up," Andy says.

"Don't kill this for me," Steven says. "We need…to celebrate. Have you still got the donkey?"

"What time is it?" Andy asks.

Steven feels the floor around him, finds his watch, brings it up to his face, strains to see it in the dull light, sees the words 'To my loving Vitek,' realizes he's looking at the back. Flips it around. "Three o'clock."

"Morning or afternoon?"

"Afternoon."

"Then it's too early for the donkey."

"Fuck that. We need to celebrate. I want to see the donkey."

"The fuck you want to see the donkey for?"

"Because it's hilarious."

Andy forgets where he is, tries to sit up, slams his head into the coffee table, doesn't quite feel it. Settles back down. "That supposed to be a joke? You making fun of me? There's nothing funny about it."

"Give me a break. You thought it was funny. Once upon a time."

"It was sick, once upon a time. Where the fuck'd you find it, anyway? I know where to get that shit nowadays…But five years ago?"

"A friend brought it back from Tijuana with a delivery. Grade-A shit, man. The perfect trip."

"The fuck was your angle with that, anyway? Giving me that shit?"

"It was your birthday."

"You couldn't have given me socks?"

"I thought you'd appreciate something novel. You enjoyed your nudie cuties. Big boobed barefooted bitches blissfully bouncing balls in Boca. So I thought you'd enjoy something more…*novel*."

Andy thinks about this. "Shit."

"Well, you did enjoy it, didn't you?"

"I said, I thought it was sick."

"So let's see it again. Give ourselves a good shock. What's a shock like when you're stoned? It must be a rush, man. Wild, man. Crack out that projector. I wanna see it."

"I seen it enough."

"How many times?"

"What?" Andy almost sits up again, remembers his mistake.

"How many times have you seen it?" Steven, eyes shut, a peaceful Buddha drifting in the serenity of an opiate haze.

"I don't want to see it. It's too early. No donkey before eight."

"Eight o'clock. Bed time," Steven says. "But we get to stay up late now. No mom or dad to tuck us in."

"We never fucking got tucked in," Andy says.

"I thought Cousin Saskia tucked you in," Steven smirks.

"Fuck you."

"She never tucked *me* in. My loss. And our loss now if you don't break out the donkey."

"I got something else," Andy says. "Something…" Almost says 'better,' stops, doesn't know why. Rolls out from beneath the table, heads to his cot, rummages beneath it for the canister. Uncovers his projector, recently purchased from old Al Koscian over at the Oracle Theater, an antique but beautifully maintained Cinegraphica, so ancient that the shutter spins in front of the lens. He begins to thread the reel. Steven squirming out from beneath the table now, sluglike in his bloated countenance.

"What's that?"

"Something I been working on," Andy says. "Sit back. Watch this."

The projector clatters to life. Numbers spliced together from half a dozen prints count down from eight to two. Darkness; light. Women dance across the screen. Flesh undulates in the sensual dungeons of the far east; bodies hit cold asphalt; shotguns explode into unsuspecting men in suits; nude, sweaty wrists are secured to iron bed frames; whips crack; images and sounds exploding with machine-gun rapidity across the screen, contextless, uncontained.

"What is it?"

"Highlight reel. The best scenes from the best stuff we show. You take out a second or two here, there, no one notices. Half the shit I get's already been hacked to bits. Occupational hazard."

The phantasmagoria continues, intermittent snippets of color infused into black and white, no order to the show, no pattern or alternation of dead bodies and live bodies, violence and lust.

"It must really piss you off," Steven says.

"The fuck? Why?"

"Somewhere out there, some bastard's got the *really* good stuff."

"ANDY? I'M sorry, but we need to talk."

Andy, sitting at the projector, some bottle-blonde onscreen obviously faking it. Startled from a daydream he suddenly finds himself unable to articulate, he turns around to find Roderick slanted in the doorway.

"What?"

Roderick, entering the booth, shutting the door gingerly behind him. "I didn't want to say anything about it before, but I noticed you go down to the bathroom earlier this evening."

"Yeah? And? A man's gotta shit." Andy sits up in his chair, the girl onscreen getting hit upside the head now with what looks like a club, knocked onto her knees. He thinks he feels something; tries to hold on to that shadow of a sensation, to analyze it, to be sure that it is real and not the phantom pain of some unnamable thing inside himself severed and dulled to sensation.

"That may be so, but you were in there for almost twenty minutes. You almost missed a reel change."

Andy, turning away from the screen, looking at Roderick, jerking his head back around to look at the screen again, needing to confront this but not wanting to miss an instant, to hold on. "Ten years I've never missed a fucking reel change. Ever. Anything I need to do outside this booth, I have it done on time."

"That may be so as well, but, it's the matter of *what* you were doing in the bathroom."

"Shitting?"

"Brian tells me that there's some profanity written in the stall that wasn't there this morning. I can confirm that. I can also confirm that you're the only person I saw go into the bathroom during the period it appeared."

Andy, dumbstruck; the old management never gave a damn when new graffiti showed up in the mens' room, let alone where it came from. Needs something to keep him occupied while he does his business; do they expect him to *read*, with the garbage they're calling "*literature*" these days?

"You really wanna try and lay off some petty ante shit like that on me? Give me a break, Tillman. You have any idea how many thousand people sleaze through this place a day? You wanna lay a trip on someone, head downstairs, go in the auditorium, take your pick. But leave me alone so I can do my fucking job."

Roderick, approaching Andy, potbelly resting against the back of his chair, the warmth emanating from the fat not unpleasant, the source revolting. "Look, Andy. I understand that people get frustrated sometimes. I do, too. Every time I think about how my father reacted whenever I tried to talk to him about who I am; how he never really accepted that. But we have to learn to deal with those frustrations in ways that aren't going to hurt other people. I've done that, too. I understand. What I'm trying to say, Andy, is, I'm not here to berate you. I just want you to know that I know, and I'm not angry."

"That's really fuckin' great." The woman's hands digging into grass now, trying to claw away, supple flesh mottled with mud and grime and the nails promising to break back at any moment, and Andy grinding his teeth into his lip and hoping that the tickling sensation churning in his gut will continue to swell.

"Andy, you can talk to me." Roderick's hands coming down on Andy's shoulders, feminine in their touch but not in the thick patches of black hair rising up off of each knuckle. "I want you to talk to me. We can help one another make this a better work environment for everyone; we can help one another." Roderick, beginning to knead, Andy leaping up, head bobbling back and forth between the images onscreen, the projector, Roderick, the projector booth door, a thousand miles across the room.

"What the fuck?"

"Andy... It's all right. You don't have to be afraid. No one knows but us. No one will know but us. It's alright if you haven't before; I hadn't, either, until a few years ago."

"What the fuck are you talking about?"

"I know why you act the way you do. Where you come from, where you've been. I know we haven't talked much, but you wrote me the entire story of your life the other night. I couldn't believe it. I knew there were others like me here, but, to find someone so close...Who *understood* me..." Roderick runs a hand up Andy's jacket sleeve.

"I'm not hiding shit," Andy says. "You're fucked in the head."

"Andy... It's OK."

Andy looks at the screen, at the bulging eyes and gritted teeth, back to Roderick, his tiny eyes soft and looking all black in the dim light of the booth, back to the screen and then to Roderick again and the sensation inside of him begins to lurch through his bowels in a slow, deathly crawl.

"Reel change in two minutes," Andy says. "Can't miss it."

Roderick, backing down. "Oh. No. Of course not." His voice soft and shaking, body retreating, eyes desperate-needy. "No. But remember, Andy...Any time."

"Right," Andy says. Watches Roderick go. Closes the projector door behind him. Returns to the screen; waits for his signal; blood runs in gentle rivulets from between clenched fingers, mottled flesh impaled on hard muscular flesh, taking and beating, owning, destroying, annihilating, the faces onscreen transforming, becoming masks, phantasms; Andy thinking that he can see the visage of Roderick in there somewhere, tangled up in the heap of all of this brutality, not on the body of either party but somewhere between them, the faces liquefied into a viscous mass of no beginning and no end, a state of eternal consistency in which the splendor of the here and now maintains.

Somewhere, deep inside, a twitch.

THE CHURCH doors open with a low, shrieking noise, Andy thinking that the sound is probably the only thing remotely new about the place; at least, it didn't make such a noise when he made this pilgrimage last year. Steps inside; almost genuflects but stops himself. Strolls around the perimeter; the lighting as poor as he remembered it, covering the nave in a soothing blanket of almost-darkness. At the votive candles, he drops a quarter into the box, retrieves an unlit candle, lights it, returns it to its original place; no prayer is uttered, silent or otherwise. His commitment fulfilled, he turns to leave, his legs beginning to jerk and twitch, urging him back to Steven, his fix, sleep. As he passes the altar, he hears the sacristy door open and the voice call out:

"Hello?"

Andy, jerking around, sees the old priest begin to crab walk from out of the sacristy, ancient beyond feasibility, hunchbacked and cataracted and holding his shriveled, gnarled arms before him like a dinosaur in some jungle movie. Father Pochowanie, still alive; Andy thinking for sure that the man would have been long dead by now. For the past six years, has always managed to come here when the place was deserted. "Good evening, my son. I hadn't heard you come in." The old man's already thick Pole accent has come to dominate his speech even further in old age, his words coming out in a muffled staccato

"I don't need nothing," Andy says, backs away. "I just came here to light a candle."

"Wonderful, wonderful. It is always wonderful to pray for the souls of the departed."

"Sure."

"Who are your prayers for, my son?" The priest pauses, begins to move again and almost topples, catches himself on the altar. Andy thinks that he perhaps ought to lend a hand; stays put. The priest continues: "The attendance at the masses so scarce these days. Let me pray with you."

"I'm not here to say any prayers. Just light the candle."

Pochowanie begins to move towards Andy, surprises him when he makes it down the few steps at the front of the altar with a fluid ease unbecoming of his movement up to this point. *"Andrzej! Andrzejek Lewinski!* Elzbieta's boy!"

"Andy," Andy snaps. "Andy Lew."

"Andrzej Lewinski! Jak sie mas?"

"This is America. I speak English."

"In nominae Patris, et Filli…"

"I didn't come here to pray." Andy backs away. "I'm just doing what I said I would. The whole fuckin' world flushes its obligations down the shitter, you're going to give me grief for doing something I promised I'd do?"

"Language, language!" The old man, indignant; Andy giggles; no longer in any shape to terrorize, even if there were any rulers around for him to rap knuckles with, Pochowanie's hands are too gnarled, his arms too feeble. An image flashes through Andy's mind, Pochowanie on all fours in the middle of the aisle, shrieking for mercy in his dog-tongue as Andy delivers kick after kick to his skull, one for every blow he suffered at the bastard's hands.

"I lit the candle. I'm done here. I just want to go."

"Elzbieta. She die this day, six years ago."

"Yeah. That's right."

"You light the candle for the soul of Elzbieta Lewinski."

"I promised her I would."

"You should pray, too. She would want you to pray."

"I promised one thing, and that's all she's getting."

"You too hard on your mother. She did all she could for you boys. It hard to raise boys without father. You should light one for him too, your father. He need your prayers more."

"Why? I didn't promise him."

"He saw bad things in the war. He not right in the head when he did that to himself. It not all his fault. There still hope for him. You need to pray for his soul. You come here, I pray with you. No one come here to pray anymore." Pochowanie begins to circle around the altar, supporting himself on one arthritic claw. "They go to other places now. Pray to the gods there. One God not good enough for them no more. They want gods they can see but who are no really there. People need to come back here. You and Saskia and Stefek, you need to come back. You are missed."

"No one who knows us misses us," Andy says. "Trust me."

"*He* misses you." Pochowanie, stopping now at the head of the altar, directly beneath the crucifix; tries to turn to face it, can only manage to swivel a portion of his upper body. Andy gazes up at the great tableau, already festering with wood rot and mold in his childhood, rendered now a desiccated, amorphous mass with barely discernible hands or feet, only the iron thorns and nails still clearly defined. Once upon a time he had knelt before it; prayed before it; cannot remember now how much of that had been genuine devotion, how much of it obligation; cannot bring himself to recall if the sense of macabre fascination with the nails and the thorns that fills him now had begun to develop then, or if it is merely a comfort to him in his present state of mind to think that there has been no before time, that this has always been the way his brain has worked.

"No," Andy says. "Trust me. No one misses us. No one." He turns to leave; can hear the old priest muttering behind him as he goes, a Latin-Polish pidgin, a linguistic portmanteau of old tongues; the dying and the dead.

"YOU'LL NEVER guess who's still alive," Andy says, shuffling through the door with the remnants of a fifth of whiskey, a palliative measure against his worsening jitters. There, on the couch, Steven in his robe, joint between his fish lips; beside him, Ludo Dombrowski, mop topped and goateed, black clothes from head to toe, eyes hidden behind a pair of tiny, round shades that reflect Andy's own gaunt visage back at him.

"What the fuck's he doing here?" Andy says, slams the door shut behind him, the force of his own swing nearly knocking him off his feet. Legs twitching worse, eyelids joining in now, skin crawling at the sight of Ludo; something about him seeming dirtier than a person should rightfully be, no matter how many days he's gone without bathing. The stench of something rancid and foul wafts into Andy's nostrils, an unfamiliar and unwelcome addition to his apartment's cocktail of odors.

"Ludo came by to see how I've been," Steven says, passing the joint to Ludo. "He's a good friend. Aren't you, Ludo?"

"Ludo got you kicked out of your fucking house," Andy says.

"Ain't my fault Samantha's got a mind like a bear trap," Ludo says, gnarly beatnik drawl sounding like he's been choking down gravel for decades. "Won't open herself to new experiences."

"You tried to fuck her in her sleep," Andy says.

"Chick's gotta let the love in, let the hate out," Ludo says, knocks back what Andy is sure is the last of the beer.

"I'll open the fucking door if you'll leave through it," Andy says. "And what's that smell?"

"They, like, shut off your water for non-payment, man," Ludo says. "It was wild. Dig it, Steven here had a serious case of the runs."

Andy digs his nails into his palms.

"It'll be fine," Steven says. "The candles will cover it up. And we'll get the water turned back on soon, won't we? In any case, I haven't seen Ludo in ages. We're catching up." Steven smiles his Buddha's smile, his face disappearing into a multitude of wily folds. "And you're looking bad."

"You know fucking well I'm looking bad. I haven't slept in two days, and now I've got a toilet full of shit I can't flush."

"Need something?"

"You know I do. Now give it up. Then you and Ludo can party on in your little punk boy love club."

Ludo and Steven shooting one another a coy glance, Andy's goose-bumps intensifying. Even in the presence of the candles, the room seems freezing. "I noticed that I was a bottle short," Steven begins.

"You were always lousy at math."

"I'm very good at keeping track of things," Steven says, the smile gone now, his face deadly serious. "You owe me. Nothing more until you pay up."

"And's Ludo gonna pay up to me for the beer of mine he drank?"

"Beer's a natural thing," Ludo says. "Comes from the Earth. Nothing natural should cost a man a dime."

"And your shit ain't made out of some kind of flowers? You're a fucking draft-dodging son of a bitch and you never worked a fucking day in your life."

"Aw, like you ever served, man."

"*Hey!* At least I *tried*. Wasn't my fault they were handing out Section 8s like candy. Point is I put forth the effort while you sit on your ass drinking another man's beer. And you know where I get the cash to *buy* that beer? My *job*, you filthy deadbeat beatnik."

"So you admit you make money," Steven says. "In exchange for performing certain duties and carrying out certain responsibilities."

"That's what a job tends to entail."

"Then you can pay for your fix."

"No, I can't, because I spend all of that money keeping you alive."

Steven shrugs. "No one's making you."

"Fuck you." Andy storms from the room, starts opening drawers in a fever-dream frenzy, overturning sheets, rifling through piles of ancient newspaper, empty bottles, crushed cans, the remnants of long neglected pornographic magazines, well-read tomes of erotic exploration rendered banal by familiarity, mounds of unwashed socks and stained underwear. "Where is it? Dammit, you tell me where it is."

"Hidden," Steven calls from the couch, coughs into his fist. Andy lumbers back into the room, stares his brother down.

"Where? Give it up."

"I don't know." The Buddha smile again. "I gave it to Ludo to hide."

Andy, eyes moving to Ludo. "Oh yeah?"

"Oh, yeah, daddy-o, I got the stash and I know where it's at. And since you're not averse to work I'll offer you this: I'll let you earn your fix by doing something for me." Ludo begins to giggle, exchanges glances with Steven. "For us."

Andy, no hesitation: "What?"

"You'll probably even enjoy it," Steven says.

"What?" Andy asks, more insistent now. Exhausted; intrigued.

Steven and Ludo giggle conspiratorially, a pair of monstrous schoolgirls concocting a polluted scheme. Andy kicks a nearby pile of bottles, sends them flying, some breaking against the baseboard, sending little shards of glass sprinkling around.

"Tell me!"

"Well, see, I been feeling a little *hard up* lately, man," Ludo says. "Samantha giving me the heave-ho left me feeling a little needy, like, *unwanted*, man."

Andy, no reaction on the inside, the words coming out by rote: "You fucking pervert. I told you: never again."

"Hey, hey man, hear me out." Ludo raising one black-fingernailed hand, turning it round and around, a bottle appearing in his palm. "I'm not asking you to go into this thing flying blind, man, no, you get to fly high. Half now...half after."

"A joke's a joke, Steven, but this is enough," Andy says, body on fire now; aches in every muscle, eyes bulging and bloodshot; would rather not, would prefer not to, not for the implications of engaging in the act itself but for having to stay awake a moment longer, to endure another second of existence.

"It's out of my hands," Steven says.

"It's all cool," Ludo says, rising up from the couch, as thin as Andy but looking even more gaunt in his all-black, a skull floating in the darkness of the room. "A game, just like when we were kids. Kick the can, skin the cat, *man*, this ain't no different."

The vial in Ludo's hand, just feet out of reach, Andy making a dive for it, a feeble grab with spindly arms that sends him cartwheeling forward when Ludo sidesteps him, tumbling to the ground, a pitiful, sobbing, twitching heap.

"That's the kind of behavior that's going to get you in trouble one day," Ludo says.

"You give it to me!" Andy shrieks. "Just give it to me!"

"Clock's ticking," Ludo says. "Another minute and I'm taking the ride myself."

Andy rolls up his sleeve. No matter. In a few minutes: the first moments of peaceful surrender, the yawning void and all of the nothingness it promises, the sweet comfort of complete oblivion. "Fuck you."

Ludo joins Andy on the floor, wraps the hose around his arm, rough, clumsy. Andy gritting his teeth as the rubber grabs his arm hair, tugs it by the stem, not entirely unpleasant, wonders how Ludo would react were he to do the same to him, wrap the hose around his head, a four foot hose, five foot, enough to envelop his face and catch every stubbly hair from his throat to his crown, wrap it tight and give a good, hard yank...

The needle going into the vein; blood being drawn out, mixing with the morphine, flooding back into his system teasingly slow, just a bit, just like Ludo said, just a bit. Andy begins to nod, lies down on his side. Absently, he turns his face to see the candles, see what visions they'll give to him: things denied to him thus far in the realm of the flesh, things he hopes to see one day, visions forming before his eyes in the flames of the table candles, entwined bodies rising up in fire and smoke, gripping one another in myriad permutations of intercourse and not-intercourse, couplings impossible in the physical realm, not quite impossible on the silver screen, in Andy's mind.

Steven picks up one of the candles from the table, watches dumbly as hot wax rolls over his thumb. "Hey, remember the time us and Cousin Saskia set Mr. Wojowicz's store on fire?"

"Beautiful," Andy mutters. Footfalls, Steven moving close to him. Andy's eyes lolling up to see the candle above him. "You could…see all the smoke, even though it was dark. Because the fire was making the sky glow orange."

From behind him, Ludo, fiddling with his belt, a metallic *thunk* as the buckle strikes the floor along with his pants: "Why'd we do that again?"

"I don't remember," Steven says.

"It was your idea."

"Andy has the better memory. Hey, Andy?" Steven angles the candle down, globules of hot wax hitting Andy on the eyebrows, the forehead. He twitches away instinctively, the pain dulled, just a reflex against a foreign body nearing the eye. "Why *did* we?"

"To watch it burn," Andy murmurs. Settles in. Begins to drift.

The film rolls on.

"HAVE YOU got anything?" Andy whimpers this into the receiver, his whole body trembling, the stench of vomit wafting out of his mouth with every word, stinking up the whole phone booth. Hasn't changed from the clothes he woke up in, his shirt torn, chinos rumpled and bloody at the seat. His body aches; can't help but think that he should be in more pain than he's in.

On the other end of the line, the static silence of open air, a phone held away from a face, the ambient noise of an empty room swirling back to him, the sound of nothingness.

"Anything?" His voice wavers.

Another second passes and then Eddie's voice, guttural and strained, comes back to him: "Maybe. I think I found something. Andy…A new issue of *Real Action Tales* came in last night. Got a story in there 'bout this guy gets taken prisoner by— get this— these women in the jungle who…"

"The new thing," Andy says. "The better thing."

"Andy…"

"Yes?"

"You're sure? The new issue… I'll give you half off."

Andy bows his head, puts a hand over his face. "Eddie. Please."

"All right. OK. Maybe. I just need a little more time to… Andy…"

"Yes?"

"I'll talk to you soon."

The line goes dead. Andy slams the receiver into the phone, kicks the wall of the booth. It doesn't occur to him until a block from home that Eddie Lawler sounded scared.

ANDY LEW, banging on the front door of Eddie's, hands chafed by the cold; lost his gloves somewhere along the way: in his apartment, the projector booth. Even with the bitter wind intensifying and bits of frost coagulating around his cuticles, he does not care; is not bothered; just needs to get in; to get *it*, whatever *it* may be.

Eddie, appearing in the window, gives a gesture indicating the rear of the store, disappears again into the pale darkness beyond. Andy turns, heads around back, loops through the side alley, is surprised to find Eddie waiting for him there.

"Eddie…"

"Don't talk." Eddie, sterner than usual, wild-eyed, none of the usual cad's joviality in him today. "I found you what you wanted. This city's a sewer. You want the garbage you talk to the rats, you want the rats you talk to the garbage men. You want what I found, you evil little shit? You take this, you understand something: You never come back here. You never set foot in my store again. I never see your face another day in my life. You come near me, you come near my store, I will kill you. I will kill you with my hands, and I won't regret it."

No hesitation: "Give it to me."

Eddie slips Andy a business card, crisp ivory, gold embossed lettering: S. DRAFT. Below that a phone number; below that, nothing. "He's waiting to hear from you. You set up the meeting. He has what you want. You're *his* now, got it? *He* gets you your shit from now on. You fuckin' burnout."

The door slams. Andy watches it a while, waiting for it to reopen, the snow sticking to his glasses. When he realizes Eddie isn't coming back, he goes to find the nearest phone booth.

THE PHONE rings three times before a voice drifts down the line, too soft to determine the sex, the speech too annunciated to pinpoint any dialect or accent: "Hello? How may I help you?"

Andy's breath, caught in his throat; symptom of the cold and his own excitement and his incrementally increasing heart rate.

"Hello?"

"Yes? May I help you?"

"S. Draft?"

"Is this Andy Lew?"

Andy nearly tumbles over; puts a hand on the phone booth wall to support himself. Like hearing a celebrity speak his name. "Yes…Yes, I'm Andy Lew."

"I know all about you, Andy. You like *movies*, don't you, Andy?"

"…yes."

"Scary movies? Movies with pretty women?"

"*Yes.*"

"Well then, have I got a movie for you. I want you to come to my office. Tomorrow. Eleven sharp. Have you got a pen?"

Andy writes the address down on his palm. Even after he's transferred it to a napkin in a diner down the block, he can't bring himself to wash it off.

"WHERE ARE you going?"

"Meeting. Work." Andy, not really listening to Steven, more focused on getting his tie right; has decided that a half-Windsor is the proper knot for this shirt collar: too narrow for a full Windsor, the meeting too important for a simple four-in-hand. Wonders if he should perhaps wear his spread collar so he can use the full Windsor; remembers that the shirt he has on is the only clean one in the apartment, the money he used to allot to his dry cleaning bills having gone to the wayside since Steven moved in. At least he still has two clean suits to choose from. Goes for the gray pinstripe: more business appropriate than the olive glen-plaid, though it would pair better with his ever-yellowing complexion.

"You don't have meetings," Steven says, hacks, spits a wad of phlegm onto the floor. "You're just a projectionist."

"I'm a senior staff member," Andy says. Checks the clock; still has two hours. Will probably leave sooner; the candles doing nothing to cover up the scent of the slowly filling toilet bowl, Steven refusing to use the john at the bodega down the block.

"You mean that you're the only person there who hasn't quit for something better." Steven switches on the television; the picture rolls. "If you worked a better job we could move into a better place. Get a better television."

"You always say there's nothing good on."

"Well, you never know. There could be one day. And then I'd like to see it clearly."

"Well, maybe Ludo has a good television wherever he's crashing tonight."

"I don't know where he is." Steven sighs; sounds genuinely disappointed. "Oh, shit man," Steven groans, clutches at himself. Andy, striding over, kneeling beside him.

"You need to go to the hospital," Andy says.

"Fuck them. I don't need their pity."

"It isn't fucking pity. It's fucking medical treatment, you dipshit. I'll call you an ambulance."

"I'm not going anywhere. They'll have to carry me. Down all three flights. They could *drop* me."

"Imbecile," Andy spits.

"Shut up," Steven mutters. "Why do you even care?"

"You're my brother."

"And *you're my* brother, and I wouldn't give a damn either way."

"Well, I promised mom," Andy says.

"What?" Steven, genuinely confused by this.

"In the hospital. The week before she died. I promised her that I would go to church every year on the anniversary of her death and light a candle for her. And I promised her I'd take care of you."

Steven's eyes loll down in his head a moment and then bob back up. "Why?"

Andy thinks about this for a moment. He has never really considered the question himself. "Well…she asked me to."

"And? I promise people shit all the time. Do you have any tuna? Any canned ham?"

"We got no food til next payday."

"Well," Steven says. "That's not taking care of me very well."

"A hell of a lot better than you can take care of yourself." Andy sighs, stands up. "I've got to go. I'm going to be late. Where are my black wingtips?"

"Under your cot."

"You *would* know where everything is in this place, wouldn't you? Hey, where's Dad's watch? You haven't pawned that, too, have you?"

"Under the sofa," Steven says. "It's only gold *plated*, anyway. Worthless, really."

"To you, it would be," Andy says. Laces up his shoes. Considers leaving the door unlocked on his way out; remembers his highlight reel; thinks better of it.

ANDY LEW sits in the waiting room of Draft's office, fingers drumming on his knees. Forgot how comfortable the fabric of this suit feels against the skin of his legs, the sense of power it instills in him to see himself clad not in ragged, fraying cotton but a uniform of respectability, someone with authority, someone to be admired; someone to be feared.

Andy scans the room. Paper-thin mauve carpeting; a bad paint job on the walls. Two doors, one leading back out into the main hallway, a bleak gray thoroughfare housing the operations of mail order catalogs, title companies, real estate brokers; the other into whatever back offices this Draft occupies. Around Andy, dime store frames holding cheap prints: Starry Night; that old farm couple; a house on a hill, a young girl splayed out at the base, all dark clad and willowy and gazing up at it, longing for it, Andy thinking about what the house must contain: chains that will bind her wrists, her ankles; implements of torture; vats of lava; perhaps something he cannot fathom; something that S. Draft knows all about.

The office door opens. Andy rises, straightening his pant legs. S. Draft looms in the doorway, a squat, massive, bulk of a man in a navy blue suit, tendons popping in the portion of his neck visible above a white silk shirt collar, the muscles of his pectorals and biceps straining at the fabric.

"Yes?" He asks. His voice is just as soft as on the phone, sexless and indistinct.

"Andy Lew."

Draft smiles, two rows of perfectly aligned teeth, the incisors tiny and cubic, the canines tapering into fine, sharp points. "Samuel Draft. Come on in."

Andy hesitates a second. In that second, ideas enter his head: that this man is a fruit, a psychotic, that he has been lured here to be fucked, fucked and killed, fucked and tortured and killed, that he will now be another of the number of people in this city who went into buildings never to be seen again, to vanish into the ether with no trace left behind, thinks on this and then strides through the door; a big, open space beyond, two rows of cubicles set too far apart, Andy thinking they could fit another two or three rows in easily, sees as he follow Draft down the aisle that each cubicle is completely empty but for scraps of paper on desks, cardboard boxes full of shredding, phones taken off the hook.

"I'm glad you could make it," Draft says, bobbing along in front of Andy, Andy thinking as he follows that he can see his own reflection in the back of Draft's bald, polished head. "I don't often get to share my passion with others. Do you enjoy sharing your passions with others, Andy?"

"No."

"You ought to consider it," Draft says. "It's amazing what you can learn about things you thought you knew everything about. People share with you, you share with them; they share with other people; all of the knowledge you've imparted gets to live on. *You* get to live on." At the end of the row of cubicles, a row of doors, all but one of them shut, Draft leading Andy on in to the open room, a closet space just big enough to contain two folding chairs, a little screen, a projector, not some 16mm setup like he was anticipating, no military issue RCA 400 but a tiny old Acme 35mm portable. "Well, go on then, have a seat."

Andy, trying to contain his breathing, excitement rippling waves of goosebumps across his flesh, wanting this to be *it*, concerned that it won't be. "You ain't going to charge me?"

Draft, smiling. "The first hit's always free."

"Yeah. OK."

Andy, taking his seat; Draft, killing the lights, firing up the projector. Andy digs his nails into his palms. Watches.

Onscreen: A gray, grainy field, and, situated in the center of it, a distorted skull; not human, Andy sees, or any animal, something fabricated in a factory, shining glass eyes staring out of the sockets, the jaw articulated by unseen strings, gently bobbing. As the jaw softly moves up and down, numbers begin to appear in the mouth, 10 counting down to two. A white flash. A jump cut. It takes Andy's eyes a moment to readjust to the darkness; when they do—

She's beautiful.

A beautiful woman. A beautiful woman bound to a chair in one of the many dungeons of the world, the awful places where the lost and the missing experience their final moments. Her hair is blonde and long, the style and her makeup dating the print to the first half of the last decade. She has clearly been furnished with clothing other than what her captors found her in, her lithe body draped in an elegant chiton, the material of which is elegantly smooth beneath the loops and knots of her bindings. Her doe eyes are wide with fear, darting about in every which direction, her arms and legs struggling to twitch against her bindings.

"What is this?" Andy whispers, turns to Draft, a quick glance, does not know what this is but does not want to miss a second of it either, catches only a fleeting glimpse of Draft's face, bearing an expression of pure awe.

Onscreen: striding in from the left, a man, what Andy *presumes* is a man, the small, lean figure obscured by a dark apron and long sleeved work shirt, a leather veil with mesh-covered eyeholes. It walks slowly, with jerking, mechanical precision, like a wind-up toy of a Russian soldier. Its hands grasp a club, something Oriental looking, cylindrical and studded with what seem to Andy like tack heads. It sets the club beside the woman; moves behind her; grips her head in its hands, forces her to look into the camera.

"Is this real?" Andy, whispering, knows the answer when he sees the look in the woman's eyes, the fear that no actress can convey, the terror that no amount of acting classes or years in the pictures can allow someone to replicate artificially.

The fear of someone who knows that she is about to die.

The projector shuts off. The lights switch on. Andy jerks around; Draft on his feet, standing in the doorway, adjusting his suspenders.

"What do you think?" Draft asks.

"The rest of it," Andy whispers. "I want it. Show it to me."

Draft, coming forward, slapping him on the shoulder, Andy thinking that the blow has perhaps dislocated something. "See? Isn't it nice to share?"

"Please."

"You understand that nothing's free. You've already asked about a charge."

"How much do you want? I'll give it to you. I'll get it."

Draft, turning his chair around, sitting down on it to face Andy, arms folded across the back. "Good. Eddie said you were serious. I'm glad to see he was right. Now, you need to understand something. This here"— Draft points at the projector—"you will never be able to afford. All right? If you worked five jobs, ate dirt every day for the next ten years, lived in a dumpster, wore the rags that you took off of bums passed out in the gutter, you would not be able to afford this. Not a single frame of it."

"But..."

"Shhhh. I'm not here to tease you. *I like you!* I pride myself on my analysis of first impressions. You've got *passion*. Other people I know, they got theirs because they *could*. They heard about it, they've got the money, why not? But they don't have the *passion*. That makes me *angry*." Draft visibly tenses, Andy wondering for a moment if the man is about to pounce towards him. "Why buy something you haven't got the passion for? Who are you impressing? Yourself? Not your friends; if they have a passion for what you're buying, they're disgusted that you're treating it like another commodity to be purchased. If they're not, they don't care; it's just another nick knack. You need to have a passion for the things you take in; that you look for; that you *care* for. You, Andy…you're *passionate* about this, aren't you?"

"Yes."

"Have you ever felt this way before? The way you feel about this? I saw a look in your eye, while you were watching it, maybe you can't see yourself right now, but I know you felt something. Have you ever felt that before? For a woman? A man?"

"I…can't remember."

"That's fine, that's fine. Now, listen: There are things that I can buy and there are things I can't. Not because I haven't got the money, but because they aren't for sale. Now, the item itself may be for sale, but for it to have *value*, it has to come from the proper source. I can go to the Salvation Army and buy a shirt that some poor, dead soul's family has donated; or I can go to Fifth Avenue and buy a custom-tailored shirt for a hundred dollars. I can buy a brand-new Mercedes; or I can buy the Benz that *Der Fuhrer* drove through Berlin. Do you understand what I'm saying, Andy? About how certain things can become more than the sum of their parts because of where they come from, who makes them, the meaning attached?"

"Yes, yes. What do you want from me?"

"Shhh. Patience is a virtue, Andy. Possess it if you can. Now you see the sort of things that interest me. This here…this isn't the only one I own."

"Did you…make it?"

"Let's say I produced it. And I wouldn't be offering it to you if it *were* the only one. I promise you, there *are* more. And they're more beautiful than you can imagine. You'll never see them. But if you get me what I want, you can see this one as many times as you'd like. I've seen it enough. I've seen *all* of them enough. And that's my problem. All I've gotten to do is *see*. I'm a tactile man, Andy. I enjoy the sensation of *touch*. Do you know that your skin is the body's largest organ? One great, big, organ, sending signals to the brain every time it lands on something. Have you ever considered that you can live as a blind man, a deaf man, a mute man, but if you were to lose your sense of touch, you would completely lose your place in the world? Everything, numb. I lie awake at night, sometimes, and think about that." Draft stops a moment, looking sullen, Andy thinking for a moment the big man might actually cry. "I want something I can touch, Andy. Something to heighten the experience. A tangible connection. I want a *body*, Andy."

Between the men: Space, immense; a moment in time frozen by apprehension, awkwardness, that second when the mind frenzies itself looking for the proper response to maintain order, to lead the conversation towards its desired conclusion.

"You…can't buy one of those?" Andy asks. "Or just…pick one up? I see bums all the time…"

"Shhh. No, Andy. I can't. Well. *I could*. But this is what I was talking about. I thought you understood. Some body from the pavement is useless to me. That's all it is. It's a body. A shell. A body that I've procured through financial means? Even if I were to hire a killer, some Mafia goon, what does he care? Another hit, another notch on his belt. I want one delivered to me by someone who has *my passion*. Who has the passion of *that man*." Draft points again to the projector; Andy imagining the shrouded figure there in the room with them now, looming over his shoulder in all of its splendor and majesty. "Someone who has it in them to take life. To hold life in his hands and to end it, so he can carry that life with him. You understand that, don't you, Andy? That when you take a life, you carry it with you forever and all time? That a bond forms between those two people? That one of them was responsible for the end of the other's life? I think about that at night, too. What that moment must be like. What it must be to be able to remember it, years, decades later. To be an old man, rocking his grandchildren on his lap, reading them Christmas stories by the fire, and just for an instant to remember that moment. I'll never know it myself." Draft sighs. "I just have to do with someone else giving it to me. Someone like me. Someone who has the bravery I don't. And whoever that person is... Will be handsomely rewarded."

"You...want me to kill someone."

"It doesn't matter who," Draft says. "A stranger, a lover. Anyone will do. But it has to be you who does it. And you have to tell me about it, afterwards. Every detail, every moment. For me to savor forever and think about every time I touch my prize. You, Andy. Your hands. Like I said, I'm an excellent judge of people. If you bring me someone you didn't kill yourself, I'll know you're lying. And...It won't be pleasant for you, Andy."

"This is something big you're asking of me," Andy says. "Maybe I could just see...a little more."

"Shhh. No. That isn't going to happen."

Andy, wringing his hands. "I've never done anything like that before."

"I figured. But this is what you want, isn't it?"

"What...if it isn't?"

Draft shrugs. "Then you can leave here. You can forget you ever saw this, or ever saw me. And you can dream every night for the rest of your life about what you could have had." He shrugs again. "Your choice. Now then." Draft going towards the door, compelling Andy to follow him. "I have other matters to which I need to attend. Business to conduct. Wheels to oil. Progress to make." Through the cubicle tunnel again; Andy thinking he can see paper scraps rustling in their boxes, on desks; does not feel any wind. At the door, Draft places his hands on Andy's shoulders.

"You should consider getting some exercise. Hit some weights. You're too tense. Tension can kill a man. Put some meat on your bones. And call me when you've got what I want. Or don't call me at all. I won't be waiting; but I'd love to hear from you."

Andy, alone in the waiting room; *Starry Night*; the girl on the hill, beckoning, somehow turned upside down now. Stench of fresh urine in the air. Andy doesn't realize until he's halfway down the hall that it's him.

ANDY LEW, feet propped against the projector booth wall, legs jiggling frantically, not with the agitated unease of sleep deprivation but with the eager working of a mind trying to come to a resolution, to decide upon a matter of literal life and death.

Onscreen: Andy cannot even tell. Blurs. Colors. Meaningless abstracts. One thing on his mind: the next course of action to take. Rode the subway back from Draft's looking for all the world like the living dead, pop-eyed and soaked in a rancid cocktail of his own fluids, staring straight ahead into some invisible oblivion beyond the vision of his fellow passengers. Even in the booth his hands worked mechanically, by rote, threading the film into the projector with no thought as to what was going onscreen; even now, as the cue arrives to switch on the second projector, he reaches over and does it with no consideration of the act, his thoughts fixated on the visage of the Executioner, what has been asked of him to see the film through to its conclusion.

Behind Andy, the door opening, "Andy?" and Andy jerking around, half-startled away from his obsessing, only vestiges of his conscious mind being dedicated to inspect this intruder, the rest of his brain still stewing in mayhem.

"Hey," Roderick says. "How's it going?"

"Fine. What do you need?"

"Just checking in. Did you have a funeral to go to? I noticed the suit."

"Lunch with a friend," Andy says.

"Oh." Roderick sniffs the air. "Do you smell something?"

"Some bum pissed on me on the subway."

"Well, that's terrible. But I'll have to ask you in the future to change into clothing that hasn't been soiled before coming onto the job."

"I was on my way in. I'd have been late."

"Maybe you should consider keeping a change of clothes here in the booth," Roderick says. "When I was a boy, my parents sent me to private school. We had to wear uniforms. And if I came home with so much as a speck of dust on my shirt, my old man would wallop the *heck* out of me. So I started keeping a change in my locker, so that if I got dirty near the end of the day, I could switch them out and then wash the clothes in the bathroom sink the next day."

Andy, incredulous: "Well, I'm sorry your dad was a sack of shit. That doesn't have much to do with me though, now does it?"

"Well, I…no, I…I guess it doesn't. But you understand where I'm coming from." Roderick, moving forward, hand on Andy's shoulder. "We really had a moment the other night, didn't we? I could feel it, too. I understand why you're irritable. You've *never*…you know, before, have you?"

"…what?"

"Been that way. It's all right. I get it. But you don't have to worry; only we know. And only we *will* know. No matter what happens, it's just between us."

Roderick's hand moving up and down Andy's shirt sleeve, gripping, stroking, Andy tensing up. From the auditorium below, the sound of screams. Andy looks over his shoulder, catches a glimpse of a knife entering flesh, another scream, the violence here looking to be protracted, brutal. The screams continue. Andy looks back to Roderick.

"You've just changed reels," Roderick whispers. "Plenty of time." His face moves towards Andy's, Andy dodging left, Roderick following the movement to meet Andy's lips with his own. Andy jerks back, topples out of his chair, his feet becoming tangled up in the folding legs.

"What the fuck?" Andy shrieks, Roderick kneeling beside him, placing a gentle hand on Andy's calf.

"Are you OK? I didn't mean anything. I thought you were ready…" Roderick's hand slides up Andy's leg, Andy looking around the booth, the reel canisters, the projectors, the shut door, his workbench with its tools for splicing and cutting and…

"I *am* ready," Andy says. "But you're right. It is my first time. I want it to be special. Something I've always dreamed of."

"Oh!" Roderick says. "I didn't mean to try and rush it. I'm so sorry."

"It's all right. It's fine." Andy clears his throat. "But I've thought about this a long time. About how I'd want it. And…it's always been here. The movies mean a lot to me. I think you've learned that about me."

"Yes, I've seen."

"Especially…*White Slaves of Chinatown*."

"Oh? I'm not familiar with that one."

"It came out last year. Probably the only good flick *to* come out last year. No dialogue; no story; just an hour and twelve minutes of whips… and chains…and beautiful, *beautiful* agony."

"Oh," Roderick says, Andy's eyes all alight with fury and exhilaration, sweat beading on his brow. "Oh," Roderick says again, understanding this time, apprehensive. "I…don't know, Andy."

"It was like a dream coming to life," Andy says. "I'd never imagined anyone else but me thought that way…and I just thought…" Andy, moving to his work table, picking up the short length of extension cord kept as a backup for the projectors. "I wouldn't be too rough. I guess…since my dad was always such a son of a bitch…I always dreamed about being the one to dish out the punishment."

Roderick, nodding slowly. "I understand."

Andy, on the inside: not a twitch, not a hiccup. He extends an arm towards Roderick, Roderick moving to him, Andy clearing away space on the work table. Knots the cord around Roderick's wrists to be the best of his abilities, wishing for the first time that he had not gotten himself kicked out of Boy Scouts, that the movies showed you the actual tying instead of just the aftermath, good as that may be.

"They're awfully tight," Roderick says.

"Good," Andy says. "They're meant to be." He surveys the tools he's taken off the work bench. Screwdriver: too slow. The film splicer: too small. The box cutters: too messy. Guess he'll have to settle for the hammer. Well, shit. Should have thought this out; spur of the moment; *shit*. Too late now. No going back.

"What are you going to do to me?" Roderick asks, mock terrified. "Please, just don't hurt me."

"I'm not going to hurt you," Andy says, thinks to himself he's going to do much worse.

"I'm sorry," Roderick says.

"What?"

"For being so terrible to you. All those times I hit you and said you weren't enough of a man."

"What the fuck are you talking about?" Andy, hand hovering over the hammer, can smell the rubber of the grip.

"Being such a terrible father," Roderick says, squirming on the table. "I'm sorry…just don't hurt me." The last words delivered with such lustful relish that Andy is taken aback, that he has slipped into the role so well, realizes this cannot be the first time Roderick has engaged in such a scenario.

"Yes…you were," Andy says. His hand wraps around the hammer; the cool rubber of the handle feeling strangely comforting in his palm. "And now you've got to pay." He waits for his arm to swing up; for it to swing back down, splitting Roderick's forehead in half, caving in the space above his nose, his eyes collapsing inward in a viscous slush of gore, waits for the hammer to arc back down for the second blow that will silence him, send his teeth down his throat, gagging noises as he chokes on the blood flowing down his throat, waits for the final swing that will destroy his brain, finishing him once and for all, his ticket to the big time, to the treasure of his life.

Waits. Waits.

When Andy realizes his hand will never move, he lets the hammer set back down. Strides to Roderick, delivers as powerful a backhand as he can manage.

"Oh!" Roderick shouts. "Please! Not again!"

Andy sighs, unties the cord. Roderick watches him, bemused, rubs his wrists once they're free.

"Andy? That…was it?"

"It was my first time. What do you expect? Now get the fuck out of here. I want to be alone."

"Oh. Oh…all right. I…understand. Was it…good for you?"

"I've had better."

"…better?"

"…with chicks. Are you happy? Now I got a fucking job to do, don't I?"

Roderick moves towards the projection booth door; a final backwards glance over his shoulder at Andy. Andy closes, locks the door behind him. When he's sure no one will hear he tips the work table over; sets on it with the hammer; doesn't stop til he's broken through to the floor.

ANDY BARGES into his apartment, slams the door behind him, sweat drenched and panting. Steven, lolling on the couch, looks up, eyes glassy and distant, body trembling.

"Where's Ludo?" Andy asks. "I need to see him."

Steven makes a noise. "*Hwah. Hunh.* I dunno."

"Well, let's get your buddy Ludo over here to fix you up. I'll go down and call him. C'mon, whose couch is he crashing on tonight? He had to have said."

"Andy, I don't know." Steven's breathing even more shallow than usual, Andy wondering what it'll degrade to in his sleep. Wonders if he cares. He rummages around the kitchen; finds the butcher knife, covered in coagulated jelly and breadcrumbs and hardened, graying scraps of meat. Not a neat job to do, anyway. Dirty works just fine. Goes under the sink, begins yanking out garbage bags.

"How'd your meeting at work go?"

"What?" Andy, confused a moment. "Oh. Yeah, it was a real shindig." Needs to get Ludo over here, *now*; a plan formulating in his head.

His only problem with Roderick: there had been no plan. That was all: there just hadn't been any plan and that was his only reason for hesitation. Has a plan now; knows what to do; how he will do it; he has formulated the perfect murder and now all he needs is his victim. *"Where's Ludo?"*

"He left. I don't know. He's gone. He started giving me shit about when I was going to move back home, wanting another shot at Samantha."

"Dammit, Steven…"

"I don't feel really hot, man."

"Well, that's pretty tough fucking shit, now isn't it?" Andy squats beside Steven. *"Maybe* if you'd give me a fix instead of pulling shit on me for it, I wouldn't have to put in the extra hours at meetings to afford it. Then I could be here to take care of you better. Or *maybe* if you weren't a fucking junkie in the first place, you wouldn't get yourself sick every other fucking day shooting up with the same fucking needle. *Maybe* if you weren't such a lousy fucking husband, you wouldn't have gotten kicked out for pimping out your wife. And *maybe* if you weren't such a lousy fucking brother, I wouldn't have to worry about any of this anyway. And you know what? Right now, I'm not worried about it." Andy stands up; already beginning to improvise. "I have my own problems to take care of right now. I'll deal with you later."

Steven rubs his stomach, sweat trickling into his eyes. "Hey, Andy?"

"Yeah?"

"We gonna see a movie pretty soon?"

"What?"

"You said you'd get me in to see something soon." Steven's voice quivers, Andy remembering what he sounded like at twelve, a chubby little whiner threatening to tattle if he and Ludo didn't get to tag along with him and Saskia. "I'd like to see a movie. Pretend you're sneaking me in. Like old times. What's showing?"

"Don't sentimentalize with me."

"I just want to know."

"Who Killed Teddy Bear and *Last Man on Earth."*

"Any good?"

"*Last Man's* wannabe shit."

"*Teddy Bear*?" Steven's eyes big as saucers, glassy, staring past Andy.

"…Not bad. It's got Sal Mineo. I gotta go, Steven."

"Hurry up," Steven says. His voice goes flaccid again, contemptuous. "Steal some popcorn for me."

"Like old times," Andy mutters. Slams the door on the way out.

ANDY, CROUCHED in the alley, freezing cold, wishing he had changed; would be much warmer in his jeans and trench coat, could replace those easier than his suit. No matter; things going to be different from now on. See how long Steven stays in the apartment after he shows him his latest acquisition; and if the freeloader doesn't get scared off by it, then he'll kick him out. Steven right about one thing: their mother is dead; nothing left of her to hold him to any promises, no stern eye or commanding voice. Leave her to the grave.

Andy watches: Through the window of the diner, the girl, wiling away her night, books spread on the table before her, cup of coffee having long ago lost its steam. Young; slight; alone. Will have those same books bundled in her arms when she leaves. No defense. If he's lucky, she'll cross the street, come towards him; he'll bolt out at her once she turns in whichever direction she's headed. If not: Will slip his shoes off at the last moment to facilitate a quieter jaunt towards her; keep his distance til she passes another alley, drag her in. Shank her between the tits, a good thrust to penetrate the breastbone, her screams silenced as the blood begins to gush up and out her throat and through her sweater, soaking it black-red in the dim light, drag her down by her hair and smash her face into the ground. No interruptions, no harassment; time enough to take her apart, stuff her in his garbage bags. Can't weigh more than a hundred and ten, a hundred and twenty; will be even less with all the blood

BEASTS OF 42ND STREET

drained. Can stash the bags inside a trash can, make a couple of trips. No one around to find him suspicious, trash pickup not until daylight. Perfect. Perfect.

Andy, shivering, fingers gnarling; looks past the girl, into the diner proper. Only the short-order cook at the register, a waitress in her pink and white uniform frumping around behind the counter. Wonders if the cook is packing a weapon. Could probably take them all out if he wanted; stun the girl with a blow from behind, vault the counter, a quick kick to the waitress' shin to take her down. The cook out behind the counter by this time, charge him head on, knife to the gut. Andy sure he could do it; has read those stories about men undergoing adrenaline rages, flipping over cars and tearing phone books in half. Is certain he's got that in him now; twitching be damned and cold be damned, craving for another fix be damned; there is something in this world waiting for him more wonderful and mysterious than any religious encounter, sexual encounter, celebrity encounter he's ever had, ever could have, and nothing will stand in his way to get it, nothing at all.

Andy rises up. Ready to make his move. The girl rising up a second later, Andy backing off. Squeezes the knife. The girl tosses coins on the table; gathers up her things. Coming out into the street now, juggling her books to tighten a scarf around her neck, the long, lovely swan's neck that Andy will soon be sawing through like a Thanksgiving turkey. The girl crossing the street, eyes downcast, trying to shield her face from the sleet. Good. Perfect. Andy's heart thumping harder, can hear it in his ears, his blood turning into pure energy inside of him. He pulls his arm back, waiting for the moment to thrust, the girl just before him now, has dropped her book on the sidewalk, crouching down to lift it, Andy breathing heavier, raising the blade, holding it above his head, body ready to strike, the girl standing, turning around to shuffle papers, Andy about to leap on to her, the girl turning to walk away, Andy ready to pounce, Andy lowering the knife, the girl walking away. Andy trembles, whimpers, drops the knife. The girl turns; Andy, halfway out of the alley, the knife between his feet, the girl staring at him in horror. Andy reaches down; knows what he has to do; that the moment has been forced upon him and he has to act. Undoes his belt, drops his zipper; his pants crumble around his ankles. Andy shrieks; the girl shrieks; turns around again and runs for it, books falling in her wake. Andy watches her go; slips back into the alley, falls onto his haunches, bare ass freezing on the concrete as he sits there and screams.

ANDY'S HAND is still shaking when he unlocks the apartment door, his body aching from the prolonged exposure to winter's night, his brain throbbing inside his head, a cacophony of images ricocheting around, stabbing at the backs of his eyes, pounding on his eardrums. The girl, dead in the alley, her blood on his hands; the Executioner raising his club high to strike; Draft, perched atop one of the folding chairs in his closet-office, knees tucked beneath his chin, naked and demonic, spinning the film reel with his own hands, Andy watching from the floor, supine, pajama clad and munching popcorn.

"It's me," Andy mutters. Slams the door, locks it. The apartment even dimmer than usual; all but a few of the candles gone out, the gray flicker of the television screen not enough to compensate for the loss of light. Steven rests on the couch, his head propped on one of the arms, staring at the screen. Andy's eyes adjust to the darkness; on the television, the American flag wafts in the breeze, black and white on the ancient set, the national anthem playing before sign off. Andy pauses, places his hand over his heart, waits for the set to cut to static.

Approaching Steven, something trudges up in Andy's guts, crawling from his toes into his shins and settling in his bowels with a terrible, revelatory power. Steven is soaked in sweat, mouth open, his discolored tongue bulging out. A rubber band dangles from his swollen thigh, the dried remnants of a torrent of blood deepening the hue of his already purpled flesh. Resting on his bloated stomach: a bloody needle, a vial of morphine. Steven's eyes roll up to Andy pleadingly; he whispers, his breathing at its shallowest since he moved in: "Need...my fix."

"Son of a bitch," Andy mutters. "What the fuck happened?"

"Fucked it up. Couldn't find anything in my arm. Hit...something."

"Your fucking artery," Andy says. "Oh, shit."

"Andy... Gimme my fix."

"Fuck your fix, I need to get to a phone!"

"Andy... Please, man..."

Andy stares down at his brother, his wild eyes, pleading, pathetic. Andy takes up the jar, uses it to refill the half-empty syringe back to maximum capacity, the contents already tinted red with traces of Steven's blood.

"Already... I already shot some," Steven mutters. "Don't need anymore..."

"Yes, you do," Andy says. "You need your fix." He snaps the rubber band off of Steven's thigh, applies it to one of his arms. Finds a single throbbing vein, tiny, infinitesimal. Andy primes the needle, jams it in; Steven lies there, eyes popping even larger now. He weakly tries to raise his hands to Andy, tries to protest; cannot lift them an inch off of the couch.

Andy shuts his eyes when he pushes the plunger down. Keeps them shut. When he opens them, he is greeted by the visage of Steven's own eyes, one wide open, the other half closed; his mouth hangs in a crooked half smile.

"Steven?" Andy whispers. He leans forward; puts his ear to his brother's mouth, his nose. Silence. Nothing.

Andy steps back; nearly stumbles over the coffee table. Sits down on the floor. He watches Steven a good long while. When he's convinced that he's dead, Andy begins his search. Drawers are ripped from their hinges; the remnants of the refrigerator are torn out, empty cartons reeking of sour milk and empty bottles smelling of flat beer tossed onto the kitchen floor, the toilet lid tossed aside and cracked, the loose floorboards of the living room corner pried up. At last Andy rolls the bulk of his brother's body from the couch and upends the cushions. There, in the corner, the fabric ripped up and sloppily tucked back down. Andy rummages inside; pulls out Steven's little black bag. Opens it up: jackpot.

In the bathroom, sitting on the edge of the stained tub, the fumes of the toilet battering his nostrils, Andy rolls up his sleeve, tourniquets himself with his belt, pops the needle in. Injects just the right amount. Once it has taken effect, he finds his trench coat, puts it on. Heads downstairs. At the payphone, he deposits money, waits for the answer on the other end.

"Hello?"

"Draft? It's Andy. I've got your body."

WHEN ANDY opens the door of his apartment, he isn't sure if it's Draft or a bandit come to rob him of whatever pitiful tchotchkes he has worth taking. The figure standing there is covered from head to toe in winter accoutrements, a black fedora pulled down over the eyes, the nose and mouth ensconced by a thick red muffler. It isn't until the man steps into his apartment without a word of welcome and deftly shuts the door, locking and relocking it with gentle precision that he knows his guest has arrived.

"I don't usually make house calls," Draft says. "Please understand that." He removes the muffler and fedora; once the stench hits his nose, he replaces the muffler.

As Draft's eyes adjust to the darkness of the apartment he begins to gaze around the living room: the newspaper clippings on the wall, the empty bottles and cans that litter the floor in even greater multitudes than they did on the day that Andy first asked Eddie Lawler to begin the hunt that resulted in this meeting. "You live here?"

"Yeah," Andy says. "There a problem?"

Draft opens his mouth to say something and then stops. "No. Not at all. I'd just pictured something...*different*."

The two men stand there a while, Draft rocking on his heels, Andy stone still. It takes Draft's eyes a few more moments to adjust before he sees that Andy is splattered from chest to ankles in dried blood, great splotches of it flowing together over his clothes to create a tye-dye pattern of gore.

"I'm very impressed," Draft says.

"You wanna see it?" Andy asks.

"Of course."

They go to the bathroom, Draft holding his hand over his muffler to combat the ever-increasing intensity of the odor. The seat on the toilet is down to hide its foul contents; in the blood-splattered tub lies Steven's remnants, painstakingly hacksawed into individual pieces for easy transport, the hands severed from the arms, the arms from the torso, feet from the calves. Steven's head lay atop the pile, the eyes shut, the mouth closed with the serene contentment of a resting Buddha.

"All yours," Andy whispers. "Get him out of here."

"Someone close to you," Draft says, real awe in his voice.

"My brother."

"And...how did it feel?"

"It...didn't feel like anything."

Beneath the muffler, Draft frowns. "That's...a disappointment, Andy."

"I figured." A pause. "I have some trash bags. To put it in."

Draft, transfixed on Steven's body, takes a moment to respond. "Oh, no. That won't be necessary. I have some men waiting downstairs to help. We've brought provisions." Draft's turn to pause. "I should go get them. They have instructions to come up here and kill you if I'm not down in five minutes."

"You know the way out."

Andy follows Draft to the living room, watches him go. Stares at his newspaper clippings as he waits; needs to get some more; needs pictures. When the knock comes, Andy opens the door without hesitation. Draft enters, flanked by a pair of men in coveralls and stocking caps, each carrying a cooler.

"Back through that way," Draft says, indicating the direction of the bathroom. "In the tub. Please, be careful."

The men absent themselves, leaving Andy and Draft and the tin reel case cradled in Draft's arms.

"Yours," Draft says.

Andy's hands reach out for it, trembling; his fingers dance across the lid of the container; and then he's snatched it away, scurrying to his cot, mounting it to sit there on his haunches, rocking back and forth.

"We can watch it while we wait," Draft says. "I might like to see it again. For old times' sake. It was my first. You always have a special sort of affinity for your first."

"Alone," Andy says, and then says no more.

Draft smiles. "I understand. I was young once, too."

It only takes a few more moments for Draft's men to exit the bathroom, carrying the coolers. Andy's eyes watch as they pass through his field of vision; then he turns his gaze back to the canister. Draft opens the door for them; on his way out he turns to address Andy.

"You won't see me anymore," he says. "So if you need to tell me it was worth it…or if it wasn't worth it…if you need anything at all…I won't be there. Oh, and Andy?"

Draft moves to Andy; reaches into his jacket; comes out with a twenty dollar bill. "A final gift to you, from me. Buy yourself a new pair of glasses. You're going to want to see this clearly."

Draft and his men leave. Once they're gone, Andy gingerly moves to the door, locks it. Then he threads up the projector.

ANDY IS not sure if he breathes through any of the film. He greets the few seconds he has already seen with the same rapture with which he viewed them in Draft's office. When the moment approaches at which Draft shut off the projector, Andy involuntarily gasps, bunches the sheets of his cot up in his fingers and whimpers.

The film runs out; the projector blasts light against the wall, a perfect square of pure white. To Andy Lew, his body trembling, his eyes filled with tears, the room looks like Heaven.

ANDY LEW isn't sure what time or day or month it is when the knocking awakens him. He staggers from his cot, finds his glasses, puts them on. Hasn't quite adjusted to them yet: their solidity; the heavy black plastic versus his old browlines; the way they stay securely on his head; the way they do not require masking tape to hold them together. Andy tries to look for the clock, can't find it; hasn't been able to find much of anything lately; articles of clothing, his father's watch, pieces of food he thought he'd left lying around; his days blurring into nights, shifts at the Colossus now marathon endurance sessions before he can get back to the apartment to bask in the presence of the reel. He has not dared watch it since that first night; afraid that the thrill might be gone, that he might see some gaffe or error to alert him to its inauthenticity, that it will leave him as empty as Eddie's fuck reels. Instead: Hours spent staring at the case, little hits of Steven's needle here and there to take the edge off, a beer chaser when the first faint pains of hunger strike him.

Andy staggers to the door, is about to open it when a familiar voice drifts through from the other side:

"Andy?" Samantha Lew asks.

"Who else would it be?"

"You sound awful."

"So do you. What do you want?"

"I want to talk to Steven," Samantha says. Andy does not bother looking through the peephole; presses his back against the door, hopes that she will somehow sense this and go away. "Where is he? We need to talk. Your brother's a piece of shit, but he's the only father those children have, and I refuse to raise them on my…"

"They're better off without him," Andy says.

"What?"

"I said he left," Andy says. "And those kids are better off without him." Samantha, dumbstruck. "What? You're lying. Steven! Get out here!"

"He left. He left a note."

"A…a note? What is this, a note?"

"I threw it away," Andy says. "It was bullshit anyway. A bunch of stuff about wanting to find himself. Beatnik garbage about how you and the kids were dragging him down." Andy stops a moment, turns again to face the door. Places his hand on the knob; takes it off. "This is probably the sort of thing that most people would leave out, but he said in the note he wants to start fucking guys. He said he tried it once and that it got him off."

In the hallway, the sound of feet staggering, the thump when Andy supposes she falls against the wall. "Oh no, oh, no, you son of a bitch. You son of a bitch."

"That's right, Steven is," Andy says. "And if he ever comes back this way again I'll be happy to kill him for you."

Samantha begins to sob; in his mind's eye, Andy can see big, fat, tears rolling down her heavy face. Andy wonders what they would taste like. He lets her cry herself out for a few seconds before he addresses her again:

"It's a lousy fucking break, but that's the sort of shit that happens," Andy says. "Look. I don't want you to get the wrong impression, that I want to help or anything. I don't need to be helping anyone right now. But I'm going to give you some advice. One time only, understand? You go back home, and you tell your kids that he's dead. Come up with something. He hanged himself. He died in a robbery. Whatever the fuck you wanna tell them. And then you raise them as good as you can. Steven's gone, and I don't think he's coming back anytime soon. He's history. No need to let your kids dwell on that."

Through the doorway, he can still hear her crying.

"The most important thing, I guess," Andy says, "Is you got to keep your eyes on—oh, *shit*."

"What?" Samantha asks.

"The last time I saw him," Andy says, putting his back to the door again, sliding down to the floor. "He was still wearing dad's watch."

OUR FINAL FEATURE OF THE EVENING:
INFERNAL BELOVED
(1977)

"How comes it, then, that thou art out of hell?"
"Why, this is Hell; nor am I out of it."
—Christopher Marlowe, *Dr. Faustus*

IN THE stagnant heat of his apartment, Andy flips the projector on. It whirs to life, a bright square of light forming on a laundered sheet nailed to the wall. Within seconds, the square is replaced by a grainy gray field, and, set in the middle of it, the visage of the skull, an effect accomplished, Andy has determined, through the sort of crude yet innovative puppetry pioneered in Eastern Europe before the whole place went Commie-up. It has long been a fantasy of his that a fellow Slav made the film.

The numbers tick to two, to one, to zero, and then there is another great flash of white light as the image onscreen is replaced by a small, undecorated room, no larger than this one, perhaps even tinier. In the center of the room is a chair; beside it, a little metal drink cart; and there, sitting in the chair, arms bound behind, mouth gagged, great, luminous eyes staring ahead from an angelic face, is *her. Her. Her*, here to help him out of one of his greatest struggles; here for him, as she has always been there for him, at an hour of need.

"That," Nicky says, awed, "Is the most beautiful bitch I've ever seen." His voice softly cracks and Andy thinks that, in the dark, he can see a tear well up in the corner of Nicky's eye.

The only sound in the air is the whirring of the projector and the collective ragged breathing of all the men in the room. She continues to stare ahead, head jerking from side to side, body writhing as she attempts to break free of her bonds. When it becomes apparent that she will not, she begins to look around her, to determine if there may be some sympathetic party within earshot whose attention she might gain. Her head is moving back towards the camera when the Executioner strides in, carrying what Andy first presumed to be an elaborate club but which he has since identified as a traditional Japanese bludgeon known as the *kanabo*, wielded in feudal mythology by the demons known as *oni*.

"What the fuck?" Chad says. Gator shushes him. The figure reaches the girl, stands directly behind her. She does not try to look up at him but stares directly ahead at the camera a moment before resuming her struggles. The figure sets down the *kanabo* against the chair and takes the girl's head in its gloved hands, rotating it up so that she is looking directly into the camera. The girl seems to understand some instruction conveyed to her and continues to look directly at the camera, body rigid now, tears beginning to flow from her eyes, streaking mascara down her cheeks. The figure lifts the *kanabo* and steps back from the chair. The girl begins to wince, tries to brace herself for the expected blow. Isn't braced when it comes, the club arcing sideways like a baseball bat, catching her in the temple and cheek. The studs on the side of the weapon split flesh, open gouges, black blood beginning to ooze down her cheek and mix with her tears. Her head flops onto her chest. The figure sets the club down, goes to the drink cart, retrieves a washcloth from a bowl of water and dabs her face, uses a styptic pencil to seal the smaller wounds, her body twitching and writhing at the burn.

"A killer," Wilson gasps, touching his fingers to his lips. "Like Sybarite."

When it is satisfied, the figure steps back, retrieves the *kanabo*. Then the club comes back up; another swing; another snap of the head. Blood flows again, her eyes boggling in their sockets, and the Executioner is cleaning her again, and it is clubbing her again, and it is tending her wounds again, cradling her head in its small but powerful hands.

Andy turns away from the screen, to watch Gator and Chad and Nicky and Aaron and Wilson, watch them watching her, transfixed, spellbound, he understands now, completely in her thrall, understands now after all these years and the times he's watched it and the times he's shown it to Gator, the power she can has, the way she can enchant a person, the way she can envelop a man, place them in her thrall like Cleopatra, Helen, Marilyn, and Andy smiles proudly to see that they are all in her thrall now and she is his.

The Executioner gently shakes her by the shoulders. It bows its head; though there is no sound it is clear to Andy now, after all these viewings, that he is speaking to her, and her barely coherent eyes attempt to move up in unison and look towards the camera, and they remain there, fixed, staring straight ahead, obedient. She is still staring when the Executioner comes up behind her and begins the final barrage, blow after blow after blow, new wounds opening on top of old ones, until there is no more jerking or twitching, until her body is very, very still and her head is slumped forward against her chest, strands of matted and dripping hair hanging over her face.

The Executioner sets the club down, and for the final time lifts her head up in his hands, chunks of skull and brain just barely visible as they ooze onto his thumbs. He holds the head up for the camera to see, to behold, to play witness, for the camera to look and see the shimmer in her eyes as it at last dulls and goes out forever.

The film abruptly runs out; the white light strikes the blanket and Andy moves to shut the projector off, switch on the lights, look at his audience. Gator leaps to his feet whooping, wiping sweat from his forehead, wiping his hands off on his tank top. "Awwww, boom, boom! What'd I tell you boys?"

Chad leaps up from his seat, moves towards Andy, and in a flash he has lifted Andy by the collar of his jacket and hauled him to the window.

"Sick fuck," Chad bellows, is ready to throw him through the glass.

"Chad!" Nicky shouts, rising. "Put him down. We can't kill him."

"It ain't killing," Chad says, "It's forced reincarnation. Rat shit here needs to come back as a jockstrap."

"Down!" Nicky shouts. Gator, giggling, has removed his gun but lets it dangle at his side. Chad looks between them, puts Andy down, stares at him, stares back at Nicky and Wilson and Aaron.

"What the fuck is wrong with you?" Chad says. "That you…have that? That you enjoy it? You're sick."

"It isn't sick," Andy says. "It's beautiful. It's the most important moment in her life. It's what we're all going to go through, every one of us. The biggest, most important thing any of us will do in our entire lives. The one thing everyone shares. And that's hers. Just…hers. Forever. For everyone to remember. To know that she was alive, that she was real, and to know…to know how it ended."

Chad shakes his head, looks all around the room.

"I said I'd be your bodyguard… I said I'd… I said I'd be your personal trainer. This shit…*this*…" His voice cracks; he pauses; opens his mouth to say something; stops; and, wordlessly, goes to the door, unlocks it, and lets himself out.

"So fuckin' beautiful," Nicky mutters as Chad leaves, staring at the projector, then back at Wilson. The two share some sort of look, Andy sees, something passing between them, Nicky asking a non-verbal question, Wilson somehow responding in the affirmative with a twitch of the head, a jerk of the eyes that only the two men understand. Then, it's Wilson's turn to address Andy.

"Our greatest apologies. We have blasphemed."

Aaron nods vigorously. Wilson moves to Andy, takes one of his hands; Andy jerks it away.

"Forgive us," Wilson says. "Forgive us for doubting. That we had to see to believe. To know that this…is what we have been waiting for. We had no clue that we were in the presence of someone so finely attuned to the realities of the modern age. That you were a man with his very own muse, like Dante's Beatrice, Beethoven's Immortal Beloved."

Andy nods. "You understand now?"

"Yes, yes."

"You get it? You really get it?"

Wilson shakes his head. "No…no. I don't think… Anyone will ever really… Truly understand all of its mysteries. But! Such is life, yes? And…such is death! I understand this now."

"And you?" Andy looks to Nicky, gaping spellbound at the projector.

"I wanted to see something like I've never seen in my life. That was it. Who was she?"

"No clue," Gator says. "Andy-man here, he's spent the better part of the last decade trying to find Miss Priss' real name, number, measurements, favorite pastime." Gator snickers.

"OK. You've seen it," Andy says. He puts out his hand. "Deal's a deal."

"It is," Nicky says. He removes his checkbook from his vest, a pen, begins to write, stops. "I've got to wonder, though, Andy…"

"You gonna try and go back on your word?" Andy asks. "You some kind of commie?"

"Ain't never gone back on my word a day in my life. But I've got to wonder. If watching that is worth five hundred…what's it worth to keep?"

"She's not for sale." Andy's blood turns to ice; almost pounces on Nicky out of pure impulse for the suggestion.

"Not sale," Wilson says. "But rental."

"No deal," Andy says.

"Hear us out," Wilson continues. "The videotape recorder, you saw it just now, yes? Playing the nature program?"

"The point. Get to it."

"We have the technology to transfer a print such as yours to a video tape. Completely safe. It won't affect the integrity of your film by a single particle. The process will allow us to make an exact copy of your film, to be preserved in our private library."

"I've seen them do it," Nicky says. "Transferred a bunch of my old loops, made me a few compilations. Best of Nicky. Ain't seen myself so clear in decades. The boys know what they're doing. And this..." Nicky taps the projector. "I'd pay top dollar to be able to fall asleep to this every night."

"She isn't yours," Andy whispers. VTR. Andy tenses at the thought; he has long been conflicted over the opportunity to so easily recreate the marvels of the home theater experience in his own home; has, too, seen some of these *video tapes*, the low quality of the picture, the way that it can warp and bend with no real way to properly adjust it.

"Wouldn't be her, now, though, would it?" Nicky asks. "This here, the real deal...well, we'd give that right back. Me? I just want a copy. Kinda like taking a picture of the Mona Lisa, isn't it?"

Andy's mouth goes dry. The correct answer, he realizes, is "no." The correct course of action is to demand these interlopers out of his apartment; money be damned; the right thing to do is send them on their way, wait the appropriate amount of time, gather her up along with whatever scant belongings he can cart with him to the Port Authority and buy a ticket to wherever it is he can afford to go, no matter how close, Newark, Philly, even if it's only to Queens he has to get away now, get as far as he can at the moment, but get away and figure things out there.

That is the correct answer.

"How much?" He asks.

Nicky crumbles the check he had been writing, stuffs it in his vest. Writes another, signs it, tears it, hands it to Andy. Andy lifts his glasses and looks beneath the rims to see the sum better; thinks his heart might stop.

"Bullshit," he says.

"*No* shit. I'm a man who knows what he wants. And I want this. It'd make a hell of an addition to my collection. And it sure seems to have inspired these boys. Can't wait to hear how it inspires their work."

"You'll...take care of her?"

"With extreme caution," Wilson says, Aaron nodding soberly behind him. "A sterile room. Freshly cleaned equipment. Film cleaner, new cotton gloves. We wouldn't dare risk compromising the integrity of so singular a work of art."

There have been times—when he has miscalculated a dose, when he's bought from a new dealer who misgauged the purity, when he's gotten greedy and shot up twice in too short a span—when it's seemed to Andy that he's transcended the physical confines of his own body and watched himself from an ascended distance. Times when he's felt he's floated to the roof of his apartment and, for some metaphysical reason, prevented from moving beyond the confines of his own living space, hovered there, staring down at his own twitching, sweating body stretched out on his cot, stains forming beneath his pits, foam trickling from his mouth; and on some of these occasions he's even watched his own body—free of any conscious will—rise up from the cot, grip its edges to steady itself, watched his body stagger through the apartment trailing pools of vomit, collapsing either beside the toilet to void the rest of its stomach or beneath the refrigerator to grope and grasp for any remaining food or beer it may find there. There are no drugs in Andy's system tonight; barely any alcohol; but it seems that he watches himself as—guided, he supposes, not by narcotics but by the freshly inked check now in his pocket—he unspools the reel, places it carefully inside of its container, and hands it gingerly to Wilson.

"Helluva party," Gator says after Nicky and Aaron and Wilson have gone. "Ought to throw more. Turn it into our own little business. Host a few little soirees, fry up a couple of rats, serve 'em up to guests on trash-can lids, make a real wad off of it."

"No," Andy snaps. "One night only. After I get the rest of that cash, she goes roadshow. With an audience of one."

"So that's it then? Hittin' the old dusty trail?"

"As in permanently."

"Can't say I'm not a bit disappointed," Gator says. "But after today's, uh, enlightenments, I think that I can wholeheartedly encourage it."

"I'd say it's been fun, but it hasn't." Andy guides Gator to the door. "Now I've got shit to figure out."

Once he is alone, Andy flings himself on his cot, uncrumples the check, holds it over his head and stares at it. Soon. As soon as she is back in his arms the two of them will be off. On board the Greyhound and riding into the sunset.

His lady and he.

DAYBREAK FINDS Andy awake and alert, not out of desperation or a deficit of smack but excitement; real, honest, alien excitement keeping him alert. Up until this point he has conceived of his flight from New York as just that—a forced exodus from the city of his birth. Now, with Nicky's check safely secured beneath his cot, more to come, the idea occurs to him that events have been moving in this direction for another purpose: He has found one of *them,* those fabled new beginnings that the gurus and the armchair shrinks are always talking about, a real, honest opportunity for a new life in a new city, a place where no one knows his name or face, where his rap sheet is clean and his work history unblemished; where the tantalizing questions that have eked away his days and nights these past twelve years will have no relevance. Her name, her age, her birthday, her loves and hates and hopes, her identity; all the things that together encapsulated the entirety of her being, what he sees go out at the end of every viewing, the truth of these things, their power, will be lost to him. They will become, as with particular types of couples, quiet secrets left unquestioned, parts of a life before there ever was a couple that neither partner wonders after nor questions; irrelevant details of another life. He has her now; that is all that will matter. No more time wasted over idle speculation; in California, all their time together will be time appreciated unconditionally.

Against all logic, Andy's grey double-breasted chalk stripe is the most used yet least worn suit in his wardrobe. He puts it on every other Saturday morning, promptly heads to his bank, cashes his paycheck, and then immediately returns home to change out of it. The suit was, some ages ago, a gift, given to him by a particular someone—now nameless in his mind and, as far as he is concerned this morning, quite dead to him—with an intimate enough knowledge of the topography of his body to have it tailored without his knowledge and then packaged in a neat white box wrapped in a black grosgrain bow. The gift had not been unappreciated, though Andy had initially found himself at a loss as to what to do with it, as he was not then, nor has he ever been in the position to be conducting the sort of business that calls for a real, quality chalk stripe. He had no idea when he should wear it, and indeed scoffed at her suggestion he just put it on to go out on the town with her, as though chalk stripe were some sort of laissez faire pattern to be worn to a ballgame or to dinner and not something more befitting of a banker. He had been trying to explain this to her when the idea had hit upon him that it would take some of the stress off of his mind if he had a nice bank suit, something to throw on with a soft shirt and a knit tie every other Saturday, something he could easily slip back out of in favor of more casual attire for the afternoon. So it was that the chalk stripe became Andy's trusted bank outfit, worn faithfully over the years and dutifully cared for, occasional alterations made to accommodate his shrinking waistline and sloping shoulders.

It is the grey chalk stripe suit Andy is wearing when he enters the bank this morning, cheeks smoothly shaved and the remnants of his hair neatly slicked. His armpits are, unusually, damp. Kept feeling the hair on the back of his neck standing up on the way here, kept feeling the little prickling sensation in the back of his skull that he gets when he knows he's being watched, followed, kept turning around and looking for the tail, got on and off at the same stop three times just to try and throw anyone off, so that by the time he arrives at the bank there are small dark circles beneath his arms, produced not by the heat but by the cold, wet anxiety that needles him even now.

As he approaches the teller desks, one of the girls spots him, does a double take, tenses up, and leans over to whisper something in the ear of the next teller. The next teller, older broad, beehive hair and a Shar Pei's worth of wrinkles, nods calmly and walks away. As Andy gets closer, the younger teller bunches up her hands, looks to the left, to the right, back to Andy. At the counter, Andy clears his throat.

"Give me a deposit slip."

The girl's eyes go saucer wide. She opens her mouth, her jaw starts slowly opening and closing as though she's stuttering some imbecile's symphony only she knows. Andy leans forward, stares the girl in the eye.

"Hey. Deposit slip. Now." He looks back over his shoulder; the following sensation has abated but he still doesn't like it, half expects his warning bells to go off full blast any moment now before he's beset by a swarm of sweaty, mustachioed men in cheap sports clothes.

The teller is slowly backing away from the desk when a larger gentleman in a blue serge suit comes up behind her, followed by the older teller. He gently taps the younger teller on the shoulder, leans down, whispers something in her ear. The girl casts one last deer-in-the-headlights glance at Andy before scampering off, replaced by the gentleman in the suit.

"Welcome back, Mr. Lew," the gentleman says.

"The hell's wrong with your girl back there?" Andy asks.

The man in the suit smiles, polite but not friendly. "She's simply feeling ill, Mr. Lew. How may I help you?"

Andy sneers. "You can help me by hiring employees who don't turn tail and run when they see one of their most loyal customers walking

through the front door." Can't wait to be in San Francisco; for all of their ostentation, at least the gays have a sense of decorum, some vague dedication to good manners and etiquette.

"Like I said, Mr. Lew, she's feeling ill." The gentleman clears his throat, offers the same faux-pleasant smile. "And a little surprised. Didn't we just see you last week?"

"The fuck business is it of yours when I come in here? I'll come in here to check my balance every fucking morning, noon, and night if I want. My money's my business; I damn well fucking earned it and until the Reds drop the big one I'll keep earning it and keep putting it in your bank, unless you want me to find someplace else that…"

"Whoah, now, son, why you gotta go trying to cause trouble for this nice man?"

Andy nearly jumps out of his wingtips; turns to see Dick Valentine a foot behind him in the same damn tan suit, arms folded behind his back. Dick approaches the teller window, leans on the counter.

"You know you've got a certain effect on folks, Andy. Especially decent ones. Now why don't you just go on about your business and leave this nice man in peace?" Dick offers a cordial smile to the man in the suit; the man turns to Andy.

"How can I help you, Mr. Lew?"

"Deposit," Andy says.

"Of course." The man pushes a deposit slip to Andy.

"Then again, your selection of companions seems to be degrading in quality these days," Dick continues. "Now it seems to me, if you're considering cutting one particularly loathsome individual out of your life, that don't mean you go trying to replace him with an even bigger piece of shit, less you're one of these sorry folks who ain't got any interest in learning from his mistakes. There's this sister I know—professionally, of course—had the shit beaten out of her by six different boyfriends in the past twelve years. Every time worse than the last. Already knew half the fuckers myself—professionally, of course. The fella she hooked up with last fall I busted back in '71 on a pedo rap. Last I heard of her, round Saint Patty's Day, was sittin' in a room up in Bellevue with her jaw wired shut. Asked her why every time me or one of the boys dragged off the nasty SOBs she didn't take the chance to haul ass in the opposite direction. Go live with her sister, find a decent man, anything other than keep diggin' even deeper into the gutter. Still ain't got an answer. How about you, Andy? You got an answer for yourself?"

Andy finishes filling out the deposit slip, passes it to the teller, takes out his check to endorse. "The fuck are you talking about?"

"I'm talking about how I suggest you cut ties with a certain mutual acquaintance and now I hear you're brothers for life with motherfuckin' Nicky fuckin' Blayze."

"Not a fan?" Andy asks.

"Not particularly," Dick says. "Can't understand why you are."

"How about this?" Andy flips the check in Dick's face, slaps it back on the counter to sign.

"The hell you talking about, son?"

"This, here? This is what he paid me to hang with him. Half of it. To show him and those freaks he runs with what's *real*."

Dick cranes his neck towards the check as Andy pushes it towards the man in the suit. "Andy, a check from Nicky Blayze ain't worth the shit he signed his name with."

"Yeah? Says who?"

"Says the mommas that his cracker ass paid off to keep his own self out of Sing Sing," Dick says. "Motherfucker ain't got a penny to his dumbass name after those kinda payoffs. 'Nicky Blayze' my ass. Seen his rap sheet. Boy's name's Blaszkiewicz."

"Mr. Lew?" The man in the suit is looking at Andy with a great deal of concern, his eyes moving back and forth between the check, Andy, Dick. "Sir? This isn't a valid check, sir."

"What?"

"The routing and account numbers are invalid, sir. They don't exist. They're not even in the correct format. If you'll look here, this is a 'Q.' I'm afraid routing numbers don't have letters, sir."

"Don't you fuck with me," Andy says, not sure if it's to the man in the suit, Dick, or both.

"'75," Dick says. "Couple of gals come down to the station, say your good pal Nicky gone and knocked up their little girls. If I remember right, one was fourteen, one was fifteen. Then again, they looked a little bit younger than that. Oh, there were some boys down at the station had a real hard on—no pun intended—to nail a celebrity. Buddy of mine, Stubbs, his name was—caught a knife in the ribs last year, early retirement, lucky bastard—it was gonna come down to him to bust Blayze. Last minute, things dry up. All of a sudden those girls maybe didn't spend a night with Nicky and a bottle of codeine. Maybe it was they boyfriends got them in the family way. And maybe, just maybe, it was cause their mommas won the lottery that all of a sudden they were wearin' brand new clothes and comin' down to the station in a nice new Lincoln. Maybe."

"You follow me all the way from my apartment just to shit on who I spend time with?" Andy asks, voice cracking.

"Follow you? I got better shit to do with my life. Was grabbin' a hot dog on the corner. Seen you walk in here."

"Mr. Lew?" The man in the suit asks. "I'm afraid this is an invalid check, sir…You're aware that's a criminal offense?" There's a little too much glee in the man's voice as he says this.

"Go…fuck yourself," Andy says, almost an afterthought.

"Don't know what kinda scam the boy's running," Dick says, "But Nicky Blayze' ain't got a red cent to his motherfuckin' name."

Andy's staring at the counter, rings of moisture expanding around damp hands. His head snaps towards Dick, eyes bulging, desperate, as the realization of the truth begins to set in. Andy's mouth hangs open, thoughts cascading through his mind at such breakneck speed that he cannot comprehend them at any intellectual level, can only experience the raw emotion that each one dredges up in him, and as the world begins to spin around him, his feet are carrying him away from the teller, away from Dick, staring sleepy eyed, out the door and onto the quickest route back to Nicky's place.

THE BODYBUILDER who opens the door, Andy notes, is not Chad. This one is less streamlined, blockier, veiny, his muscles, Andy thinks, not developed to be aesthetically pleasing but to tear the seams out of jackets and frighten small animals and announce to the world a general desire to terrify the living shit out of anyone unfortunate enough to lay eyes on him.

"The fuck you want?" The bodybuilder asks. His pectorals bounce rhythmically.

"Nicky. Now." Andy hisses this as he slips past the bodybuilder. The light of early afternoon seeps in around the edges of the drawn curtains, fighting against the red track lighting for luminescent dominance. There's an air of urgency here today that Andy hasn't felt in the place before, a sense of things *happening,* most of the revelers he's seen here before now absent and those that remain bustling about in great haste. Some carry great bolts of fabric over their arms, black, it seems, judging by those that pass through the slivers of light coming in from behind the curtains; others are carrying tall, cylindrical candles, not far removed in dimension or design from those Andy watched burn to nubs in the church of his long suppressed childhood. In the center of it all stands Nicky, looming over Wilson and Aaron as they consult some great leather bound book. As he approaches them, Andy realizes the entire living room has been cleared—no couch, no hookah, no television set— except for what appears to be a brand new projector.

"Nicky!" Andy shouts. He hops into the sunken living area, winces as weight comes down on his injured ankle. Panics slightly; might've come into this too rashly, too passionately. Should've shot up just a little beforehand, dulled his senses, prepared himself for some really hardcore violence. He slips a hand into one pocket of his suit, tries to casually fumble for some errant baggie or pill he might've left there after a previous wear. No such luck.

"Andy!" Nicky says. The thin, hateful smile spreads across his face. Gator's eyes widen; Wilson and Aaron look to one another nervously, close the book. Wilson hands it to Aaron, nods, the taller boy disappearing with it somewhere in the back of the apartment. "Pleasant surprise. You're going to love this. You've arrived during a most momentous occasion. Today's my graduation." Nicky reaches down to the floor and comes up with a framed certificate. In the dull light, Andy can make out the inscription: UNIVERSAL LIFE CHURCH—DOCTORATE OF METAPHYSICS—NICHOLAS BLAYZE.

"A surprise, from Wilson. He and Aaron decided that I'd passed the final test; that I've finally reached the highest levels of enlightenment. Now, I'm certified to preach to the masses." The dead chuckle, accompanied, this time, by a dry rattle in the base of his throat, a wet sounding cough. "Think I'd prefer to be called 'Dr. Blayze' from now on. Or you think that has too formal of a ring to it? May be too intimidating. Maybe 'Dr. Nicky.'"

"That certificate cost you $12.95 plus shipping," Andy says. "And it's going to cost you your life if you don't give her back. Now."

Nicky smiles serenely; beside him, Gator's eyes continue to bulge from their sockets, sweat beads dripping down his face. "I'm sure that this is the result of a misunderstanding."

"I don't care if it's the result of a fucking lung cancer test. You're giving her back." In his pocket, Andy's hand fumbles with the switchblade, his thumb slipping off the trigger, moving back into place, slipping off again. "The check bounced. Deal's off. Give her back. *Now*."

"I understand why you're confused," Nicky says. He slowly begins moving towards Andy; instinctively, Andy steps backwards, almost stumbles. "Something I realized early in life, idiots get confused easy. One of the reasons they're idiots. And Andy, sorry to tell you, in case you haven't heard it already, friend, you're one of the biggest fucking idiots I've ever met in my life. I had something like that—*her*—I'd never let another man lay a single fucking finger on it. But sell it? Give it away? That has got to be one of the stupidest fucking things I've ever seen a man do."

Andy nearly pounces forward. "Where the fuck is she?" Andy turns, begins to move up the little flight of stairs out of the living room.

"Grab him!" Nicky barks. Andy has barely made it a few feet before the bodybuilder has gripped him from behind, arms as thick as tires forcing Andy to the ground, locking him into a half nelson. A few shouts of surprise erupt from the room, turn into giggles and peals of laughter as Nicky's guests watch Andy squirming to escape the bodybuilder's grip.

"Gator! Are you going to let him do this to me? Get him off!"

"No can do, Andy-man," Gator says. "Not gonna mess up a good thing." Gator steps forward, kneels down to look Andy in the eye. "Shouldn't have kept that shit from me, man. There's something I can't abide, it's other folks risking my ass without my knowledge, you know what I mean?"

"You fuck," Andy whispers. "You piece of shit, festering cock sore, cum guzzling..." Gator turns his back, strolls away; Andy turns his attention to Nicky, screams: "She doesn't mean anything to you!" He tries to twist his arms to free himself, jerk himself away, even attempts in a feeble moment of pure desperation to dislocate his own shoulder the way he's heard some of the escape artists do it, pop it free from his socket to make himself more flexible; would inflict any amount of bodily harm on himself now to get to her; would, given the time, chew through his own arm.

"She means everything to me!" The roar coming up out of Nicky's throat is deeper and angrier and full of more malicious power than Andy had expected; cowers instinctively, hates himself for it. Trembling, stuck,

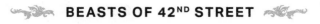

here, while she's somewhere nearby, mere feet away. "You cunt. You stupid, fucking cunt. You really have no idea, do you? When Gator laid it all out for me, told me about his little bitchboy friend jacking it to a dead chick, I couldn't believe it. But you really don't know, do you?"

"The fuck are you talking about?"

Nicky squats down in front of Andy so the two men are eye to eye and whispers the words he had hoped would never pass another man's lips but his own: "Samuel Draft."

Andy goes rigid, stops squirming. "The fuck did you say?"

"Ahhh, you get it now, don't you?"

"Get what? You heard it from Gator. He told you about me and Eddie."

"I heard it from Joe Tuesday," Nicky says. "Ring a bell? On his way down when I was on my way up. Must've made twenty, thirty flicks back in the day. All the boys in the business wanted to be Joe Tuesday. Abs like a washboard and he came every time. No stunt cocks for Joe Tuesday. Got to work with him two, three times my first year in the city. Shit. The luck I had. Barely off the bus and here I'm pulling four ways with Joe Fuckin' Tuesday. Took me under his wing. You have any idea what that's like?" Something vaguely resembling sympathy passes over Nicky's face, disappears just as quickly. "Course you don't. You wouldn't be here. But *I* had that. Had the man of all men teaching me how it's done. Owe my whole fuckin' career to that man. My whole fuckin' life. Man left the world a little too soon. Know that?"

"Blew his brains out in '75," Andy says, thinking he might even have the photo somewhere in his collection. Figures it best to play along for now, not antagonize his captor any further, accidentally instigate him into ordering the bodybuilder to snap his neck.

"Blew his fuckin' brains out," Nicky says. "A man like that. I was with him the night before. Yeah. That's the story you won't read in the smut rags. Nicky Blayze and Joe Tuesday, getting high and getting by the night before he sticks a twelve gauge in his mouth. Never forget that night. Bunch of reasons. You got a night you won't ever forget?"

For a moment it seems Nicky might be genuinely interested in the answer to this; Andy does not respond. The moment passes.

"Yeah, me and Joe and enough ice to get an elephant tweaking, and he's getting really nervous, nervous like I haven't seen him before. Joe's a calm guy, even when he's on ice. Real orderly. Some guys smoke, they stab their girlfriend, knock over a bodega, Joe's the kinda guy cleans his bathroom, rearranges his closet. Not tonight. Tonight, Joe's getting all creepy. Starts telling me shit like I never heard before. Normally it's, 'Let me tell you about the time I banged Sylvia Kristel,' 'Let me tell you about the time I got high with Harry Reems on top of the Empire State Building.' Tonight, it's dark shit. Weird shit. Says he's a fraud. Says he got burned out years ago, stopped being able to get hard without popping a Percodan first. Says he stopped tasting food, his hands are numb all the time. Says he thinks he fucked his soul out and he didn't have one left anymore. No idea he went in for the spiritual shit, but I'm not judging. Says he got desperate, that he didn't know how to do anything else but lay bricks and chicks, and he'd fucked his back up too bad in a car wreck to go back to bricks. Saw shrinks, a guru, even his fuckin' Rabbi. Says he got twenty different answers from ten different people, still, no dice. Then he says one night he's in the phone booth in the lobby at the Lyric, sitting in his own piss, needle still hanging out of his arm, double feature's about to start, and he thinks he might be in one of them, wants to see himself fifty feet tall. And the phone rings. Well, Joey's high so what does he do? Joey picks it up. And what do you think he says he heard?"

Andy's muscles tense; he does not know the geography or topography of this story, the particular terrain that Nicky Blayze is about to take him over, but he does know the destination.

"Him," Andy says.

"Him. Fuckin' him. Weird voice, Joey says. Says he didn't know if he was hearing a chick or a cat at first. But he does hear his name. 'Mr. Tuesday, I understand you have a problem. Well, my name is Samuel

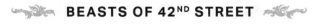

Draft, and I'd like to help.' Joe thinks it's the smack at first. Maybe he took too much, maybe not enough. He hangs up, starts to nod off. It rings again. Picks up again. 'Mr. Tuesday, I'm offering something very generous, and I think you'll be very interested in how it can potentially revitalize your career.'"

Nicky has gotten twitchy now, Andy sees, not the sort of movement brought on by nervousness, drugs, even agitation, but the kind endemic to a man who's absolutely terrified and doing everything he can not to betray that. He shuffles his feet, paces, toys with his own hair; anything to prolong the shakes, weak knees, an absolute and complete breakdown.

"Joe's scared now. Knows that this ain't the smack, the ice, the booze, knows it's none of that. He tells me he knows it's 100% real now. I ask him how he knows, why he doesn't just think it's bullshit like he's gotten before, hearing music that isn't there, seeing spiders on the walls. Joe, he tells me there's times in a man's life when he just knows something. Knows he's met the woman he's gonna marry, knows he's gotta get out of a dive because trouble's coming. Tells me he knows this is the real deal. And he tells me that Samuel Draft gave him an address in Midtown; and he went there; and Samuel Draft showed him something. Something he doesn't wanna describe. Something he says he knew right away he couldn't live without. Know why Andy?"

Of course he does.

"Because he *feels* something again. For the first time in a long time he *feels* something again. In his balls. In his *heart*. He says he *tastes* what he sees. And after that he knows he has to have it. And Samuel Draft tells him he *can* have it. If he's willing to pay the price."

"What did he want?" Andy asks, genuinely curious.

"Joey wouldn't say. But he says he did it. He says he did it, and he says he regrets it every day of his life. Except, he says, while he's watching it. While he's watching it, everything else goes away. The room gets brighter. His dick gets harder. The air smells sweeter. Everything's peachy-fuckin'-keen. Says he's blowing loads on set like he hasn't since he was twenty. But he tells me, now, when he's fucking some bitch, on set or at home or wherever the fuck, he tells me he's starting to see *her*. Even if he keeps his eyes open. He doesn't tell me who—just '*her*.' 'She's all I can see anymore,' he tells me. Crying. Fuckin' Joe Tuesday crying."

Nicky pauses a moment; in the silent space Andy notes that Gator has perched himself on his haunches and taken to chewing on a piece of beef jerky, sipping from a can of beer, totally disinterested in the story; the behavior of a man who's heard this a dozen times before and has lost all interest in the narrative. Nicky digs his fingertips into his forehead, breathes; continues:

"And then he shows me. He asks me if I want to see what the fuck all of this is about, and, I don't know whether he's gone totally fucking batshit on me so it's 'Sure, Joe, let's see what all of this is about.' And he shows me *her*."

"*Her?*" Andy asks. Though he does not articulate it, the meaning is clear: *her*, or another *her*?

"No," Nicky says. "A brunette. But still fuckin' beautiful. And Andy, next to what Joe showed me, the shit on your reel is fuckin' *Sesame Street*. Joe and me watched it. Twice. First time to show me what he was talking about, second time so I could make sure I really seen what I just saw. Oh, but Andy, I fuckin' saw it. Joe didn't want to talk anymore after that. Gave me a popper for the road, told me to come by the next morning. Said he wanted to show me something else. And I saw that something else. Door was unlocked when I got there. Both barrels, under the chin. Pulled the trigger with his toe. Neighbors were probably too fuckin' high to call it in themselves. I'm the asshole getting on the line to the cops because I don't want some snitch putting me at the scene, taking the fall. I looked around while I was waiting for them to show up. Always thought they left a note of some kind, 'Goodbye world, why I did it.' Nothing. Nothing but a burned up reel in a trash can. Nothing left but a big hunk of black plastic. Two empty bottles of Ronson's next to it. Guess he wanted to make sure it was gone."

"So sell it to the fucking *Enquirer*," Andy says. "The fuck does this have to do with me?"

The thin smile, the chuckle, a soft shake of the head. "You got no clue what the fuck it really is, do you? What it *means? Well,* how about this?"

Nicky peels back his vest. Even in the dim red light Andy can make out an unmistakable lesion on his ribcage, another just above his waistline, near his right hip; bulbous and raised from the flesh, like great bloody blisters begging to be punctured. He recognizes them well from the living skeletons shambling around outside the baths, the hard-luck cases begging for one or two final rides before they go screaming into the abyss, and they'll try hard not to spread it to you, too, or maybe they'll try extra hard *to* pass it along if they're feeling vindictive. Kaposi's sarcoma—the tell-tale early sign of the gay cancer currently ravaging 42nd Street and trickling across the nation.

"Yeah. Figured you'd know what those were. Popped up a few months after Joey bought it. Tried to brush it off. Bruises. Blisters. Shot something up while I was high, drunk, didn't remember. Yeah. Then the other boys and girls I know from set start dropping off. I hear the stories. How it starts, how it goes. No idea who the fuck it was gave it to me; would snap their fuckin' neck if they weren't probably already in the fuckin' ground. But that ain't where I'm going. Our lady friend is gonna make sure of that."

"*What the fuck are you talking about?*" The question comes out as more of a shriek than Andy had intended.

"You think you've owned a simple film all these years," Wilson says, strolling forward like a general, back erect, hands clasped behind him, sunglasses tilted down on the tip of his nose. "Who do you think Mr. Draft is? *What* do you think he is? Perhaps he *was* a man...*once.* Now, he is so much more. And the gifts he offers so much more than you can apparently comprehend. You have been in a possession of a *totem,* Mr. Lew. A gateway. A beacon. A means to communing with something whose power you haven't even begun to understand. Something which had to be given willingly in order to maintain its efficacy. And give it you did. And now, the dark conjuring can begin."

"You're some fucking mutant geek!" Andy snaps.

"My spirit is much older than my body would indicate. True, I have lived on this earth for only twenty-four years, but my and Aaron's studies in the art of *magick* have given us the wisdom of souls millennia old. I'm afraid we gave false testimony to you, Mr. Lew. While Aaron and I may be composers, that is not our primary vocation. You see, my *terrestrial* name is Wilson Rawton; my *true* name—my true station—is the Great Black Magician Melsondorph the Powerful. Aaron and I lead the Congregation of the Infernal Dawn." He spreads his arms wide, gesturing to the other, anonymous figures scurrying about the apartment, not hangers-on or sycophants, Andy realizes now, not moochers or ass-kissers, but something at once far more pathetic and far more dangerous: cultists.

"We welcome all who seek us out," Wilson continues. "And offer our services to all who request them— like Mr. Blayze did. Now, Aaron and I shall conduct the great working with your sacred totem to call forth Mr. Samuel Draft, and all the glories he has to offer us."

"That isn't how it fucking works," Andy says, realizes too late that Nicky's own fear has slipped into his voice, that he may almost be sweaty enough now beneath his strained and tearing suit to slip out of it, slip out of the bodybuilder's grasp. The sweat of terror rolls down his forehead, hits the rims of his glasses, streaking the lenses, rolls through his eyebrows and into his eyes, stinging them, blinding him. "You can't *call* him. *He* comes to *you*. You said it yourself: *he* called your jackoff buddy. *He* arranged to meet me through Eddie Lawler. Gator—you heard both sides, tell them!"

"Boy has a point," Gator says between mouthfuls of jerky. As he speaks, Nicky pulls back and delivers a blow to Andy's face that cracks the bridge of his glasses, sends one half tumbling to the floor, the other precariously balanced on Andy's ear and nose.

"Joe Tuesday was no fuckin' jackoff. And I ain't gonna die. If he ain't gonna come to me, then I'm placing a call myself. I'm Nicky fuckin' Blayze. I'm not gonna kick it in some fuckin' quarantine ward, surrounded by queers, turn into a fuckin' ghoul, need a closed casket. They're gonna use their fuckin' book and that fuckin' film, and they're gonna call him up. And Samuel Draft and me, we're gonna come to an understanding. He gave you what you wanted, Joey what he wanted, long as you did whatever he asked? Well, I'll do whatever the fuck he wants. And then he's gonna fix me. I'm gonna be whole again. And me and Samuel Draft are gonna fuck together across the universe for the rest of eternity."

"Yeah? And you, what the fuck are you getting out of this?" Andy addressing Gator now, Gator's opinion of the whole matter seeming to mean more to him for some reason, can understand how a desperate terminal case and a few idiots taking their dice games too seriously could have come to this place but not him. "You think this is the real deal? Think you're gonna get to meet the fucking devil or some shit?"

"Honestly?" Gator licks his fingers clean, takes a swig of beer. "Got kinda bored, Andy-man. I just wanna see what happens."

Andy's eyes move across all of them, Nicky, Melsondorph, Gator, every nameless piece of walking garbage in the room, understands at last what he's gotten himself into, that for all of the pimps and rapists and Pinkos and pedophiles and Democrats he's encountered in his life, lived amongst, for all of the filth even now packing the streets of this dirty town, he has finally found the worst, these jackanape scumbags with the fucking gall to steal a man's woman and to use her for their own selfish, twisted ends. Andy grits his teeth; he flexes every non-atrophied muscle in his small body; he wills the sight to worsen in his eyes, the sensation to drain from his limbs, he wills his heart rate to slow and his respiratory rate to drop, he wills every process in his body to redirect itself to giving him strength, to letting the adrenaline surge in him like a mother rescuing her child from beneath a car. He will break free of this bodybuilder, scramble up his back, snap his neck like he's seen so many times before in the movies, use the momentum to bring out his switchblade, lunge forward, and start taking them all out like a whirling dervish of blood and terror. He will do it for her. He can do it for her. He must do it for her.

Andy twitches in the bodybuilder's grip. The man's muscles are so large, his strength so overwhelming, that Andy cannot even more an inch. Not a centimeter. He cannot get an arm free, a leg to move. Not for anything. Not even for her.

Andy would like to think that the loud, wailing sob he hears next comes from somewhere else in the apartment. Somewhere dark and lonely and forgotten that no eyes will ever see again.

Nicky chuckles, looks to Gator. "No wonder Andy's so hung up on bitches. He cries just like one." Nicky turns back to Andy, smirks. "Now here's what's gonna happen. I'm gonna beat the shit out of you. Then, when I'm done, I'm gonna beat the shit out of you again. And then you're gonna leave here, and you're never coming back. And if you do, I'm gonna fucking kill you. And she's gonna watch."

Andy doesn't feel the punch that connects with his throat and sends a little spurt of blood out of his mouth, matting the bottom of his mustache to his upper lip. He doesn't feel the backhands to the face, the hurricane of kicks to his abdomen that send vomit coursing down the front of his suit, doesn't feel it when a quietly smirking Gator comes forward with a left hook and takes out a molar. What he feels he cannot articulate; cannot think of words or actions that could properly convey the vast and interminable emptiness swelling inside of his chest, the sense of loss, loss greater and more profound in its intensity than the loss of his father, the loss of his mother, the loss of Saskia, Steven. He is losing blood and he is losing vision and as he is at last dropped onto the floor and he sees a fuzzy, fading Gator stand above him and undo his fly and he feels the warm stream strike him in the face he is losing consciousness, and none of this can compare, none of this can compare...

TIME LOSES relevance for Andy Lew. He does not recall how he makes it back to his apartment; does not know how much time passes in between the lapses in consciousness, the fits of vomiting. When he at last discovers that the congealed blood and bile on his clothes have stiffened so much that it's difficult for him to rise and make it to the bathroom, he realizes he needs to get out of the desiccated remnants of his bank suit. The growth in the mirror indicates that at least a good few days have passed since his audience with the despicable Nicky Blayze. No matter. No matter at all, really, about this, or anything. Once, in some forgotten long ago, he had floated through life blind, tunneling ahead like a mole rat moving towards the precipice of a cliff, knowing all the while that the next fistful of dirt may lead to the abyss, powerless to stop, driven by pure instinct towards some meaningless and final goal. Then *she* had come along; and while his pursuit had never slowed, his trajectory unchanged, he had gained, through her presence, the certainty that now there would be some abject meaning to the pursuit, however vague; that he would from here forward propel on towards the end with a modicum of purpose, and that, reaching the end, in the throes of his final plummet, his having known her would grant unto him a great clarity, that all of this had been for something, something after all.

In the wake of her absence, he is, after all, only moving forward still, blind still, towards the end, still; yet now with greater trepidation, though greater speed—for he has known her, and had her in his life, and now that she is gone he must live with the full knowledge of what he can never possess again.

The first several weeks pass without incident. Andy has enough smack in his apartment to see him through that time; knows where he needs to go and what he needs to do when the supply starts to dwindle, to obtain just enough to keep him sane, from tearing out his own nails, from yanking what remains of his hair from his head. His superficial wounds heal to the extent that they can in his malnourished state; once he's eaten up all of the chips and pretzels and canned ham left over in his apartment, his diet becomes whatever he can afford after the latest score. His glasses beyond repair, he digs around the apartment until he finds his old browlines, still held together with masking tape—the pair he wore when he first laid eyes on her, the lenses through which he first saw her face; a final memento. He fashions a cord out of old boot laces and ties them around the temples, lets them dangle from his neck when he nods off, so they will never be apart. His lovelies try to comfort him in this time, Andy lying on the floor amidst the refuse of a life once lived, Elizabeth and Sylvia and Kitty and all the others peering down at him from their own lowest moments, whispering soundless platitudes in his ears, reaching out to him from their own dark places to take his hands, hold them, soothe him.

Andy has no idea when the trouble starts, when the first series of incessant knocks from an angry landlord come to his door. Has he been given any leeway? A few days or weeks or even a month past the day the rent is due? Or none at all? He contracts into the fetal position on his cot and brings a blanket over his head, a pillow around his ears to drown out the shouting. Then the shouting is gone. Maybe he will be given some more time, if he has been given any at all. Maybe the next time the door will come down and Dick and the goon squad will come tumbling in to carry him off to some dark and awful place.

It is not, Andy thinks, too much longer after the landlord's visit that the phone calls start.

"I've been thinking," Rod-Rod drones, sounding a little nervous, Andy thinks, from deep down in his smack haze. "That maybe...well, maybe you might still have a home here...after all? Why don't you come down here and we can...talk about it." Andy lets the receiver drop from his hand, flops down onto his haunches and lolls his head. Can hear the tinny, distant voice of Rod-Rod asking, "Andy? Hello? Andy?" before a final, "Shit" and the line going dead.

Next, the little Red whore decides to darken his doorstep.

"Andrezj? What's happening, Andrezj? I'm worried, after your last call. I haven't heard from you."

Andy-manages a guttural, "What?"

"Last week, waking me up at two in the morning. Sobbing about some girl? What's happened, Andrezj? Have you been seeing someone? Is that…is that what the money was about? Why you really needed the money? This girl, who left you? Andy, I know what you think about things, but, if you're actually…. If you've actually gotten some girl in trouble, you know, that isn't anything I'll judge either of you for. If that's what it is, I can help you take care of it, still, if that's what the two of you want. If that's what's going on?"

Andy stares at the receiver.

"Andy? I'm worried. I've never heard you cry so…I want to come see you but I've lost your address. It's been so long, and I can't find any of the old birthday cards you sent me. Tell me your address, Andrezj. I'll come today."

"You're just like her," Andy whispers into the phone. He stares hatefully at the putrefying remnants of his chalk stripe suit, now torn into haphazard shreds and stapled to the wall above his cot. "You all just leave me." He's fearful at first that he cracks the phone when he slams the receiver down into its cradle; realizes he has no one he particularly cares to call, anyway; no one he particularly cares to hear from, either. Hopes it is broken.

Disappointed to realize the phone isn't broken when next it rings, Dick Valentine's smooth basso reverberating on the other end.

"I know our friend ain't gone, though we don't see much of him anymore," Dick says. "Thought for a while maybe you'd finally found your balls, whatever box in the back of your closet you stuffed them in. Then I realized our acquaintance just gone and holed hisself up at that prick's place every free moment he's got. You all had some kinda falling out? They done something to you?"

Andy hits the phone down harder this time.

When it next rings, Andy is contemplating cutting the cord out of the wall; surprised, frankly, that his service hasn't been discontinued at this point along with the water, long since shut off, allowing the toilet bowl to flow over and the bathtub to begin reeking with the waste piling up there. Finds himself reaching for the phone anyway, stuporous, his hand closing around the cracked and deteriorating receiver and bringing it to his cracked and deteriorating lips.

"Yeah?"

"This Andy?" The voice on the other end is unfamiliar, eager. "Andy Lew, this Andy Lew?"

"Who the fuck wants to know?"

"Andy Lew with the movie? The one that got taken?"

"…yeah."

"You want it back?"

Dormant adrenal glands fire back to life. Time begins to move into high gear, the entropic sludge of these past few whatevers giving way to heightened reality.

"Yes. Yes."

"I know where you can get another one."

"There is no other one. There's just her."

The brief silence on the other end of the phone is broken with sudden violence. "The fuck there isn't. There's more. I know. I know, ok? Trust me, OK? Look, you want it or not?"

Andy speaks. The answer to the question he asks is meaningless, be it death or torture, brought onto himself or a stranger or Saskia or anyone, be it mutilation, disembowelment, the answer is meaningless because the answer will, of course, be…

"What do I have to do?" Andy asks.

ANDY WAITS.

Clad in his denim jacket and a green paisley shirt and a pair of his cleanest jeans—casual enough for the clandestine encounter, chic enough to be presentable if—*when*—the reunion occurs— he shifts from bootheel to bootheel, partially from the still shooting pain of his unhealed injury, partially from excitement, partially from fear. The alleyway he has been instructed to go to is in a region of the city he is not accustomed to visiting, no more violent than his native Deuce yet no safer, either. There is, Andy thinks, a particular inborn safety in knowing your own turf, as desolate and wretched as it may be. He knows he may get stabbed, mugged, hassled at any moment on 42nd but that is the exact point, he knows, and per experience and the wisdom of having lived for so long there he knows how to react in just such a situation. Here, down this open tunnel like nothing they have over in Manhattan, with its high dark walls plastered with ancient playbills and posters for films long gone from the theater and old newspapers, missing posters and wanted posters and flyers begging for the safe return of pets, here in this brick and concrete memorial to the lost, forgotten, and forsaken, he does not know exactly how he should react should violence come his way.

Yet, there is no place he would rather be tonight, not in his booth or his apartment or at the Last Chance; there is no other place he belongs but right here and now and, what is more, he can feel it not only in his body, in his muscle and his rushing blood but he can feel it in the air around him. There is an energy tonight that only comes along once in a while on truly momentous and heinous occasions, when the indifference of the universe switches gears and there is a purposefulness to events, when life itself begins to drive things forward towards some desired goal.

Andy has felt this before. He has felt it the night he first saw her. This is why he shifts; this is why he waits as the minutes tick by on his watch, and he twists his hands into tight and bleeding knots in the pockets of his denim jacket. He waits because he knows.

He knows that he will see her soon.

How many seconds, how many hours go by that Andy waits, waits down this alleyway growing hotter and danker, the lights growing brighter and the night growing darker and Andy's foot and back aching ever more, how many nameless faceless people drift in and out and by while he waits, waits until the waiting begins to take physical shape and it begins to hurt him, the waiting worse than the pain in his foot or the pain in his heart, the waiting an unbearable taunt, that they will be reunited, that his prayers will be answered, that all he wants in this world will be given to him if he waits just another moment, just another moment, just another moment...

When it seems he can bear no more, when he is ready to punch a wall, scream, claw at his own face, drop trou and stroke or simply do *something* to purge himself of the frustration growing inside of him, Andy's eyes fall across the face of a sweaty young man standing stationary at the entrance to the alleyway. It's some twitchy, fey pug ugly in a leather jacket with no shirt beneath, and while the image at first conjures memories of Nicky, Andy can see as the young man begins to steadily approach him that this is not one of Blayze's ilk: the kid too dirty, hair too greasy, his whole countenance too generally repugnant. No, Andy sees, this is who he has been waiting for, another of his own kind, quick and shallow breaths revealing the protuberance of his narrow ribcage, his glazed eyes and twitching facial muscles betraying an ice head in the throes of a hardcore tweak.

"Andy Lew," the kid says, and it hits Andy not just that the boy knows his name but that there's something familiar about him. He begins taking a mental inventory of the cloudy faces that populate his deteriorated brain, trying to place him: a regular to the Colossus or Last Chance, a regular trick, one of Saskia's pretty boys finally gone to pot like all good little Commies? Nothing clicks. Andy digs his hands deeper in his pockets, tensing his fist around his switchblade.

"...you," Andy says, uncertainly.

"Andy Lew," the kid says again, a little chuckle behind his voice this time. "Andy Lew. Andy fuckin' Lew."

"We've established that I'm me," Andy says. "The movie."

"The movie, sure, right, of course," the kid says, tilting his head back towards the sky but letting his eyes remain fixed on Andy. "You want your movie, of course, sure, right. You want it back. You want the people who took it to be punished."

"Yes," Andy whispers.

"What'll you do for it?" Now, the kid is the one whispering, his voice barely audible over the din of traffic, the noises of the city. A thin trickle of snot drips out of one nostril, and he wipes it with the back of his sleeve.

"Anything," Andy says. "I told you and I meant it. Anything."

"Steal for it? Would you ever *steal*, Andy?"

"I've been stealing since I was eight. Is that what you want? A robbery? Is that what this is about? A bodega, a bank, what?" Andy fumbles in his jacket, comes out with his switchblade. "I've got this. I'm ready. Where, who?"

"That was a trick question, Andy, I know you'll steal, oh, I know know *know* you'll steal, I just wanted to see if you'd admit it. If you had the guts to admit it. You got guts, though, huh, don'tcha, Andy Lew, Andy fuckin' Lew? I like that. I don't like you, but I like that at least you got the guts, you got the balls, the great big motherfuckin' balls, huh, Andy?" The kid seems to suddenly just now see the switchblade and steps back. "Hey! Throw that away. That's not what we're here for. We're here about the movie. Throw it!"

Without thinking, Andy tosses the knife aside, raises his hands palm-up, shows he's no threat; running on fear now, that he will never see her again, that this sniveling, snot nosed twerp is his last, best hope for a reunion and like a mother whose child has been taken at gunpoint he is responding as he is told to respond, taking orders, will give away his weapons, his dignity, whatever is necessary for her to be safe with him again.

"Anything else, you got anything else, Mr. Big Man, Mr. Andy Lew, Mr. Switchblade?" The kid rushes at Andy, performs a hasty and ineffective frisk, slapping at his jacket pockets, his legs. Under other circumstances, if he were carrying more, packing a pistol at the small of his back, a second knife in his boot, the kid would miss everything.

"That's it. Now come on. I threw the knife away. I'm here. I told you I'll do anything. The movie."

"You watch it?" the kid asks. He's getting twitchier, more animated; must've smoked not too long before coming here, Andy realizes.

"Have...*you?*"

"Really something, ain't it? Really something special? Oh, and when the bitch buys it at the end...isn't it just so fucking *sweet?*"

The idea of this little cretin watching her revolts Andy, nearly makes him gag deep down on his palette; probably woefully inexperienced, probably has no idea how to properly treat her, how to thread a reel correctly or perform a proper cleaning, probably fondles her with his bare, filth-caked hands instead of caressing her with gloved hands as she deserves, needs.

"Well, ain't it?" the kid demands. His voice drops in pitch; more threatening than Andy would've anticipated, not the blind, dope-fueled rage of a speed freak but real malice coming through, the sort of deep-seated hatred that some men carry with them and employ as weapons when it suits them.

"It's amazing," Andy says.

"You like it? Huh, you like it? You get off to it?" With every question the kid's face becomes more contorted, redder, veins becoming more pronounced, eyes bulging more, the words coming quicker, spittle starting to fly off the tip of his tongue, little flecks of it landing on Andy's glasses, striking his face, until at last, desperate, frustrated, shaking, Andy cries out:

"Who the fuck are you?"

The kid screws up his face, chuckles, not mirthful but joyless, incredulous, the sarcastic mockery of someone just presented with a question so certifiably ridiculous that there is no proper response but complete disdain. Then, in an instant, the expression is blank, stone, the twitching stopped, his eyes fixed firmly on Andy's.

"Who am I? *I fucking made it.*"

The hot summer air turns frigid, Andy's open palms wrapping around the sides of his jacket to hug it tight around himself, shivering there in the alley as though it were winter and the multitude of insects swarming around him now were instead bits of frost and snow intensifying the cold. His knees quiver, buckle, threatening to give out from beneath him at any moment. A dearth of vehicles on the street casts the alley into blackness before traffic picks up again and Andy and the boy are once more intermittently illuminated in the undulating reflection of headlamps. The pipsqueak standing before him is too young to have made the film; cannot be a day over twenty-five, if that; he is too nervous and strange and other than the rage he has demonstrated there is nothing in his demeanor or bearing to indicate the artistry or discipline or imagination required to have given birth to something of such awesome proportions. Yet there is something unmistakable about the way the boy has said it, the confidence in his voice, the assurance.

"You...made it? It's...*you*...in the movie?"

"I thought you fuckin' watched it."

"I have."

"So you know."

"I...don't. I didn't. I..." Andy opens his mouth but finds himself lost for words; can only shake his head in dumbfounded response.

"You that fuckin' bad with faces, or you just that fuckin' high? Or did you even really fuckin' watch it, you ratfuck greedy bastard? You even give a shit what goes into something like that, huh? Do you? You got any fuckin' respect for an artist whatsoever?"

"I... I..." Andy stammers, terrified to offend him, to bring shame or dishonor upon himself here in his presence; to act foolishly or disrespectfully before the master.

Then, from behind, an explosion.

Somewhere out on the street, a car collides into another, a fantastic rear-end from the sound of it: the sudden, abrupt crunching of metal and burst of glass, the familiar sound of a low-speed but nonetheless catastrophic fender bender, and, moments later, the even more familiar sound of the resultant argument, curses made, accusations hurtled. One of the stalled vehicles casts a steady, uninterrupted beam of light into the alley, landing directly on the boy, spotlighting him; and now, fully lit, recognition at last kicks in, how Andy knows this face, solving at least the perimeters of the puzzle, if not filling in the remainder.

"You're Terry Hawkins," Andy says. "You're from *Last House on Dead End Street*."

The kid's brow knits. "My name's Rog Watkins, asshole. At least learn the names of the fuckin' people you steal from."

"Steal...?"

"Yeah, Andy, my movie. Directed by Victor Janos? Written by Brian Laurence? Starring Steve Morrison as Terry fuckin' Hawkins? Me, you prick, all fuckin' me. My writing, my directing, my movie, my asshole friends covered in cow guts for three weeks. My. Fucking. Movie. That. You. Fucking. Stole."

Andy looks towards the place where he threw his switchblade; moves for it; isn't fast enough. In a moment, Watkins has snatched it up, flicked it open, backed Andy against the alley wall.

"No theater will carry it, the distributor said. You'll get paid once tickets start getting sold, they said. And so I wait. I wait and I wait and for five fucking years *I wait,* and you know what they tell me every time I call them up, the worthless sons of bitches? The same damn thing. No one will play it. And then lo and behold, what in the *fuck* do I see on the marquee one day? Well, if it isn't my fuckin' movie that no one will play."

"Rod-Rod ordered it!" Andy protests. "He got it from the distributor! We asked for it!"

"Oh yeah, you asked for it. And when I called my distributor, what do I hear? That no one's going to see it. Zero sales. A total loss. Which is why there were lines out the fuckin' door every time I passed by. Now, I figure, someone's burning me, but, how many people, and who? So I pay your little Rod-Rod a visit. Oh, he had plenty to tell me about you. Sick shit. But, you know, as far as far as I'm concerned, nothing as sick as robbing a man of his due pay. Yeah, Andy, jig's up. He told me. That you compile the sales reports. I know the scam. Pocket the money yourself, show a loss. The hot-shots get the big bucks and the artists keep on starving."

Andy's mind races, the desperate phone call from Rod-Rod making sense now, trying to lure him down to the theater. It's the age old Deuce distributor con: send prints to theaters under the table, collect the receipts, claim total insolvency; half the auteurs on 42nd too strung out to bother keeping tabs on their own films, more still too desperate trying to scrounge up money for their next feature, even more still dead within a year or two of making the sale. In the event anyone's ever sober and alive enough to realize their film is playing 42nd and comes looking for receipts, the distributor claims ignorance, passes the buck: the theater is underreporting grosses. Andy can see in his mind's eye this tweaking, nasty little freak storming Rod-Rod's office, screaming fire and brimstone, probably pegged Rod-Rod for the little candy ass he is and started claiming the movie was real, probably threatened to give him a power drill colonic; and Rod-Rod, in his terror at the thought of physical harm, anger at Andy for his transgressions, perceived or real as they may be, passing the buck even further, to the point where it can go no more, the very bottom of the corporate social economic ladder, right into Andy's lap, to serve as the ultimate and final scapegoat.

"Well, guess what, Andy, I'm hungry, you know, I'm a fuckin' hungry starving artist, and I need to get myself a meal so where the *fuck* is my money, Andy? Where the *fuck* is what you stole from me?"

"It's bullshit! It's all fucking bullshit! I didn't steal your fucking film and that's the truth! Rod-Rod Tillman is a fucking lying, two-faced back-stabbing pinko *shit* and if you want any money you go straight back to him, but I don't have *shit!*"

Wads of spittle are flying out of Watkins' mouth now, low, feral grunts and ululations coming up out of his throat as he makes shallow jabs at Andy with his own switchblade, always stopping short of the adam's apple, the face, the chest, Andy feebly keeping his hands up in front of his face, backing himself as hard up against the wall as he can. Under other circumstances, he might try to duck and run, perhaps kick at Watkins, try and nail him in the shin with his bootheel, put up some sort of offense; in his weakened state, his ankle still raw, malnourished, his soul diminished by having come so close only for salvation to slip away, for him to essentially lose her a second time, there is nothing he feels he can do. If he runs, Watkins will be on him in a moment; he will be on the losing end of any fight and take it even worse for having put up a struggle, slow and savage rather than quick and fierce. A fight means wounds to the palms, abdomen, perhaps the groin if Watkins is feeling vindictive enough; a fight means being knocked onto his back and having his face penetrated a multitude of times with his own weapon, his cheeks sliced open, eyes gouged out, the knife going into him again and again until shock sets in or enough organs have been punctured or he bleeds out. Acquiescence is the quickest route to a quick end. With luck, the knife will penetrate his throat, open his jugular, and he'll be gone within moments, sinking deeper into the blackness until the blackness is all there is; with more luck, Watkins' tweaker rage will allow him to penetrate the breastbone, sever his aorta, and he'll be gone within seconds; no different than a needle in the vein, really, a prick of pain and then oblivion, although it will be final this time, one last intrusion of cold steel into flesh and then it can all finally be over.

There is nothing left to do; nothing Andy wishes to do. She has been taken from him; she is in the grasp of men more dangerous and organized than he; his one apparent chance at a reunion has proven to be this cruel trick. She is gone. She is gone and they will never be together again and if that is the case then why not here, why not now, why not at the hands of a true artist?

There is nothing left to do but cower here in this dark alley, surrounded by the images of faded marquee idols and pets who disappeared into the night and girls who never came home, nothing left to do but cower and hope for a quick and merciful end.

Against Andy's expectations, Watkins chooses not to employ the knife; is, perhaps, not as homicidal as he let on; perhaps has reconsidered the ramifications of actually taking a human life, at least one to which he can be directly tied; has perhaps considered that if Andy turns up dead the police will at least make a cursory attempt to interview the last people to have interacted with him, that they will probably make inquiries of Rod-Rod as his last employer, and Rod-Rod, having already demonstrated himself of weak will and easy treachery, would finger Watkins immediately. Instead, with a great, strange, trilling cry, Watkins tosses the knife aside with one motion and brings his fist into Andy's gut with the other. Andy doubles over, clutching himself, retching, the scant pieces of pretzel and canned ham in his stomach erupting immediately down the front of his shirt, his jacket. In this weakened position it is easy for Watkins to grip Andy by the back of the head, work his fingers into the thinning hair there, get good enough a grip to begin repeatedly smashing Andy's face into his raised knee, Andy's nose crunching, torrents of blood joining the vomit in soiling his clothes. The assault continues like this for a moment, a canine cascading out of Andy's mouth in a torrent of blood and puke, until Watkins loses his balance and, toppling forward, catches himself on the wall, releases Andy, allowing him to tumble to the ground. Now, braced against the wall, Andy prone before him, it's all too easy for Watkins to begin kicking him, quick, sharp blows to the hips, the ribs; Andy certain he feels one crack, the symphony of his own body crumpling accompanied by a chorus of grunts and swears and incoherent sounds of rage, until everything suddenly goes black.

Almost.

The effect is disorienting at first; while a great deal of light is abruptly sucked from the alley, Andy certain that he is about to go over into unconsciousness, that life is slipping away, he realizes that his eyes are still open; that he is generally still in control of his faculties; that he is still partially bathed in the sheen of headlights. The next realization: Watkins is seeing the same thing, because the kicks have stopped, the screams have stopped, the whole assault has stopped, and looking up, Andy sees him gazing about in confusion, staring out of the alley, into the street, Andy following his gaze to see that the streetlights have gone out, the electric signs have gone out, other than headlamps there is no light in the street whatsoever.

It's a blackout.

"Oh, fuck," Watkins mutters. "Fuck, fuck, this is bad, this is very bad. Why is this happening?" He places his hands over his ears, sways and weaves in the alley. "Where's the light, where's all the light, what did you do with the light? This is bad."

Watkins hovers over Andy a moment, staring down at him, Andy turning his head enough to look back up and return his gaze; can see in the man's eyes the total, abject terror of a speed freak in the final throes of absolute paranoia, logic and reason long gone, reality completely subject to the whims of the drug gripping his brain.

"I'll...be back," Watkins says, his voice cracking. His eyes loll around in their sockets, looking at Andy, out into the street, up to the heavens, his overtaxed and fevered mind struggling to reconcile the reality of the blackout with whatever tortured delusions are coursing through his head. "I'll be back and...and..."

And Watkins is gone, charging out of the alley, into the street, disappearing as a panicked and frightened little silhouette lost in a sea of criss-crossing light beams.

Andy coughs, more blood coming up but the intensity of the flow beginning to ebb. Fire consumes his body, his nose burning, jaw burning, chest and ribs burning; feels like what he imagines it must be like to be burned alive like the Medieval fanatics going to the stake, sublimating their lives to whatever divine concepts they've cooked up in their desperate minds. Cannot decide if it is for the better or for the worse that probably none of his injuries are fatal; that he will probably survive tonight, and tomorrow; that, lacking the resolve to place razor to wrist, to seek out an overdose, being generally an individual incapable of bringing an intentional end to his own life, he will go on living for days, weeks, maybe years to come deprived of her presence, her company, her-

The image comes into focus slowly for Andy, gazing up at the wall beside him, the posters there, the portraits of the damned. At first it is just another blur, a gray-black blob cast half in shadow; then, from Andy's vantage point, it begins to come into focus, eyes and a nose and the broad, white teeth of a radiant grin taking shape, a lovingly rendered if not grainy photo beneath the crudely scrawled black legend "MISSING." The poster is homemade and very old; looks to be a photocopied third or fourth generation, judging by the grain, the degradation of the text and picture. Yet, as Andy rises to his feet, the pain subsiding, disappearing, his body suddenly feeling rejuvenated, better than he has felt in perhaps years, he is certain.

Andy places a hand on either side of the poster, smearing blood and grime over a missing cat and a one-sheet advertisement for *Poor Pretty Eddie.* He gazes into her eyes, rendered blurry by copies of copies of copies down through the years, but still as clear and vibrant to him as they have always looked; revels in that smile, the smile he has only guessed, obscured from him by her bindings; and though he cannot see it in the picture, though, from the angle of her face, it ought to be visible, must be the quality of the picture, might not have shown up due to lighting or some other photographic fluke, he knows there is a birthmark just above the jawline on her left cheek.

It's her.

Her.

MISSING: SYLVIA TOLHURST

Sylvia Tolhurst, aged 20. Sylvia left for the bus station on the morning of November 23 1958 but never came home. She is blonde, gray eyed, five foot three and 118 pounds. If you have seen her please call…

A phone number is written at the bottom of the poster in the same quivering handwriting as the rest of it.

Andy wipes his hands on his jeans, checks them, ensures that they are pristine before he gingerly peels the poster from the wall, making small rips and tears around the periphery but leaving the photo and information intact. Once he has successfully removed it from the wall he cradles it in his hands, not wanting to grip it, risk staining it; stares down into the face, *her* face, her beautiful, beautiful face, come to him now in his hour of desperation and need, come to him when he had feared he would never bask in its warmth again, come to him now to tell him to keep going, that the fight is not over; and at once all of the fear is gone and the fight is back in him, and deep within the fetid recesses of Andy Lew something bursts and, his lip trembling, tears leaking from the corners of his eyes, he opens his mouth and utters the words that, until now, he has only been able to articulate once before and long ago, one forsaken night in the back of a gently rocking car, when they were offered but not returned to him. Words that, though they have gone unspoken for so long, have remained at the tip of his tongue since he first laid eyes on her, words whose meaning has only intensified through the years until now; words he regrets having not spoken to her when he had the opportunity:

"I love you."

He says it and he means it, has always meant it, and in saying knows that she has known all along, that despite it going unspoken these many years she has understood, accepted, and that is why she has come to him tonight. That is why she has risen up to him here and now, out of the darkness, the reason why she has returned to him, even in this indirect way, why her shade has presented itself to him, to give him the necessary strength, the necessary guidance to find her, to rescue her, to descend like Orpheus into the netherworld and bring her at last once and truly home. She has felt his suffering in his absence; she has watched the indignities and humiliations and beatings he is willing to sustain for her; she has seen him prove his true love so she has brought him here tonight, used the strange alchemy of Watkins and the stolen reels and treacherous Rod-Rod to provide him with the final key to her great mystery, which, now solved, can propel him forward, empower him with a new resolve.

"I love you," he says again, tears welling up in his eyes, spilling down his face, washing clean rivulets in the blood. He loves her. He loves her like he has loved no other and if that means death then so be it; he has acted cowardly; he has allowed baser men than he with no passion in their hearts to possess her, use her, keep her, while he has wallowed in his own misery. She has needed him and he has not shown his love; has not been willing to make the necessary sacrifices; has been too afraid to put his own life before hers. No longer. No more.

Nicky, Gator, Melsondorph, his dipshit assistant whatever the hell his name is anyway, the bodybuilder, Eddie Lawler, Rod-Rod, Samuel Draft himself. None of them will stand in his way any further. None of them will keep him from his lady love.

Andy brings the image to his lips and gently kisses it, the sparse hairs of his mustache scratching against the paper. Then, carefully folding it first in half, then into fourths, finally eighths, he places it safely in his wallet.

Andy Lew feels around on the ground until he finds his switchblade. Then he limps out of the alleyway on an ankle that has already begun to feel healed; gazes out into the abyss of this newly formed New York, this city of eternal blackness. Had expected a few blocks to have suffered the outage; finds instead a vast abyss laid out before him, traffic lights gone out and signs gone out, the outline of skyscrapers gone completely black barely visible against the inkiness of the night sky.

It's a two mile walk north from here to Nicky's place. Andy flicks open his switchblade, ensures that it still works. Closes it and secures it in his jacket pocket. The last time he traveled there, it was out of desperation, panic, weakness.

Tonight, he cannot be stopped.

ANDY WALKS.

His journey begins uneventfully; though the pain has subsided from his ankle, his ribs, his head, though the blood has stopped flowing from his nose and his mouth, he is still limited in speed by the agility of his body, by muscles atrophied from long hours sitting in the booth, on the subway, laid out on his cot at home. He moves as quickly as his stiffened hips and grinding knees will allow; he moves as quickly as he can with the crowd.

The crowd: minimal at first, the usual aggregate of New Yorkers en route to their homes, places of business, worship, liaisons with lovers or appointments with dope pushers, growing steadily as the blackout wears on, as minutes pass and it becomes apparent that the energy will not be soon returning, that Con Ed has at last been overtaxed and the grid is well and truly fucked, customers spilling out of restaurants and shops, employees freed by bosses not inclined to pay them for time spent squatting in the dark, motorists even beginning to abandon their vehicles, taking the ludicrous step of locking up and securing the windows and trunks before slipping into the growing mass of humanity now drifting up towards Midtown. Andy moves, one with them, another pedestrian trapped in the night simply trying to make it to his destination for the evening; keeps his hand on his switchblade; has been through blackouts before but this one different somehow. Can't quite place his finger on it; an energy in the air, a tension, a nervousness among the homeward bound, individuals looking askance at one another, hands in pockets like Andy's, gripping unseen weapons, keys between fingers, those unarmed attempting to present the appearance of being so. There is a dreadful anticipation hovering above them all: that this is only the beginning; that it is the harbinger of something more; that this is not something so routine as a normal blackout, a fluke of the electrical system, the result of some errant electrical storm or a dipshit spilling his coffee on a console.

Andy hears the first cries come up at roughly the same time he sees their source: flames licking the horizon, a band of dull ochre dancing across the night sky, tiny rows of dancing waves, going this way and that; some in the crowd hesitating, unsure whether to go forward or turn back, others still retreating, the rest, like Andy, moving forward; and then, more flames, joining the rest, cries erupting out in the distance now, whoops and hollers and manic laughter, coming, Andy sees, as the crowd sees, trying to maintain its silence, its distance, from a group of looters that has set fire to a bodega, young men pouring out of the front like ants erupting from a drowning mound, cash and food and glass bottles in hand, silhouetted against the growing flames. They do not molest or harass, attack, mug, maim; the crowd is a passing nuisance to them, bodies to be dodged as they race into the night with their newly obtained goods, broken window glass crunching under sneakers; and as soon as one group of looters has vanished they are replaced by one, two, three more groups, the night growing brighter as more storefronts are set ablaze, flames licking out of open doorways, shattered windows, intensifying the heat of this already forsaken summer. Andy feels as though he's passing through a gauntlet of furnaces, dodging charging bodies as they rush past him; and as he watches a spindly young man in a sopping wet undershirt toss a Molotov cocktail into the front of a liquor store and run, not looking back, not making any attempt to gain entry, not part of any group with eyes set on material gain, he realizes that the fires are not the means to an end, not a byproduct of the carelessness of the people shattering glass with bricks and bottles or tearing newspaper machines out of the ground and using them like battering rams, the destruction is the end in and of itself.

Dick Valentine's rats have at least reached maximum capacity.

Andy walks. He walks through a sea of destruction whose tide has only just begun to come in, whose waves gain in intensity with each passing moment, seeming to ebb and rest before rising up again with even greater force than before, groups of men and women, boys and girls turning their rage now to the abandoned cars in the road, cars parked at meters on the street, windows smashed with pipes and boards, burning wads of newspaper tossed inside, dozens of hands rocking and swaying them and at last gripping their chassis and struggling to flip them over until they at last gain enough momentum to send them crashing onto their roofs; impacts like explosions, the untouched windows bursting like grenades and sending shrapnel of broken glass fragments into the streets and onto the sidewalks. When they have completed their task, shouts of joy erupt before the miniature groups disperse, or waft together on the breeze with the little embers of burned paper drifting now over the street, onto the next car, onto the next victory; they pass a man in a striped t-shirt and skivvies firing his gun wildly into the front of an electronics store, exploding the screens of televisions like skeet.

Andy walks through what has become an ocean of fire and music, the latter provided by the multitude of transistors radios that have begun appearing amongst the travelers, held by handles at waist level, ghetto blasters mounted aloft shoulders; The Sex Pistols intermingle with Joni Mitchell with Sabbath with America with Hendrix with Seals and Croft, "Kashmir" seeming to rise up above it all, an anthem for the apocalypse. Intermingled amongst the dissonant songs, occasional news reports: Andy keeping his ears attuned, listening for reports of greater destruction, shootings, stabbings, bombings; under other circumstances he would find a perch someplace, crack open a beer and enjoy the show; perhaps measure out just enough of a dose to give himself a mellow high with which to enjoy the festivities: front row seats to the end of the world. He has seen this all unfold in his dreams, excepting the incongruous displays of camaraderie and empathy that have intermittently unfolded around him; curled up on his cot, lost wholly to slumber, he has seen the city engulfed in flames just like this, the crowds running through the streets just like this, the city lost to absolute and complete abandon, all restraint and pretensions towards civility thrown to the wind as the good old people of New York eat themselves alive. He has awoken from many such dreams as this with a sense of serenity, disappointment that the dream is over but glad that it was ever experienced to begin with, has peeled his gunked-up briefs off with a certain wistfulness and regret at the knowledge that as the day goes on, the memories would fade, until the images of the dream were barely half-remembered. Tonight, cannot relish the chaos too much; cannot hope for absolute pandemonium when Nicky's place must be spared at all costs; when no harm must come to the building before he arrives there, before he can rescue her. Tonight, every act of destruction, every lit fire, every overturned car threatens to bring the chaos that much closer to her.

On the radio: the apocalypse, unfolding in slow motion. Panicked reporters tallying the rapid escalation of violence, the city having devolved into anarchy. Warzone, the word is used on multiple stations by multiple reporters for various parts of the city: The Bronx, a warzone; Brooklyn, a warzone; Harlem, a warzone. Andy listens for word of his beloved 42ⁿᵈ; can hear no reports.

Andy walks. He walks until he reaches Nicky's building, looking much smaller than it did the first time he approached it, when it seemed to be a spire reaching up into the clouds like the keep of some ancient feudal lord holding sway over the land. Here, now, the city burning down around it, it's just a cheapjack flophouse located on good real estate. Andy removes his switchblade, opens it. Everything he has seen tonight, the looting, the fires, the whole rotten thrust of it all really meaningless, really, ultimately meaningless. Let his fantasies come true an hour from now; let the Chrysler and the Empire Building and Laguardia and Penn and JFK all be smoldering ashes tomorrow; let the blackout never end; let the sun never rise again over Manhattan; let the riots rage on and on and the island burn and burn and sink like a stone into the East River until a thousand years from now it as fabled as Atlantis— Andy will watch it all with the contentment of a sage, with her clutched safely by his side. He will gladly go down into whatever encroaching darkness this is all promising to bring; he need only to retrieve her first.

Andy walks upstairs.

IT TAKES Andy a long while to make it up to Nicky's floor, nearly fifteen minutes by the luminous hands on his watch, both from the toll it takes on him as well as simple precaution. He is able to find the door to the stairwell in the lobby from the headlights shining in off the street, but then he's shrouded in total darkness, having to grip the railing and feel his way up, counting off floors as he climbs, occasionally groping for doorways on landings to double-check his progress, slipping into hallways and inspecting door numbers by the faint glow of distant fires coming in off the street through windows. Occasionally, he'll pause to catch his breath, taking in the sight of the fires burning below, the flames rising higher, the dull yellow of headlights joined by reds and blues now as police cruisers begin to drift into the madness. Little figures looking like black ants leap out of them, attempting to quell the chaos, men unprepared for what's unfolded before them this night, the crowd unresponsive, still swarming, still churning, turning on the uniforms the same way they have the stores, the cars, the city. Bricks and bottles are thrown, occasional blows, punches, a few of the rioters forced to the ground, wrists cuffed behind backs, officers attempting to drag them to vehicles now overturned and smoldering in the street. Beautiful; all of it so very beautiful but immaterial right now. Andy watches not out of a

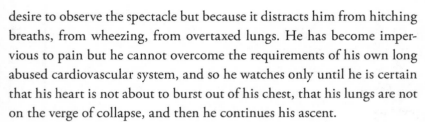

desire to observe the spectacle but because it distracts him from hitching breaths, from wheezing, from overtaxed lungs. He has become impervious to pain but he cannot overcome the requirements of his own long abused cardiovascular system, and so he watches only until he is certain that his heart is not about to burst out of his chest, that his lungs are not on the verge of collapse, and then he continues his ascent.

The hall is silent outside of Nicky's apartment; Andy not expecting bossa nova music or the howl of an electric guitar but had anticipated some chatter, people bustling about inside, Latin incantations maybe or Russian, perhaps, depending on what sort of godless Melsondorph really is, had anticipated that the freaks really getting off to this: instead, absolute, deadly quiet. Andy approaches the door; had not anticipated how he would gain entry; wonders if the switchblade point is fine enough to function as a lockpick. Surprised when he tries the door and discovers it open. Turns the knob slowly, opening the door centimeters at a time; can't afford to make a noise; can't risk being seen slipping in if the guard is up. Hopes they're distracted by the fires outside, some orgy Nicky has arranged to commemorate the occasion.

The inside of Nicky's apartment looks little different than it has on previous visits, the firelight from the picture window serving to light the place only a slightly different shade of red than he's used to. As his eyes adjust from the darkness of the hallway, a scene begins to unfold before him, a picture forming of the events that have transpired here this evening, Andy assumes this evening, the scent of blood fresh enough that it can't be more than a few hours old, the bodies still intact enough from what he can tell that they haven't begun to rot yet. The bodies: at least four of them, three cultists scattered about the apartment wearing dark robes, the fabric Andy saw being hustled around the last time he was here. The three cult members are splayed out in various places, look to have been gunned down while running, gaping bullet holes oozing blood from cheeks and the backs of heads, hair matted against skulls with brain matter and bone fragments, arms and legs splayed out in broken doll poses; and, on the wall above the sunken living room, his head pointed towards the floor, feet aloft, the bodybuilder, a multitude of knives driven into him, one in either palm, one in either wrist, several more in his ankles, another in his ribcage, a crown of knives driven into his skull round the forehead from ear to ear, so that the image he presents is of an over-muscled, inverted Christ, the loin cloth replaced by white briefs growing dark with blood trickling down his body. Andy can just make out esoteric symbols scrawled around him on the wall, familiar inverse pentagrams accompanied by things he supposes to be some sort of runes; and in the center of the room itself, replacing the television set, Nicky's projector, looking lonely and disused.

Andy begins to move towards the projector, looking this way and that, surveying the bodies even as he listens for the sound of human footsteps, whispers, looks for signs of living beings still occupying this place, lying in wait for some intruder to add to the body count. Hears nothing; sees nothing; continues moving towards the projector. Perhaps the authorities were here; perhaps someone heard the gunshots, phoned the pigs, Nicky and his sick crew dragged away just as it hit the fan outside. No time to put up crime scene tape, outline bodies, cart them away; no time, Andy hopes, if this is the case, to retrieve evidence. If this is so, then she may still be in the projector…

Andy is feet away from the projector when he's hit with the dropkick, a combat boot striking him in the side of the skull, sending him tumbling to the floor. He scrambles onto his back, pulling his knife, thrusting it upward as a humongous shadow descends on him. Andy grits his teeth and hisses as he attempts to drive the knife up and into his attacker, waffle iron hands wrapping around his wrists to force the blade back towards him. As the figure's face moves closer to his, its identity slowly forms; and, Andy guesses, so does his own, the grip on his wrists slackening as recognition sets into the blank face now only inches from his.

"Rat shit," Chad says, frowns. With a sudden, quick jerk he pins Andy's wrists to the ground, looms over him, Andy squirming beneath

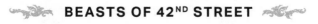
him, trying to get in a good groin strike with his knee. "I thought you were one of them."

Chad leaps to his feet, stares down at Andy, Andy detecting a certain choked quality to his voice, as though he's been crying for a long time.

"Where are they?" Andy asks. "What the fuck are you doing here?"

"I came to make things right," Chad says. "I was meditating when this happened. The blackout. I thought it was a sign. Māra: the bringer of death, murder and destruction…he's come. It's the end of the five thousand years of peace. I thought it would come later. The Moral Codes are disappearing: it's time for the reign of the Amoral Concepts. Dharma's leaving. I wanted to go too…I thought I could if I made things right. If I stopped them. If I…" Chad looks down at his own hands—the instruments, Andy guesses, he had intended to use on Nicky, Melsondorph, whomever else he'd come here to administer his own particular brand of brutality to, the image taking shape in Andy's mind, their bodies beaten until they're pulverized, flesh and bone and muscle all liquefied into one satisfying paste.

"But I got left behind," Chad continues. "Again."

"Enough Krishna Krishna bullshit," Andy says. "What happened? Where are they?"

"Why should I tell you?"

"Because I've got the balls you don't. And when I get wherever they went, I'm killing them."

"Yang bringing order," Chad mutters.

"The fuck?"

"I got here as they were leaving," Chad says. "I only got parts of the story. Melsondorph said the blackout was a signal to begin the ritual. They hooked the projector up to a generator. But the exhaust started to make people sick. Nicky got mad. Told him to keep going. Melsondorph got nervous. He broke something on the projector. Nicky got madder. Melsondorph said that the ritual could still work even if the film didn't play. He tried. It didn't. Nicky got mad. He asked if they needed blood. Melsondorph said maybe." Chad gestures to the bodies around them by way of explanation for how the remainder of the evening turned out.

"Where are they going?"

"I couldn't find out," Chad says. "I got nervous. I was afraid…they would ask me to come. And if they did…and I said no…" Chad turns and looks at the bodybuilder on the wall, bites his own fist. "That could have been me."

"Well, it isn't, so take the panties out of your mouth," Andy says. Stands up, moves to the projector to inspect it, looking for signs of damage to the film, a torn frame left behind, residue to indicate some sort of burning, melting; can find none; hopes that, at worst, they have only caused superficial scratches he can potentially clean out.

Chad shuffles to the window, stands before it, staring out at the night. Quiet little sobs occasionally echo from his direction. After a moment, he begins to sway back and forth before the window, seeming to dance in harmony with the flames in the distance. Andy thinks; he has come too far now to let it end here, in this half-assed abattoir with its dead jackoffs in dress up robes; knows that she would not abandon him now, here, like this, that it is simply another test, another weigh station en route to their glorious reunion, that she is telling him to prove himself to her, that he is not just fury and force but intellect, that he is capable of solving this puzzle.

"Chad?"

"Huh?"

"Was Gator here?"

"Gator shot them," Chad says. "When Nicky asked. He was…laughing." Chad's voice cracks.

Andy moves towards the door. Knows now where they went. No need to waste any more time here. Looks over his shoulder at Chad, still dancing before the window, becoming one with the fire; leaves him here to await the coming of Māra alone.

He's headed back to the beginning. To a place that Gator Hyatt knows has a working projector of its own; a place that he also knows has a loose door, easily pried open with a crowbar.

THE CITY has begun screaming by the time Andy makes it back downstairs and resumes his trek further north. The fires are so multitudinous now, so intense and fueled by the kindling not only of the buildings they consume but the accelerant of Molotov cocktails and gas soaked rags that they almost replace the usual lights; and joining them in equal force is noise, noise like Andy has never heard before, the city never quiet but never this loud. Usually it is the din of humanity, a collective of voices all murmuring and muttering and catcalling and shouting and begging but now the voices are howling, hollering, bellowing, chanting. He pushes the cacophony to the back of his mind; cannot let it overwhelm him. Half-remembers something from one of Saskia's books, the ones she used to try and read to him a lifetime ago, her beloved fancy boys and their sad-sack ruminations on the world: miles to go before he sleeps, miles to go. Two more miles. Has made it two already by this point; can stand two more. Two more miles to his sweet reunion; two more miles until he will have the taste of blood in his mouth.

The further he goes, the brighter the fires, yet the darker the city becomes; the flames seeming to no longer cast light but shadows, throwing swaths of darkness in their wake. Strange sights appear before him: here, a soot-covered hobo, his face black with ash and grime, genuflecting before a building so conflagrated that its original shape can barely be determined; here, a lingering figure in the midst of flames, standing stationary in the window of a smoke-bellowing structure, consumed by flame but not affected by it; Andy unable to tell if it's a mannequin, a statue, if he is so sleep and food deprived that he has begun to concoct visions in his mind.

Then, as he approaches 42nd Street, something begins to happen.

It starts with a diminishing of the fires, more buildings intact as he moves, fewer looters, the crowd thinning out; then, the furor begins to diminish, the screams and shrieks growing quieter, sparser, less intense until they are all gone; car horns cease to honk and police sirens fade into the distance until Andy at last finds himself back on a Deuce like none he has ever stepped foot in before, a realm familiar to him in its architecture but wholly alien in its ambiance. For the first time in a life lived here, Andy finds the place quiet as a tomb—no arsons, no looters, no screams or fights, no thwarted muggings or angry mobs; it could be the final street left in existence at the end of the world, a lonely oasis waiting to sink into the void and its denizens wanting the last few moments in the existence of mankind to be peaceful ones. Andy would have anticipated this to be the epicenter of chaos; would have laid reasonable money— if he had it— on this being the spot where it was really all going down, bodies dragged from buildings and bludgeoned in the street, bodies intertwined amongst the flames, thrusting and gyrating even as their flesh and muscle dripped from bone, explosions lighting up the sky like volcanic rocks thrown to the heavens during an eruption.

Instead, silence.

Not absolute, complete silence, not the absence of sound, but the quiet, Andy guesses, of a country evening, all footfalls and patter, the occasional friendly call: here, a pimp in velour splendor leaning in a doorway, flanked on either side by leopard print beauties, extending one hand not in wrath but invitation, the other clutching a battery operated lantern, yelling out in a rich, calming, baritone, "If it's too far from home, you come on in here tonight, ain't no charge. Ain't no one gonna hurt you, you be safe in here tonight. Got me some coffee for the ad-dults, chocolate for the kiddies, we ain't doin' our usual business tonight. Come on in, you be safe here." A hot dog vendor passes out free wares from his car, collecting no money, buns and wieners disappearing into the gullets of displaced tourists and vagrants and runaways alike. A woman screams

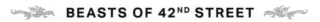

out, some stationary motorist trying to wait out the event in her car suddenly dragged through a broken windshield by a pair of giggling men, and as they try to pull her towards an abandoned storefront two longhairs in denims, whom Andy is certain he has seen pushing ice, are suddenly on them, letting out enraged shouts, cries of disdain and cries for justice, and as they shriek for mercy the assailants themselves are gripped beneath the arms and behind the knees, screaming as fists begin to descend into their faces and abdomens, and the motorist is up and on her feet again and running in the opposite direction as the iceheads still continue to drag her tormentors off towards some undefined hell. A hooker in her crop top and massive heels offers a guiding hand to a young mother in pearls and double-knits, clutching her crying infant. A pair of young boys crouch beside an elderly man encamped on the sidewalk, clutching a flimsy cardboard sign in fear, its implorations for change now obsolete compared to a desire for safety; and the boys guide him away, gently, one offering him a beer, the other laying his jacket around the frail man's quivering shoulders. Under other circumstances, Andy would be more befuddled, disgusted at such saccharine displays; tonight, it makes all the sense in the world. Things gone topsy-turvy, the civilized parts of the island gone over into madness and here, where Andy could have anticipated a portal to Hell itself cracking open in the street and spewing forth all of its fiery horrors, a glimpse of the beginning of civilization, the Neanderthals learning to cooperate, setting aside their clubs and spears to break bread and plan the cooperative future of the species; and if this can be so, if the impossible can be made to happen, if the beasts of 42nd Street can take this evolutionary step towards becoming real human beings, then his mission can succeed, too, guided by divine will as it is, not God or Chad's Buddha or any other celestial being showing him the way but the woman who waits for him there, mere feet away, at the Colossus Theater, the marquee still seeming to glitter in the dark.

Andy casts his eyes up at it, gets a glimpse of what they've been showing in his absence. Mainstream garbage, of course, the work of

Rod-Rod and the unimaginative stuffed suits at corporate, thinking in their estrangement from the Deuce, tucked away safely in distant corporate offices, that this place wants the same drivel as the rest of the world, the same cookie-cutter bullshit they play in Peoria. The double feature running now: That Sidney Sheldon garbage and the geek flick about the war in space that the nerds down at Playland Arcade have been losing their shit over. Pathetic, Andy thinks, making his way to the back entrance, can't imagine who the hell would turn out to see this dreck. Not Colossus material at all.

Tonight, he'll put on a show worthy of the establishment.

AS ANDY approaches the red metal door of the Colossus, he opens his switchblade, prepares to use it to pry the thing open; scans the ground, surveying the random bits of debris scattered about, formulating a Plan B in the event the blade isn't sturdy enough, if it snaps off while he's trying to open the door. Knows that Rod-Rod has long ago abandoned this place, seen everyone out safely and locked up and probably hauled ass to the Bacchus Baths, where Andy knows he's sequestered himself before in times of distress; knows that the front door will be useless to him. Needs some bit of rebar or a discarded screwdriver or bit of metal to serve as backup; has not come this far to be kept away from her by some flimsy inch of metal, with its shitty lock and ill-fitting frame.

Andy is feet away from the door when he hears its familiar mechanical groan; as it swings open he ducks behind a garbage can, peers just over the rim to see Gator sashay out, stripped to the waist, his body looking especially frail and slick this evening, sweat beading up all over his torso and forehead. When he inhales, Andy can see the entirety of his spine and ribs bulging against the thin layer of flesh and muscle covering them; thinks he's lost weight since the last time he saw him; wonders if he's taken to the needle himself, or if he's somehow achieved the great

Deuce dream and discovered a method for surviving solely on being a reprehensible piece of shit; if he's managed to eliminate the need for food and drink and is now sustaining himself on sheer vileness.

Andy holds his breath, watches in silence as Gator looks up to the sky and the faint, waning crescent moon that hangs there, casting no light, a thin, taunting smile in the nearly starless sky. Seemingly pleased with the sight, he unzips his pants, begins to urinate on the ground. Behind him, Andy can make out the dancing glow of candle flames coming from the stairwell. Slowly, he rises; keeps his ears pricked for the sound of the urine stream ceasing; has the upper hand as long as Gator's literally got his dick in his hands.

"Andy-man!" Gator's eyes register shock as Andy approaches him, quickly stuffing himself back into his jeans, a damp spot forming at his crotch as he tries to zip up, wet hands fumbling with his fly. Andy keeps his own hands tucked into his armpits, eyes locked on Gator's; has known him long enough to be able to be able to detect the subtle cues before movement, to be able to read the thoughts forming in his mind as they present themselves in little twitches and glances. "The fuck you doing here, man? Last time didn't clue you in?" Gator looks over his shoulder, places a conspiratorial hand on Andy's shoulder.

"You come back here to get your ass kicked again, man? Cause, uh, let me tell you, 'tween the two of us, after last time, you and me are square, even if I don't ever wanna have to smell you again in my life, right? You did me wrong, man, don't necessarily mean I wanna see you turned into ground beef. But Nicky, man? Ooooh, boy is on the war path tonight, I tell you what. Seen some wild shit tonight, man. Suggest you skedaddle before he sets his sights on you, gets any ideas about turning you inside out or whatever other shit comes to his mind. Boy's got a violent streak like I didn't know; not that I mind, necessarily, but…"

"I've seen," Andy says. Though it is not a conscious choice he thinks he might be softly smiling. "*Your* handiwork, too, the way Chad tells it. Though I'm not surprised. All your stories about hunting trips."

"You seen Chad?" Gator suddenly seems concerned.

"I've seen a lot tonight. And I've come a very long way to get here. And right now you're going to answer one question for me: Is she up there?"

"All right, listen man, was trying to do my good deed for the decade, lettin' you walk away from here, but if you're gonna keep up with the bullshit, I'm gonna have to do something about it." Gator's brow knitting, a tone of irritation in his voice. "I have got a good thing going here, man, freakier the better, you know, and Nicky and the dynamic duo up there are about as freaky as it gets, right? Now we had our fun, but you got an expiration date on you, always have, and I left you on the shelf a long time past it. In terms of personal entertainment, you're, uh, what I'd call a limited engagement, right? And Nicky, he's gonna run longer than fuckin' *Grease* at this rate, and I don't want him bouncing me on account he thinks I'm still associating with certain, uh, undesirable elements. So, not gonna say it again: *get.*"

"It was all always a joke to you, wasn't it?" Perhaps it's the slow approach, limited vision in the darkness, perhaps it's the bourbon and weed Andy can smell coming from his breath from a yard away, but Gator doesn't even realize that Andy has made it almost nose-to-nose with him, is standing so close he can see the stubs of hairs on Gator's scalp from where he hasn't shaved in a few days.

"What?"

"Your little hunting trips. Tell me…When you put down those freaks back at Nicky's. How did it feel? What was it like? What did you say?"

"All right, I've had about enough of this bullshit. Gave you the chance, Andy-man, can't be held accountable…"

Gator is reaching back into his waistband, for the gun Andy guesses he has hidden there, but his reaction time is slow, is going for the weapon out of impulsive frustration, had not anticipated having to reach for it, Andy having already formulated his plan of attack when he chose to address Gator in the first place. One of Andy's hands grips Gator's wrist, letting rage fuel it, rage against the years under the bastard's thumb, the

indignities he suffered for him, rage against his having brought him to this point, introduced him to Nicky Blayze, stood idly by during his humiliation; and the rage is powerful enough to still Gator's hand, his eyes going wide with shock as he realizes he is being overpowered, that the situation has suddenly slipped out of his control. Gator's eyes growing even wider when, with his other hand, Andy thrusts the switchblade up into his abdomen, making a rough sawing motion as he drags it across his waist.

"*Andy-man.*" Gator gasps the words, his voice dropping into a whisper as the breath leaves his lungs. He begins to gag, his free hand gripping Andy's elbow, trying feebly to prevent the progress of his blade.

"All a fucking joke," Andy hisses. "You never understood. Someone like you never would." Andy feels wet warmth on his hand as Gator's blood gushes out over it, soaking the cuff of his jacket, spilling onto his jeans. He keeps digging the knife in deeper; lets his hand slip inside, become enveloped in Gator's innards. "Running around the ghetto, killing, like it was a game. That's what always pissed me off the most about you, you know that? You always wanted to *watch her* but you never *appreciated her*. Because it was a joke to you. It's never a joke. *Death is beautiful.*"

Andy jerks his hand up and out, tearing a gaping *z* in Gator's midsection; organs that Andy cannot and does not care to identify come bulging out of him, Gator releasing Andy's wrist and attempting to stuff them back in, the expression on his face indicating that he knows as well as Andy does what an obsolete maneuver this is. The ministrations of Gator's fingers appear to do more harm than good, some long, sopping strand that Andy guesses are a portion of his intestines sloshing out of him with a wet, gelatinous noise, trailing down his groin to his knees and finally striking the pavement with a damp sound like a dropped sponge hitting the kitchen floor.

Andy releases Gator's wrist, reaches behind and plucks the revolver from his waistband; steps away to survey his handiwork from a more aesthetically pleasing distance. Not like pushing the plunger into Steven.

Andy's heart races, head rushing, the faint colors he can make out in the dark more vibrant than they would otherwise be; his hands on fire with the sensation of Gator's blood, the smell of it rich in his nostrils, electricity coursing through his veins.

This time, it's everything he hoped it would be.

Gator stares at Andy, his eyes and the tendons in his neck bulging, his tongue lolling out of his mouth as he makes pathetic little gagging and wheezing sounds, swaying there in place in an ever expanding pool of his own blood and viscera. It takes longer than Andy would have guessed for Gator to drop to his knees, splashing in the gore, splattering himself in it; and then blood is trickling out of his mouth, down his chin and onto his bare chest, and the gagging is becoming more infrequent and the few breaths he is able to get in become more shallow. Then, his eyes roll up into his head, and with a few final convulsions he tumbles forward, hands and legs twitching, twitching, until he is absolutely still, and a singularly vile piece of Deuce trash has at last been taken out.

Andy only waits until he is absolutely certain that Gator will not be getting back up; then he performs a cursory inspection of the revolver. It looks to be a .38, from his limited experience with firearms; opening the cylinder, he sees there are six chambers and that there is a bullet in every one of them. That is all he needs. Stepping over the pile of human waste that used to be Gator Hyatt, Andy heads into the stairwell of the Colossus Theater.

CANDLES. ANDY had anticipated from the glow behind Gator that there were candles in the stairwell but had not realized how many. There are candles everywhere, at least one on every step, two or three on others, the landing festooned with them, Andy wondering how long it took to make this happen, how many of Nicky's goons were put to work arranging and lighting them. All of the candles are red, and the drippings coming off of them, forming little puddles here and there, give the impression of spots of blood spattered all about the stairwell, as though a massacre has occurred here, too; as though the candles themselves have been made to suffer.

From above, the hum of a generator, just drowning out electric guitar music coming from somewhere down the corridor, the same six notes he heard at Nicky's apartment all that time ago, repeated over and over again, a mordant oscillation; realizes they are not making use of the booth but have set up shop in Andy's screening room so that they can view the film up-close. Reaching the top of the steps, looking into the open projector booth, itself stocked with candles, Andy can see that just as they have co-opted his screening room they've similarly made use of his hole, an exhaust tube crudely attached to the generator and run out through it, lest ceremony climax in the acolytes succumbing to fumes. Andy pictures the image in his mind's eye, what a feat it must have been to have transported the generator here, wonders if they drove or walked, if a dozen men in robes paraded it through the city streets, held aloft like a casket en route to burial, only to have the lot of them turning purple and swollen as they suffocated in the output of their labor, the room filling with toxic smoke, throats closing, eyes watering, a pile of robed morons waiting for him when he arrived. A beautiful image; too bad it will not be that easy, that simple, that clean.

Andy follows extension cords down the corridor away from the booth, pauses outside the door to the screening room; over the generator he can just barely make out voices inside, words spoken, an occasional shout, a pause and then more speaking, another shout. He contemplates his options; is wholly inexperienced with a handgun but, at this range, does not figure he needs to be terribly accurate to hit someone. This will be close-quarters combat; the reason he keeps his knife open in his other hand. Will use it on anyone who gets too close; will attempt to pick off who he can from a distance; hopes that there aren't too many acolytes left, that the massacre back at the apartment has scared a good number off, or that Nicky has taken to picking them off again here.

He has made it. He has finally made it.

It's time to bring her home.

Andy opens the door just a crack, to survey the situation before he makes a full charge. Wires snake from the generator into the spare projector, gently whirring, the tormented image of Sylvia Tolhurst's final moments playing out against the wall; around it stand Nicky, Melsondorph, and Aaron in a triangular formation, Aaron holding open the book from the apartment while Melsondorph plays the guitar, Nicky looking on with an expression of impatient fury. His suit—bought two sizes ago, now hanging loosely on his body like a polyester toga— is soaked in sweat and his hands caked in blood. He periodically dabs at his dripping forehead with wadded up toilet paper, cursing under his breath. Melsondorph, too, sweating, more nervous than Andy has ever seen him, lacking any of the arrogant self-assurance with which he has carried himself until this moment. Throughout the booth, four acolytes in the same dipshit robes, looking very much like their compatriots back at the apartment—bullet riddled, splayed about, their blood streaking the walls, one looking as though he has been beaten to death, his head caved into a fibrous pulp. The general ambiance is of total disarray, of something gone terribly wrong in the presence of someone eminently powerful, those beneath him now desperately attempting to rectify the situation.

"Where the *fuck* is he, cocksucker?" Nicky hisses, jams a flattened palm into Melsondorph's chest as he frantically scans the book. "No more excuses!"

"I've recited...properly...from the grimoire," Melsondorph says, stops playing, allows the guitar to hang from his neck. Andy notices that his voice is not as shrill as he is accustomed to hearing, his elocution lacking the stiltedness of their previous encounters. He sounds, instead, very much like what he is: a terrified kid absolutely in over his head. "We've made the proper invocations. The proper sacrifices..."

"You sure about that? You totally fucking sure? Because if you need another sacrifice, I think we got a few to spare."

Aaron stands erect, hands Melsondorph the book, adjusts the tie he wears hanging loosely around his neck. He steps towards Nicky, opens his mouth to speak; Nicky comes out with a pistol, jams the barrel in Aaron's mouth, pulls the trigger. The bullet blasts one of his eyes out of its socket, trailing optical nerves and brain bits behind it. Aaron collapses into Melsondroph, snagging the guitar, tearing it from his body and snapping the neck as he crumbles to a heap beside the projector.

"How about now, huh? That enough? *Try again.*"

Melsondorph's hands tremble; he visibly struggles to keep a steady grasp on the book. His voice wavering, words coming out in broken, halting stutters, he begins chanting, trying to chant, sounding more like a skipping record than an archmage or magician or whatever the fuck the little idiot fancies himself.

"We...we invoke...we invoke the forty unknown...unknown sailors...the...the power of the nighttime sea...the dark forces trapped within this...this vessel as a beacon of your unholy power..."

At the last word, his voice deteriorates into a quick, low moan and he begins to weep, fat, sloppy tears smattering the book. "It isn't working... it isn't *going* to work...I don't...I don't *know...why...not...*And Aaron... we needed the music...it's part of the invocation. And now...This ...this was all supposed to be *fun,* man. We were going to meet a demon. It was all supposed to be *cool...*"

"Cool? *Cool*? I'm fucking dying, you little pissant. You wanted to be *cool?*"

Nicky aims the gun at Melsondorph; he tenses, raises the grimoire up in front of himself as a feeble defense. "How about I put a slug in your fucking kneecap, that cool enough for you?" He gestures at the dead cultists, at Aaron, a pool of blood spreading out from his ruined eye socket. "That *cool* enough for you? This ain't a joke, you two-bit wannabe fuck. This is my *life!* You told me you were an expert in this shit. You said you studied it. So what the *fuck* is going on?"

"I…I don't know. I…thought that I…I…I just want to go home now," Melsondorph says, and, hugging the book to his chest, begins sobbing uncontrollably. "I'm just gonna…I'm just gonna go now, OK?" His body quivering, he slowly squats to the ground, places the grimoire on the floor. "You can keep the book. You can…I won't say anything…" Turning towards the door, Melsondorph spots Andy, gasps.

"You! He's got a gun! I'll do anything, just, please— *Get me out of here!"* Abruptly, Melsondorph springs for Andy, a desperate, cartwheeling sprint. The scream and the sudden movement startles Andy, doesn't have time to process the words he's hearing, doesn't particularly care; just another threat, another liability, another mutant standing in the way. As Melsondorph cascades towards him, it is Andy's instinctual response, the only response, the right response, to open fire with Gator's gun, once, twice, three times, figures half for him, half for Nicky; and, whether out of fury for his sorcerer's ineptitude or a sense of betrayal, whether out of a desire to hit Andy or perhaps out of sheer impulsive rage, Nicky, too, opens fire with his own weapon. Melsondorph's body is riddled, one of Andy's bullets hitting him in the front, jerking him one way, one of Nicky's striking him in the back, jerking him the other, and again and again so that he does a mordant little dance in the firelight, until his whole torso has been shredded up and he falls dead to the floor.

Andy and Nicky hold their guns on one another now; Andy's breath quick, feels like it's getting faster by the moment. At some point the projector has run out and with the music gone there is now only the sound of the generator humming, the sound of Andy's own labored breathing and a shallow, gasping rattle coming out of the base of Nicky's throat. Staring him down now, Andy realizes for the first time how much Nicky has deteriorated since the last time he saw him; gaunter, frailer seeming, his gums blackened and a sarcoma visible here on his cheek, another on his forehead; a condemned man ready to take down anyone with him in the vain belief that others' deaths will somehow mollify his own.

"You can't have her," Nicky says, the hand holding the gun shaking, positioning himself behind the projector, a coward unto the end, using a woman as a shield. His eyes periodically dart between the gun and Andy, Andy hesitating to fire, already afraid that gunpowder and candle smoke may have damaged her, doesn't want to take any greater risks, wonders why Nicky himself is holding back; realizes that Nicky has lost track of how many times he's fired, the reason he keeps looking at the gun, is trying to remember, afraid that he may be down to only two bullets, one bullet, perhaps no bullets left at all, and if there are any remaining, he must make them count.

"You can't have her," Nicky says again, coughs into his elbow, a wad of something coming out, mucous or blood or perhaps both. "I came too far for this. I'll…I'll kill you. Yeah. Yeah, maybe that's what he wants." Nicky's head whips around the room like a charismatic attempting to call down the Heavenly host. "That what you want, big man? Samuel Draft? You want me to put one in this little fucker? Huh? What the *fuck* does he have, huh, you cocksucker? You give *him* what he wants, and you ain't even gonna show your fuckin' face to me?" Nicky looks at Andy again, gritting his teeth. "I'll kill you, and I'll kill Gator, and I'll kill the whole fuckin' world. I'll kill every last fuck on the planet, and then it'll just be me and him."

At once, there's a sudden rush of noise, like a sheet flapping on the clothesline, like a great gust of air blowing through a vacant room; both Andy and Nicky going rigid at the sound, unexpected and violent, a threat from some heretofore unknown party; and it's Nicky who realizes the source first, a double take towards the floor that would be ridiculous to Andy under other circumstances, but which is utterly horrifying to him now.

Unseen to either man, in his tumble to the floor, one of Aaron's pant legs has brushed against one of the candles littering the room; and, given the time, the fire has ignited the cheap material—a poly-cotton blend in an unfortunate ratio, Andy guesses—starting small but spreading rapidly and fiercely so that now his entire body has become consumed by flames. It quickly becomes apparent to Andy how foolish this all is, the candles everywhere, using the spare room instead of the projector booth, built to safety specifications with concrete floors and steel shutters back in the nitrate film days when a fire meant a potentially apocalyptic conflagration. Here, in this repurposed closet, meant only ever to hold soda cartons and expired candy and host secret liaisons between teen employees too horny to wait till the end of shift, there are no such precautions. So it is that the fire spreads quickly, lapping across the floor, the wall, and ultimately, to Andy's horror, the wooden table on which the projector sets, transforming it into a veritable altar of flame; and though she makes no sound, though she is silent in her suffering, like Joan at the Stake, in his mind Andy can hear only screams, screams, terrible screams as she melts inside of it.

And now there is screaming in the room, a shrill, caterwauling scream coming out of Andy, Nicky silent, backing away from the fire, spreading now to consume the entire room, the robes of the cultists going ablaze, Wilson's body, the pages of the grimoire curling and turning to ash as the room fills with bilious, blackening smoke.

She is gone. She is gone from him now not just in the temporary sense, stolen, locked away, but *gone,* her great, glorious passage from this realm into whatever waits beyond the veil lost forever to time; and the culprit only feet away from Andy now, the source of this great crime, this violation, the man who took the woman he loved away, cowering behind the flames, behind the thick, growing cloud of black smoke that's begun to choke his lungs.

Andy fires the gun wildly, his final three bullets going astray, unable to aim properly with the smoke or the fire or the apoplectic fury that has overtaken him, and as Nicky scrambles away through the fire on his hands and knees, Andy charges him, knocking over more candles in the process, finally landing on Nicky with his switchblade, thrusting it blindly; Nicky, meeting his attack, slapping at Andy's wrist with more strength than he would've guessed, so now they are both disarmed, each beginning to swing at the other.

It only takes Nicky a few blows to knock Andy off of him, still has the advantage of height and some weight on his side, and as Andy attempts to rise, Nicky is on top of him, just an outline in the now suffocating smoke. Andy is unable to make out any features but a frail shape in the growing blackness. Then, Nicky's hands are around Andy's throat, squeezing, throttling, thumbs pressing down on his Adam's apple as he pounds the back of his skull into the floor again and again, grunting, the world growing ever darker.

Out of the blackening void that is growing around Andy, another sound; something very low and far away and at the same time very close, from just behind him, from above him, from all around; a growl, animalistic, inhuman in its reverberations, too deep, too sustained, like a tiger about to strike, the growl growing in intensity until it almost seems to explode into a quick, deafening roar. Then, Nicky is off of Andy, lifted, it almost seems, pulled up into the air and vanishing into the smoke.

Andy struggles to open his eyes, gasping for breath, struggles for the last remaining oxygen in the room; cannot see Nicky; can only *hear,* the panicked shriek, heavy footfalls; something being dragged; desperate, garbled, inarticulate begging. Then, somewhere in the distance, the sound of something very large striking the ground followed by a tumbling, a rhythmic *thunking* that repeats and repeats until it at last ceases, followed once more by that roar, sounding triumphant now rather than aggressive, an apex predator having established dominance over arrogant prey that pretended to its throne.

Andy rolls onto his hands and knees; crawls in the direction of the door, makes it out into the corridor, gagging. The fire has already spread to the hallway; the walls here, too, have become engulfed, the floor, some of the candles nothing more than oozing puddles now. Andy continues to crawl, more purposeful this time, making his way towards the stairs, moving at a pace quicker than the fire, trying to outrun it, trying, even more so, to outrun its eventual rendezvous with the generator.

Reaching the top of the steps, Andy rises to his feet, hurries down them; stops mid-way, frozen in his tracks by the sight below, seeing now the source of the tumbling.

At the bottom of the steps lie the mortal remains of what *was* Nicky Blayze, twisted and broken now into a pulpy mess that more closely resembles a pretzel than anything human.

He begins to contemplate the implications of this, what he has just experienced, if there was, in fact, any roar at all, if his own overtaxed mind generated it in his moment of near-death terror, if there were any-one—any*thing*—else present in the room with them, if the sound he heard was the structure of the building weakening in the fire, if Nicky, in a panicked attempt to save himself, tore out of the room and tumbled down the stairs? Then, Andy remembers that these are considerations to be made later. He scurries the remainder of the way down the steps; pauses briefly to take a final glimpse at Nicky, the crushed skull, the bent neck, the limbs jutting in directions never intended by God or nature; supposes it could have happened in a fall.

Could have.

Or, perhaps, in a way he never intended, Nicky Blayze found exactly who he was looking for.

For the final time, Andy Lew flings open the door of the Colossus theater and staggers out into the night.

ANDY HEARS but does not really care when the fire finally reaches the generator and a great explosion tears through the Colossus, spewing flaming debris onto a still otherwise silent 42nd Street, a sudden burst of light like a flashbulb in the night sky; a few throngs of onlookers scurrying either away from or towards the sound, random shrieks and sounds of surprise and, it seems, at least one "Fuck yeah!" echoing along the silent avenue as he staggers back towards his apartment. The Colossus, like so much to him now, is history which cannot be retrieved. He is certain that, at some point, fire crews will arrive, suppress the blaze; the concrete booth will survive, as will, he guesses, most of the lobby and the structure of the auditorium, although the seats will have long burnt to a crisp. Remodeling crews will be brought in, the place gutted, refurbished, made new again, perhaps even into another movie theater; perhaps it will retain the name; but the place he has known as The Colossus is gone now, gone into this pitiful night, gone with *her* to the realm of the lost and forgotten from which nothing can ever be retrieved.

Unlike his last trip back home after a failed expedition, Andy remembers every detail of his journey back; every agonizing moment it takes for him to make it back to his apartment. Pain ebbs into him by the second as the adrenaline begins to leave his bloodstream, becoming harder to walk as his ankle begins to throb, as he becomes acutely aware of the difficulty breathing through his crushed nose, made all the worse by the smoke inhalation, by the sharp stabbing in his ribs, one of which, he is sure, has punctured a lung. The world grows even darker as his vision begins to fail him, certainly from the accumulated head trauma he has suffered this evening, and probably the harbinger of a concussion. Glancing down at his hands at one point, he sees that they are singed, some of the sparse hairs having been burned to the follicle, pustules and welts rising up on his flesh from where he must've made passing contact with the flames en route out of the Colossus. Had he retrieved her, were he cradling her in his arms right now, were he planning to slip her into the projector and turn on the record player when they got back, this would all have been worth it; would have willingly sacrificed all this punishment to his body and much more. Now, in her absence—in the wake of her ultimate destruction—knowing that no force in this realm or the next will ever bring her back to him, it feels a terrible joke, a cosmic prank, that he should endure so much suffering and reap not a single iota of a reward from it.

Andy does not bother to remove any of his clothes when he finally collapses onto his cot, letting blood and sweat and whatever else he is leaking stain the fabric of his sheets. Shock has kept him relatively composed until now, his emotions swirling round and round inside his brain but without any outlet through which to express themselves. Alone, now, at last, in the sanctity of the final place he can call his own, they at last break through and the violent sobs come on, occasionally exploding into high-pitched wails and shrieks, snot bubbling out of his nostrils and coagulating in his mustache. Andy sobs and shrieks and sobs more until finally it all becomes too much, until his body is no longer able to maintain consciousness, and he drops off into a dreamless sleep.

IT'S MUSIC that awakens Andy, soft and soothing, the guitar singing to him of good times past, memories of the two of them together flooding his mind, and, in those seconds before the horrors of last night come rushing back to him, it almost seems as though they were a dream, and he will rise to find her waiting for him there beneath his cot, safely in her canister— Nicky and Gator and all of it just a cruel concoction of some tainted batch of smack, a poor meal before bedtime, the machinations of his own disordered brain. Then, his eyes open fully, and he realizes that he is really hearing the song—*their* song—despite being certain he did not put it on the player before passing out; would not have had any reason to do so with the power not having come back on yet. He sits abruptly; pale light shining in through the window indicates that it is sometime in the early morning hours, when the day itself is still straining to wake itself up, the sky white and raw with exhaust; and silhouetted against the glaring light, perched on the edge of his cot, staring out the window with a look of detached fascination, sits the unmistakable figure

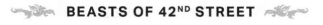

of Samuel Draft. He's much larger than Andy remembers, seeming to have grown in both bulk and stature over the years, muscles still apparent beneath the fabric of the loosely tailored black silk suit he wears, shirt open at the collar, an undone patterned tie draped around his shoulders. Beneath the sound of the music, Andy becomes aware of a faint squealing sound; looks down and sees that one of Draft's polished captoes is pinning the tail of an errant rat to the floor, the thing making a futile effort to free itself, not attacking Draft's foot but attempting to scurry away as though in fear of what lurks behind it.

"It's beautiful, isn't it?" Draft says, his voice the same indistinct, sexless whisper as all those years ago. "Last night, I mean. I rarely get to come out and play. *Really* play, I mean. I enjoy my one-on-one time with people, but, sometimes, it's great to get a whole party going. And last night was some party, wasn't it? I'm just sorry it's going to be a while before I can have that kind of fun again. That was the kind of blow-out that's years in the making." He sighs, his great shoulders rising up so much that he appears to double in size before he exhales and his body relaxes down to something more closely resembling human proportions. Andy trembles; tries to find the appropriate thing to say; opens his mouth; chokes.

"Shhhh. It's all right, Andy. You don't have to say anything. I really came to talk, not listen."

"Was that...you?" The words finally escape Andy's throat as a dry, choked rasp.

"Was *what* me?"

"In the screening room. With Nicky. Did you...?"

"Andy, Andy. Don't ask questions you already know the answer to."

"But...why?"

"She wasn't his to take, Andy," Draft says, smiles; his canines seem to have become more defined over the years. Then his lips close and his face crumbles into a disapproving frown. "But she wasn't yours to give away, either."

"I can do it again," Andy says. "What I did the last time. What I did to Gator…Anything you want. Anyone you want. Please. Please, give her back to me. I'll never let it happen again, I swear…"

"Swear on what, Andy? What means enough to you that your swearing on it would matter? I've seen the way you treat the things you love."

Andy sobs. "Why couldn't you let me die then? Why not just let me burn, let Nicky kill me, let…let *anything* happen to me?"

"I can't say I cared much for the company you've been keeping," Draft says, rises, plucking the rat up by the tail as he moves towards the window, holding the thing at arm's length. "They were dilettantes. Lukewarm. But there's one thing I could agree with them on. You can't trust a man who doesn't like animals. You know what my favorite animal is, Andy? The tiger. They're solitary. Other animals, they run in packs, they mate, they get burdened. Pups to care for, other mouths to feed. A tiger mates when it needs to, and then it gets on its way. Nothing to distract it from the hunt. Because that's a tiger's life: the hunt. One great, big, long hunt for the next meal. Once in a while, though, a tiger does something very strange. They'll adopt a pet. Did you know that, Andy? Tigers are one of the only animals to keep other living things as pets. This is true. Jackals."

Draft studies the rat, swaying as he grips it between his thumb and index finger, as though he's never seen one of the things before. "A tiger will turn a water buffalo inside out, shred a wild boar to death, but they'll tolerate a jackal. The jackal follows the tiger around like the god he knows he is. He cleans up after the tiger. Eats his leftovers. The jackal needs the tiger to survive. And the tiger likes this. He can kill anything he wants, but, to have something dependent on him? Something desperate and weak that relies on him to survive? Well, that's something else, isn't it? And you know why else the tiger likes the jackal, Andy? They're unpredictable. Other animals, they're stupid. The tiger knows exactly what they're going to do, how they're going to react to a given situation. The jackal…well, I'm not going to flatter them. They're not particularly bright, either. But they've got guts. You never know with a jackal. And the tiger appreciates that. Because he gets very bored very easily."

As though he's doing nothing more visceral than tossing away a cig-arette butt, Draft swings the rat like a baseball bat into the wall; there's a squeal and a crunching sound and he drops the heap on the floor. Satisfied with this, he goes to the record player, lifts the needle, restarts the song; hums along with the first few bars before reaching into his jacket and coming out with a little red velvet box. He moves towards Andy, smiles.

"Don't worry. I'm not going to propose. But I am going to be leaving the city soon. Like I said—it's going to be a long time before I have the kind of fun I had here last night, and I've got to do something in the meantime. Since we won't be seeing one another for a while, I thought you deserved a little going away present."

"You said I wasn't going to see you again," Andy says. "The last time."

"Special circumstances. You surprised me last night, Andy. I thought what you gave me the last time was all you had in you. You're more enter-taining than I anticipated. So that's why I'm here now. And that's why I'm giving you this."

His hand trembling, Andy accepts the box; slowly opens it, unsure of what awaits him inside, if it's some sort of trap, if acid is going to spew out of some mechanism and spray his face.

Nestled inside, tucked into a small, black pillow like an engagement ring, is a single frame of film, pristine in condition, not a scratch or pit or burn mark to be seen on it.

Her.

Her, returned to him, in all her beauty; one of the three frames in which her birthmark is visible; *her*, at her most unique and brilliant.

"I thought it was the only one," Andy says through welling tears.

"I wouldn't look a gift horse in the mouth."

"Where's...is there...the rest? All of it?"

"Maybe. Maybe this is clipped from your reel. Maybe this is all that's left."

"Maybe?"

"She wasn't yours to give away. I told you that. What you had was very, very special. So I shouldn't be here at all. But you *did* impress me, Andy. I can't stress that enough. So, I'm making a personal compromise. I'm not going to give you anything else. Not right now. But I am going to let you look. In case there is more. In case this is clipped from another reel. I'm going to let you look, and I'm going to watch. You won't even know that I am, but, I want you to remember that: I'll *always* be watching. Watching you look in every dive bar in this country. Every back alley. Every lousy place like Eddie Lawler's you can dig up. And if…if I decide that you've looked hard enough…if I decide you've *really* earned it…if I'm *entertained* enough…I'll show you where you *can* find it. *If* it's out there."

Andy's at last drift away from the frame of film, to Draft's. "But… I've worked so hard already. I've done so much. I've gone so far. *Please.* Just let me have her back. *Please.*"

"Don't insult my intelligence, Andy. We both know that's not an option at this point, is it?"

After a moment, Andy's eyes return to the film.

"Where do I start?" he asks.

"What did I say about looking a gift horse in the mouth?"

"Please…that's it. That's all you need to tell me. Just …give me a place to start."

Draft contemplates this; strokes his chin. "I would say West is a good place to start. Of the Mississippi. I don't think I can narrow it down much further than that."

With that, Samuel Draft drifts towards the door, opens it, prepares to step into the hallway. Before he does, turns back to Andy, adds: "Anything more specific would spoil the fun."

The song runs out as Draft leaves the apartment, Andy still gazing at her, eyes transfixed, rises and goes to start it over. Raises the needle, drops it; realizes the turntable has stopped spinning. He reaches for the light switch, flips it on to better inspect the player; the lights failing to come on, he realizes the power is still off.

THE NEW York Blackout of 1977 lasts for 25 hours and it is a grand wonder that any part of the city is still standing when at last Con Ed is able to fully restore power and the police—to the extent of their capabilities—are able to restore what passes for order. Even as cuffed bodies are jammed into the backs of wagons to be carted away for booking and sanitation workers and shop owners alike take to the streets to begin sweeping up the glass and debris, the city has already begun an effort to tally the damages. Twenty-five fires remain burning in Bushwick as the sun rises over the city; thirty-five blocks of Broadway have been destroyed, two of them burned beyond recognition. Widespread looting, arson, and battles with the police will continue throughout the day; by the time evening falls, over 1,600 stores will have been robbed, 1,037 fires set, 550 police officers rushed to the hospital in the process of arresting 4,500 individuals for the crimes of assault, robbery, and arson. Con Ed manages to get the power back on in Queens and parts of Manhattan by 7:00 am; it will take them until noon to restore 50% of their customers and until 10:39 PM until the city has been 100% brought back online.

And amidst the nocturnal holocaust, 42nd Street stands largely untarnished, her citizens holding their own, watching with curious detachment as the rest of their ostensibly saner brethren lose their damn minds. The Deuce's sole structural casualty: the already lamented Colossus Theater, the sight of some of the evening's more unusual carnage. By the time firefighters manage to put out the blaze, the bodies they will discover inside have been burned beyond recognition, most bearing evidence of bullet wounds that speak to some sort of mass murder. The sole immediately identifiable victim is Michael Hyatt, an NYPD vice detective who holds the dubious distinction of more officer-involved shootings than any man on the force. In the days following the blackout, it will be revealed that at the time of his death, Hyatt was the subject of an ongoing internal affairs investigation looking into, among other allegations, accusations of corruption, racial profiling, police brutality, solicitation, drug use, drug distribution, and murder. The case will be unceremoniously closed, his body buried with full police honors a week after his death. Only four officers will attend the funeral, and no civilians.

Another body retrieved from the Colossus will eventually be identified through dental records as that of Nicky "Blayze" Blaszkiewicz, a porn star of some local renown. A subsequent search of Blayze's apartment will turn up evidence of a similar slaughter perpetuated there, this one with occultic overtones. In the absence of further evidence, it will enter 42nd Street lore that on the night of the Great New York Blackout, Nicky Blayze— having either gone completely insane or committed himself too fully to the chic brand of celebrity Satanism currently *en vogue* (probably both, the more astute tellers of the tale, will say)—inadvertently burned down the Colossus theater in a botched sex magick ritual intended to summon either Satan, Baal, Babalon the Scarlet Woman, Asmodeus, or some lesser demon. That they have stumbled onto something vaguely approximating the truth will matter to few. For the dice players and street preachers and more articulate pimps and runaway teenagers given to teenage gossip, it's the sensationalism of the tale that matters. With no survivors left to stand witness to the truth, on 42nd Street, one story is just as valid as the next.

No survivor but one.

Though Andy Lew has no intention of sticking around to make sure the details of his last night at the Colossus theater are recorded accurately for posterity.

He is a man looking forward to the future, after all.

Retrieving a suitable outfit from his closet, he leaves his apartment soon after the departure of Samuel Draft, in search of a place to make himself something approaching respectable. He does not give the place he has called home for the bulk of his adult life a last glance, does not indulge in any pathetic sentimentality. The apartment has been a place for him to sleep and live relatively unmolested; it carries no further importance to him, and as such, is unworthy of any fond farewells or long, lingering last looks. He does not even bother to lock the door on his way out; hopes that, when his landlord finally arrives to toss the place, the scant value of what he's left behind—the record player, the projector, a poorly function-ing television set, the cassette player, some nice shoes— will be enough to dissuade him from using whatever means are at his disposal to track him down. He wants as few pursuers on his tail as possible in his new life; the one he knows he'll have looking over his shoulder is quite enough.

It takes Andy part of the morning to find a Y where he's able to get himself cleaned up. Considering the previous evening's events, his bloodied clothes and brutalized body pass under the radar; he is, after all, just another poor son of a bitch who got caught up in the night of the century, just an unfortunate store owner or bystander whose business was ruined by marauders, who was in the wrong place at the wrong time, who really just needs a good, hot shower and a moment to contemplate what's happened before he heads back out into the world. Some kind soul—a nurse or volunteer doctor or bleeding-heart Jesus freak or who-ever the fuck it is that runs these places—gives him some bandages and gauze with which to put himself back together, takes a shot at clumsily resetting his nose. Then he's into his fresh clothes and back out onto the street—on to the final business he will ever conduct in New York City.

It takes him a while to find a pay phone that's functioning; wor-ries as he drops the first coins in that they won't take, that the call will abruptly cut out, that he will have blown the scant change he brought for just this purpose on nothing. Glad when the receiver on the other end clicks and a voice answers, "Hello?"

"It's Andy."

"Andy? *Mój Boże*, are you all right? I've been watching the news. I'd wondered if you're all right. *Are* you all right? Since our last call…"

Saskia prattles on, inquiring as to his health, his general well-being, his mental state since their last conversation, half-serious inquiries as to whether he himself was in any way responsible for the previous night's disaster. A lifetime ago, he would have sat rapt, listening to the sound of her voice, the content meaningless, satisfied only that it was meant for him and he happy to receive it. Now, her rambling is just noise, a delay to his real business.

"I didn't call to chat," Andy at last interrupts. "I called to say goodbye. You won't...you won't be hearing from me again. Ever."

A heavy sigh. "Now there's the Andrezj I know. Of course. Things are back to normal then, are they? I won't be hearing from you again until the *next time* I never hear from you again."

"I'm going away," Andy says. "I don't know where. But I won't be back. I just wanted to ask you to do something for me before I left."

"What's that, Andrezj?"

"Forget me."

He puts the phone back on the receiver, waits the appropriate amount of time, and places his next call; feeds additional coins in as the call is transferred from reception to this desk to that desk, Andy sighing heavily, counting what he's got left in his hand, making sure to save enough for what's coming next. At last, the voice he has been waiting to hear comes on the other end:

"This is Detective Valentine."

"It's done," Andy says.

"What's been done? Who is this? This some kinda joke? I got a city damn near burned itself to the ground, you want to talk to me, you best be specific..."

"It's Andy. And the thing you wanted done is done."

"The thing I wanted...oh, sweet merciful Heaven, that was *you?*"

"He won't be a problem anymore."

"I asked you to take the garbage out, not slice open the bag and spill it in the damn street. You have any idea how this looks, the questions they askin' down here right now? And that other shit…boy, you best better tell me if you had anything to do with the rest of that mess."

"Does it matter? The job's done. I expect you to hold up your end of the bargain. He's gone. And in a few hours I'm going to be gone, too. I want the extra peace of mind no one's going to come looking for me."

"You got some balls, trying to call shots after a job like that. You got some damn big balls."

"That isn't an answer."

There's a long pause on the other end of the line; Andy tenses, furious at the prospect of having to spend another coin solely on the basis of Dick Valentine's indignity. Finally:

"You got twenty-four hours. Twenty-four hours to haul your sorry, smack-riddled ass out of my city while I try and pick up the pieces. And then I pay a visit to your pad. I'm satisfied you're gone, some photo negatives go in my fireplace. A case stays open, no suspects. One suspect cleared, though. And we all go on with our lives. But let me tell you this, and you best listen good: I think you gone and hung around my city, or I think you come back, want to be a pain in my ass again…I can't say that 'kindness' is gonna be a word in my vocabulary next time."

Feeling this to be a declaration that does not call for any sort of confirmation or rebuttal, Andy hangs up. Rubs his face in his hands. His heart rate has accelerated again, his breathing quickened; this is a moment he has both been anticipating and forestalling since the idea first formed in his mind. Besides Draft's mandate, this has been the action which has dictated the course of his morning; the reason he selected this particular blue suit, pale shirt, knit tie in which to make his flight from the city. Even though she will not see him, he wants to be presentable; wants to feel, at least, as though he will be making a good physical first impression as well as verbal and emotional, that he is presenting himself at his very best.

Andy retrieves his wallet, unfolds the piece of paper inside. Dials.

It's a few rings before someone answers. The voice is not old but it is tired, the sort of tiredness that comes from exhaustion, from weariness, the voice of someone who has perhaps endured more than they were ever prepared or meant to bear.

"Hello? Hello, who is this?"

Andy chokes; takes a deep breath. Cannot blow this.

"Mrs. Tolhurst? Is this...Mrs. Tolhurst?"

"This is she. Who is this?

"Are you...is this...are you Sylvia Tolhurst's mother?"

Andy can hear the woman's breathing become rapid on the other end of the line.

"Who is this?"

"My name is Andy, ma'am...Andrew. Andrew Lewinsky. I...I'm calling about your daughter. I wanted you to know...I wanted you to know that I'm going to find her. I don't think it would be a good idea for me to bring her to you when I do, but...I'm going to find her, ma'am. And then I'm going to take care of her. I'm going to make sure she's safe with me again. I promise."

"Oh, my God. Sylvie, you know my Sylvie?"

"Yes, ma'am. And...and she got taken away, but, I'm going to fix it."

"Is she...do you know if she's safe? Who are you? What...what is this?" There's elation in her voice, panic, uncertainty, the whole unfathomable cocktail of emotions a person experiences when they've waited a lifetime for knowledge they'd always hoped for but never believed would really come.

"I...I'm in love with her, Mrs. Tolhurst. I love her. And...I'm sure she loves me, too. And..." Andy looks at the photo on the missing poster in his hands; at the beatific smile; at the birthmark he has carefully added with a felt-tip pen to give it the utmost level of accuracy. "And I think that's why she came back to me. And that's why she's going to help me find her."

"But...I don't understand. She's safe? She's alive?" The woman's voice has begun to quiver now, tears audible in it.

"What? No, she's dead."

"She's…oh, my God, I don't understand. You're…you're sick, you're sick and this is a joke…"

"I'm not joking, ma'am. She's dead. But I'm going to find her. And I'll make sure I protect her when I do. I wanted you to know that, too, Mrs. Tolhurst. That I love your daughter, and I'm sorry for not watching out for her before, b-ut we're going to be together again. I'm going to make sure of it. And then I'll never let her go. And I'll never let anything happen to her ever again."

And Sylvia's mother is sobbing on the phone and tears are rolling down Andy's face, too, and when he hears her final wail and the phone slamming down, he hopes that in spite of everything he's somehow assured the old woman, made a good first impression.

AGAIN, ANDY walks.

As the looting continues, as police drag thieves and arsonists and vandals through the streets in handcuffs, as the city still struggles to right whatever it was, exactly, that went wrong in the first place, Andy walks, unseen. To the police, he is a legitimate businessman struggling to go about his day, to regain some sense of the normalcy that is currently evading every New Yorker. Others see through the suit and tie and know what sort of man is playing dress-up with respectability, and they stay away.

Andy walks until he identifies a car abandoned during the night which has yet to be retrieved by its owner; a car sufficiently unguarded, unwatched by any police, undamaged enough to be inconspicuous.

It has been some time since he has had to employ the skills of lock-picking or hotwiring, and, as he sets about his task, Andy is initially skeptical that he can achieve his goal in brief enough an amount of time before someone spots him and interferes, be it the vehicle's rightful owner or some officer of the law. Is pleasantly surprised when he discovers that none of his technique has left him over the years, that, within the space of only a few minutes, he is behind the wheel and inching his way Westward towards the Lincoln tunnel, his foot perhaps a bit too leaden on the gas and too sharp on the break. No matter; the traffic, of course, is heavy anyway, and his sojourn out of the city will permit him ample opportunity to recall the proper operation of a motor vehicle. Too long since he's been behind the wheel; too long since late nights with Steven and Saskia prowling 7th in the Village, looking for trouble and finding it.

Memories. Just memories now, memories he must put out of his head. He can no longer afford their distraction or their burden. There is only the future ahead of him. There are only the worst places in the world for him to seek out and endure: bars and sex shops, dives and flop-houses, back alleys and basements and long, dark nights where no light will ever shine and desperate, blue-lit mornings where time will seem to have stopped and he will find himself freezing cold in some wood-paneled motel room in a town whose name he cannot remember in the latest stop on a journey whose destination he does not know. There is only the demon on his shoulder, whispering silent words of encouragement into one ear even as he laughs in the other, invisible eyes watching him always, *always*, eyes Andy thinks he might feel on him even now, gazing at him from the backseat. There is only the road ahead of him, the eternal, end-less road, which he will drive and drive and drive until his feet ache and his hands tremble and he has driven into a thousand blood-red sunsets and then he will drive some more. For he knows that if—*if*— he ever reaches the end she shall be waiting for him there, in all of her splendor and glory. He knows that there is the hope—that great wickedness the Greeks called *hope*—his journey may—most likely won't, *probably* won't, but *may*— one day be over. Then, he can be with her once more; and they can die and die and die together again and again, forever and ever.

Her.

His infernal beloved.

MISSING REEL

(EPILOGUE, 1965)

*"Abashed the devil stood and felt how awful goodness is and saw
Virtue in her shape how lovely: and pined his loss"*
— **John Milton, Paradise Lost**

"ANDY?"

Roderick enters the projection booth cautiously; over the course of the last few months, approaching Andy Lew has become an exercise in constant awareness. The mood swings were startling at first, violent fits of rage followed by crying jags locked in the employee bathroom; then came his habit of shutting out the lights in the booth, sitting cross legged on his chair, quietly smoking in the darkness. It has occurred to Roderick on several occasions to simply fire Andy; rid himself and the company of him before he becomes a liability. Then he remembers that the onset of these episodes coincided with their rendezvous in the booth, and he rethinks his options; cannot help but believe that somehow, this is his fault.

"Yeah?" Andy calls from the darkness. Only the outline of his body is visible against the faint light being cast back by the projector.

"The reels just came in for the new feature," Roderick says. "I need you to come down and get them. Make sure they're clean."

Andy grunts. Over the past few months the quality of films coming into the Colossus has mildly improved; once in a while, he will be broken away from his meditations by some particularly heinous vision that stirs his conscious mind to attention and he will fixate for a few moments on the image onscreen, a snippet of sheer visceral awesomeness to arouse a faint twitch deep within him. Nominally, though, the films have maintained their quality of awfulness, deceptive posters in the lobby promising thrills that never come, dreams left unfulfilled. To maintain his sanity, Andy will sometimes bring *her* with him, nestling the reel beneath his workbench, urinating in empty soda cups so he never has to abandon it to potential theft. When he is certain that Roderick is busy downstairs and will leave him alone, he will open the canister and spool out a few feet of film, holding it before his face to gaze at the images of the skull, counting down towards the feature presentation, imagining what it will feel like to once again thread it into his projector and watch the show.

"We're going to need them checked out ASAP," Roderick says. "It's foreign so we need to make sure the subtitles are legible." He figures Andy has gotten the message but is unsure how to end the conversation.

"What've you got?" Andy asks.

"At Midnight I'll Take Your Soul."

Andy grunts again. "I'll be right down."

"OK then," Roderick says.

"OK," Andy says.

As Roderick is about to leave the booth, the projector cuts out, the faint light illuminating him going dead, casting the booth into darkness. Roderick opens the door; in the stairwell, complete, pitch blackness.

"It's a blackout," Roderick says. His voice trembles.

"A blackout?" Andy stands up, feels his way to his workbench, retrieves his reel. Then he heads towards the door. He pushes past Roderick, guides himself downstairs. Roderick follows the sound of his footsteps; by the time they reach the lobby patrons have already begun to shuffle out of the theater, lighters and the tips of cigarette butts creating tiny auras in the darkness. Ushers with flashlights dart around, panicked in their confusion and inexperience, trying to corral the patrons into groups, instruct them to return to the auditorium, to go home.

"A blackout," Andy says, moving towards the front doors. Beyond them, the entire city dark, a massive, yawning void given life only by the beams of car headlights cutting swaths through the night. He places his hand against the glass of the door; imagines that he can take this darkness into himself, hold it there.

"Andy!" Roderick, whispering to him, illuminated in the castoff glow of an usher's flashlight that he's begun to wring his hands. "Andy, I've given the boys instructions to clear everyone out. I'm going to be getting out of here soon. If you need me…if it's an emergency…I'll be at Bacchus Baths, just down the block. Could you…If it isn't too much… could you watch the booth?"

"Sure," Andy says. He continues looking out the doors; might as well bide his time until the real show begins. Hugs the reel against his body and ascends to the booth. The city without power: without its creature comforts, without the lights and the security they provide to keep its honest citizens honest. He will retreat to the comfort of the booth for the time being; he will listen for the sounds of honking horns and confused shouts to become bellows of rage and the report of gunfire. He will occupy his time concocting scenarios in his mind of what he will find when he comes back down, rivers of gore running through the streets, the bodies piled high, walls of police officers with rifles gunning down wave after wave of rioters in a futile attempt to restore order before daybreak. He dreams of the films they will make of this; of the fantastic art that this night will produce.

It is a long time before Andy hears the first noises from below; he thinks, initially, that he cannot really be hearing what he is hearing, that his ears must be playing tricks on him. And then he is drifting down into the stairwell, lighter in one hand, reel in the other. When he reaches the bottom of the stairs, he knows that he is terribly right, and does not bother to open the door into the lobby.

Two dozen or so voices join together in a butchered rendition of *Auld Lang Syne*. Based on the volume, Andy figures they must be coming from the street; old and young, male and female, some joyfully inebriated. Giggles permeate the song; when it ends, there is a round of applause and a wave of laughter before someone starts up with a song that Andy does not recognize. Another wave of laughter sweeps the crowd and more voices join in, louder than before, welcoming more revelers to come outside.

Andy retreats back upstairs.

In the booth, Andy rummages around his workbench, finds a flashlight. Hunkers down on the floor. As he flicks the light on and off, a memory runs through his mind, a split second image; he and Steven, twenty years ago, beneath the covers of their bed in the old apartment, the sheet propped up in the center fort-like, passing a lighter between them. Though Andy cannot be certain, it seems to him that the object of their fascination was a calendar, the girls scantily clad, if at all, the curvature of breasts teasing the eye from behind strategically placed leis, buttocks concealed by carefully positioned hips; behind them all, the airships of their father's war, flying fortresses prepared to rain down death upon the enemy; the boys dreaming of the day that they would be old enough to leave behind such infantile inquisitiveness and find out for themselves what this was really all about.

Andy opens the canister and pulls out a length of film. He holds the flashlight behind it, far enough away so as to not pose any threat. With his thumb and forefinger, he carefully shuffles through the frames; the skull; the appearance of the girl; the coming of the Executioner. Then he winds it back into its case, closes it up. Puts his flashlight away and lays his head down on the reel canister. Staring towards the ceiling, he slowly drifts away to sleep and dreams.

END CREDITS

(ACKNOWLEDGMENTS)

WHILE I can safely take credit as the sole author of the Andy Lew saga, the character properly has three parents in addition to myself.

The first is my wife, Kayleigh. She initially saw Andy's potential when he was merely a supporting villain in the short stories about life on 1970s 42nd Street I used to submit to our college's literary journal (the same stories which initially attracted her to me, which probably speaks volumes about our relationship). It was her fascination with Andy Lew that first led me to realize he had life beyond being just a sniveling, death-obsessed projectionist who occasionally harassed my protagonists. Her desire to know more about him is what led me to write the short story that eventually formed the basis for the "Passion of the Damned" segment of this book, which in turn led to my own desire to fully flesh him out into his own complete narrative.

Andy has two more parents, though, and they too played an important—albeit more recent—role in his development. Unlike my previous book, which I started and finished in an uninterrupted, frenzied, six-month writing binge, *Beasts* was temporarily hampered by a period of writer's block from which I feared I would never emerge. That creative logjam was eventually broken by the introduction of two very unique men into my life.

"Mad" Ron Roccia gave his namesake to *Mad Ron's Prevues from Hell,* a trailer compilation I researched for a FANGORIA article. During the course of the interview I conducted with him it became apparent he and I shared a like mind: a grindhouse projectionist for 35 years, he spent years collecting prints and trailers from the real 42nd, and regaled me with tales of his time on the Deuce in the bad old days. He quickly became a reader of my work, and his firsthand experience of the milieu and enthusiastic support of my writing proved invaluable to getting me back into Andy's world. Additionally, he provided me with many of the technical details present in *Beasts* (including the different brand names and vintages of different projectors), and ensured that I accurately represented projection work as it existed circa 1977.

Jason Alvino is a fellow writer. A New Yorker born and raised, Jason has a unique, deep connection to the city of his birth, and his enthusiastic interest in Andy's story and his creative feedback gave me the encouragement and perspective necessary to see him through to his Faustian climax. Between my wife's encouragement and Mad Ron and Jason's enthusiasm and feedback, I was at last able to bring Andy Lew to his fullest life, and I'm indebted to them for helping me see this book through to its conclusion.

Thanks to my parents and my brother, who still love me even though I write shit like this.

Thanks, too, to all the people who helped make my first novel a success, which of course led to demand for a second book. I hope you still like me after I unleashed Andy Lew onto the world. This means—in no particular order— Izzy Lee, Joshua Millican, Bradley Steele-Harding and Dan Gremminger, Jessie Hobson, Matt Konopka, Scott Wampler, Rebekah McKendry Ph. D., Eric Ogriseck, Leigh Monson, Katie Rife, Mark Miller, Christian Francis, Matt Konopka, Katelyn Nelson, Jon Abrams, Andrew Allan, Kasey Lansdale, Cory Brown, Monica Kuebler, Dave Alexander, Hannah Foreman, Phil Nobile Jr., Chris Grosso, Barbara Crampton, Kelli Maroney, Autumn Ivy, Mike Vanderbilt, Jason

Jenkins, John Squires, Matt Wedge, Sadie Hartman, Jess Hagemann, Robert Ashcroft, Tori Romero, Mick Garris, Jay Kay, Heidi Moore, Herman Raucher, Isobel Blackthorn, Jennifer Bonges, Blu Gilliand, and so very many others whose names I'm sorry aren't coming to me at the moment.

Thanks to the Mad Ron Quartet—Mr. Roccia, James F. Murray, Jr., Nick Pawlow, and Jim Murray—for bringing the world *Prevues from Hell*. It was a constant companion during the latter stages of this book's composition, and is necessary viewing for both young horror fans and horror fans who are young at heart.

Thanks to Brian Keene, who kindly put me into touch with Cemetery Dance's Brian James Freeman, who in turn handed me over to Kevin Lucia, who saw in *Beasts* something worthwhile where so many other potential agents and publishers saw something that needed to be killed with fire. It's through their grace that Andy's damnation has found its way into your hands.

Thanks to Kat Rosenfield for putting me in touch with Yfat Reiss Gendell, who's helped me level up tremendously and finally become a real writer.

Thanks to the people of The Fedora Lounge and citydata.com, whom I pumped for information regarding 1970s New York in general and the 1977 Blackout specifically. Unfortunately, I lost your names in the process of transferring data to a new computer and hope you forgive the slight. If I interviewed you for this book and you don't see your name here, please reach out to me for inclusion in a future edition.

Thanks always to Bill Landis and Michelle Clifford, whose *Sleazoid Express* was and remains a seminal text in both my own personal education and grindhouse history in general. It's one of the greatest regrets of my life I never got to correspond with Mr. Landis, whose documentation of life on 1980s 42nd Street was instrumental to my growth as a writer. It's my hope that the dedication of this book to his memory goes even a small way towards honoring his legacy.

Like Andy at the end of his journey, I'm running out of steam—and, I fear, space. A final thanks to all those I've woefully neglected or forgotten here, not out of ingratitude but rather my well-documented inability to remember names. You're here in spirit, if not in name, and your influence is felt and appreciated.

Photo by Kayleigh Overman-Fassel

PRESTON FASSEL is an award-winning writer whose work has appeared in FANGORIA, Rue Morgue, Screem, and on The Daily Grindhouse, Dread Central, and Cinedump.com. He is the author of the first published biography of British horror actress Vanessa Howard, *Remembering Vanessa,* which appeared in the Spring 2014 issue of Screem. His debut novel, Our Lady of the Inferno, won the 2019 Independent Publisher's Gold Medal for Horror and was named one of the ten best books of the year by Bloody Disgusting.

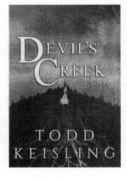

Printed in the USA
CPSIA information can be obtained
at www.ICGtesting.com
LVHW092154201123
764499LV00037B/729

9 781587 678530